Volume 14, Number 2

"Winter is the time for comfort, for good food and warmth, for the touch of a friendly hand and for a talk beside the fire: it is the time for home."

—EDITH SITWELL

From one of our greatest contemporary writers, 17 stories that "evoke a magical world populated by flying rabbis and disembodied souls, voyeuristic prophets, and lascivious angels."*

"He writes with piercing zeal."
—*The New York Times Book Review*

"In the tradition of great Yiddish writers such as Isaac Bashevis Singer."
—*The New Republic**

A "heedless rush of heady language and comic brio . . . Stern's prose fuses the magical and the mundane, with an offhandedness that makes the normal seem odd, and the truly odd seem matter of fact."
—*Bookslut*

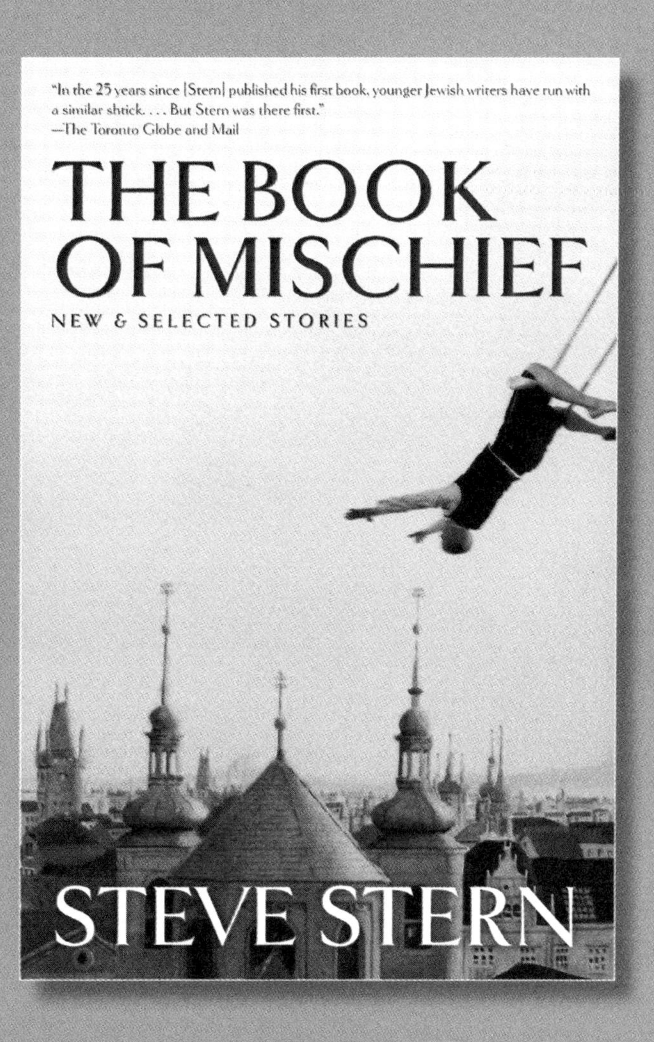
"In the 25 years since [Stern] published his first book, younger Jewish writers have run with a similar shtick. . . . But Stern was there first."
—The Toronto Globe and Mail
THE BOOK OF MISCHIEF
NEW & SELECTED STORIES
STEVE STERN

"How to make a Steve Stern story: stir in a large dose of Isaac Singer and early Roth; add a magic pinch of Marquez and Millhauser; shake with enthusiasm; serve in a plastic Marx Brothers cup. Drink deeply while laughing."
—*Shelf Awareness*

"Stern's characters are subtle, slyly humorous and at times poignant. . . . An intricate and clever web of stories."
—*Kirkus Reviews*, starred review

GRAYWOLF PRESS

www.graywolfpress.org

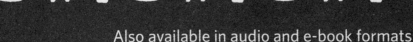

Tin House
MAGAZINE
Save 50%
off the newsstand price
Subscribe today, only $24.95
Missed the first 53 issues?
Fear not, we've hidden a limited number in our closet. Log on to www.tinhouse.com for more information.

Tin House MAGAZINE

EDITOR IN CHIEF / PUBLISHER
Win McCormack

EDITOR Rob Spillman
ART DIRECTOR Diane Chonette
MANAGING EDITOR Cheston Knapp
EXECUTIVE EDITOR Michelle Wildgen
POETRY EDITOR Matthew Dickman
EDITOR-AT-LARGE Elissa Schappell
POETRY EDITOR-AT-LARGE Brenda Shaughnessy
PARIS EDITOR Heather Hartley
EDITORIAL ASSISTANTS Desiree Andrews, Lance Cleland, Emma Komlos-Hrobsky

CONTRIBUTING EDITORS: Dorothy Allison, Steve Almond, Aimee Bender, Charles D'Ambrosio, Brian DeLeeuw, Anthony Doerr, CJ Evans, Nick Flynn, Matthea Harvey, Jeanne McCulloch, Christopher Merrill, Rick Moody, Whitney Otto, D. A. Powell, Jon Raymond, Rachel Resnick, Peter Rock, Helen Schulman, Jim Shepard, Karen Shepard, Bill Wadsworth

DESIGNER: Jakob Vala

INTERNS: Saga Briggs, Lauren Lederman, Maya McOmie, Kendall Poe, Christine Reilly, Devon Walker-Domine

READERS: Shomit Barua, Stephanie Booth, Kevin Burnside, Ramona DeNies, Polly Dugan, Tim Faiella, Ann-Derrick Gaillot, Mark Hammond, Stacy Heiney, Heather Hodges, Bryan Hurt, Sarah Marshall, Shannon McDonald, Lisa Mecham, Leanna Moxley, Cynthia-Marie O'Brien, Hannah Pass, Eleanor Piper, Corinna Rosendahl, Jeremy Scheuer, Annie Rose Shapero, Neesa Sonoquie, Jennifer Taylor, JoNelle Toriseva, Louise Wareham Leonard, Anna Weatherford, Linda Woolman

DEPUTY PUBLISHER Holly MacArthur
CIRCULATION DIRECTOR Laura Howard
DIRECTOR OF PUBLICITY Nanci McCloskey
COMPTROLLER Janice Carter

Tin House Books

EDITORIAL ADVISOR Rob Spillman
EDITORS Meg Storey, Tony Perez, Nanci McCloskey
EDITORIAL ASSISTANT Desiree Andrews
ASSOCIATE EDITOR Masie Cochran

Tin House Magazine (ISSN 1541-521X) is published quarterly by McCormack Communications LLC, 2601 Northwest Thurman Street, Portland, OR 97210. Vol. 14, No. 2, Winter 2012. Printed by R. R. Donnelley. Send submissions (with SASE) to Tin House, P.O. Box 10500, Portland, OR 97296-0500.

Visit our Web site at **www.tinhouse.com**.

Basic subscription price: one year, $50.00. For subscription requests, write to P.O. Box 469049, Escondido, CA 92046-9049, or e-mail tinhouse@pcspublink.com, or call 1-800-786-3424. Additional questions, e-mail laura@tinhouse.com

Periodicals postage paid at Portland, OR 97210 and additional mailing offices.

Postmaster: Send address changes to Tin House Magazine, P.O. Box 469049, Escondido, CA 92046-9049.

Newsstand distribution through Disticor Magazine Distribution Services (disticor.com). If you are a retailer and would like to order Tin House, call Dave Kasza at 905-619-6565, fax 905-619-2903, or e-mail dkasza@disticor.com. For trade copies, contact Publisher's Group West at 800-788-3123, or e-mail orderentry@perseusbooks.com.

EDITOR'S NOTE

Putting together a literary magazine is a joyful yet Sisyphean task. Just when you've pushed the boulder up the hill to the printer, back down it rolls. And with it go all the characters you've lived with and loved for months, all the small moments of joy and revelation, all the humor and sadness. From the bottom, you begin again, from scratch, always from scratch. Just as writers must court failure in order to transcend the known, we, too, are always looking to challenge ourselves. We search stories for that peculiar mix of the new and the ever-old true, but told anew

In this issue, we found it in young writer Helen Phillips's story "Flesh & Blood," about a woman who can see through people's skin. We saw it in veteran Stuart Dybek's fractured take on the operatic life in his story "Tosca." And in Benjamin Percy, too, no stranger to fictional and personal risks, who writes here of his monthlong liver detox (spoiler: no meat and no alcohol do not tame Percy's inner beast).

Two books after being a New Voice in *Tin House*, Monica Ferrell returns to our pages with the poem "Oh You Absolute Darling." Always searching for fresh writing, in this issue we are happy to introduce three New Voices: David Feinstein, Sam Ross, and Eric Burg.

The venerable writer William Gass, interviewed here, says, "So you try, but you probably will fail. It's a business. Failure is what happens." He's echoing Beckett's famous saying, "Ever tried. Ever failed. No matter. Try again. Fail again. Fail better." To risk, to dare—that is his, and our, challenge. We're proud of this issue, but as always, we're never completely satisfied. We do, however, hope that we have failed better with this, our fifty-fourth try up the hill.

CONTENTS

ISSUE #54 / WINTER READING

Fiction

Poetry

Interview

Features

Lost & Found

Readable Feast

THE BARBER'S HAIRSTYLE GUIDE
TECHNICAL JOB FIELDS
NAVY

FICTION

Soliloquy for a Chair

When we were born you wouldn't believe the fuss that was made over us: so many, so fit, so simultaneous. People drove by our mother's house and dropped off gifts and small change. We were tiny, especially when we were folded up. Crowds waited—patiently, I must say—to see us, maybe through a window when we were carried across the parlor, or during the few hours every day that people were permitted to walk through the kitchen to look at us lined up on the linoleum pretty much as we are here, only with not so much gray hair. Ha ha! I'm the only one of us with a sense of humor.

William Gass

We're still together, as you can see, even after all these years: that's Deadly Reckoning on your left, the one of us who received so much press; and Barry Buttock is next—we got around to calling him that on account of his constant complaining about the burdens he bore every day of his life, well, we were all weighed down from time to time (I always told him he hadn't a leg to stand on—ha ha!—he'd say he had four); then Excessively Neighborly is on Butt's left, neighbor to me, always wedged in as we customarily were, but he seemed to enjoy it; then I'm in the middle—I was always in the middle—positioned below the paper pinned to a coat hanger hook, the one that has curled like a burnt worm for being so long in a room moist with razor washings and shampoos; now we come to Commander Prince Paul, who looks to me pretty much like the rest of us but one who fancies himself some sort of exiled African royalty, compelled for political reasons (that he pretended threatened his safety) to endure our life of required labor and enforced comradeship by parking against the wall of Walter's barbershop in Natchez, Mississippi, waiting, the guys say, like the taxi girls down the street, to be of use, but fearing (as the Commander insisted) to be found out and snapped into shackles on the spot.

We sit amid our particulars but they are good as gone in the dark that washes through the front window.

We were all born together, despite Prince Paul's preposterous mytherations, and healthy as bean sprouts, but Perce was without the entirety of his equipment—a front strut—though it never seemed to interfere with his duties, which he carried out with as much enthusiasm as the rest of us . . . not much—ha ha!—yet an infirmity that sharp-eyed customers were bound to notice.

They'd pick up a comical magazine from Walt's rack to stay busy-headed while they were waiting their turn, and then leave it in Perce's lap when a barber became available, since some folks didn't want to settle down on a chair with no front strut. Perce wants me to say that all of us were fitted with those safety braces once but then, in addition, we are to claim that Perce lost his strut in a terrible accident, and that now, because of this unfortunate omission, we are to say that nobody makes use of him, just politely shies away and puts their reading on his lap instead of lowering their anatomy. If it suits him in his heart to say it went that way, why not say it went that way, say I.

The last in line, though he would hate to hear it put in those terms, is Natty Know-it-all, who got his name by being just the opposite, not quite there as to brainy particulars, and slow as faucet drip to learn or find, execute or opine anything. "I've half a mind to spin a top," he'll sometimes say—ha ha! It does make us laugh a lot, cause he couldn't spin a top if his life depended on it. Just not built for mental tergiversations. Honest as the day is long, though. Honest even all night. All night. The neons have a nervous flash. All Nite they bite air. Honesty's smaller hours go to those who pass them in their sleep. We have no sex life, though we've seen plenty of yours, and we are grateful not to have to suffer the same miseries. If we continue to be of use, you will multiply us. Since many languages assign genders to things, we have voted to be pronounced "he" not "it" or "she," as if we were all ships or fences.

Nights get me. Neons or not. We sit amid our particulars but they are good as gone in the dark that washes through the front window. It smothers what little light we might have saved up for ourselves during the day and makes for a silence that is peculiar to electric things and glass shelves. We die through use—we do—buttons into buttonholes—occasionally there's a trauma but mostly it is the quiet wear of unremarked routines—life's a chair's hinge, I say, trying to seem wise—they tell me to tell that to my screws. Our workaday seats get rubbed thin by ass squirm and body heat. But we also die during nights of inaction and enforced rest, when rust's slow debilitations pick at what we are and what sustains us with more repetition and determination than a tap drip. Neons or not. All nite they bite. When we close up shop we sit as we always sit: still waiting to be sat on. Of course the sleep of metal has its merits, but I find myself missing the company of our daily things, now that the passage of people has ceased. During business hours we can overhear the shaving gear and the howzitlook mirror carry on a conversation, mostly about the hypocrisy characteristic of spoons, or the dental complaints of combs because they have so many teeth, or the swish of brooms who collect the resalable clippings made by the hair-cutting gear; or we can attend to a pair of shampoo sinks or to trays of tedious utensils as they rattle on all day while razors, scissors, or toilet sprays yap about like pups or buzz and bicker like the electric heater. Make your little noises, fellows, I let one leg say to the others, now that silence seems total, and the reflected flicker from a passing headlamp suddenly runs the floor like one of our mice.

We've been called the seven dwarfs. I don't know why. People just say things sometimes.

You might also have been wondering why a bunch of folding chairs would call their first employer "mother." Well, we do it just for fun, and because we like to display our wit and boast of the way our legs snap open. Fate was being ironic when it assigned us to a mortuary for our first full tour of duty, deeply so, since that's what mothers mainly do—give birth to an infant who will be able to restock the general supply and keep death ungratefully in business. The big black lady who fed the mourners cookies on small glass plates, oiled our joints, because "around death, the quieter we be, the better, like those who have crossed over, it shows respect."

When we were cut out of our cardboard casing, we did not know how much of the world might someday sit down upon us or surround us with a selection of its business noises, but we were fortunate in fate's choice for us—a barbershop—since a barbershop was then closer to the center of things than almost any place readily available.

Six non-holidays a week, at eight in the morning, Walter would flip from CLOSED to OPEN the card that dangled from the doorknob. Then we would wait for the little ring the door gave out when the first customer came in. It was comforting, if business was brisk, to hear the snick of the scissors, the whisk of the hairbrush, and the skid of the barbers' razors when they were rubbed amorously along the length of their leather strops. Some guys disappeared behind the daily paper, others lost face in a roil of white lather; a few would immediately begin broadcasting their complaints about the behavior of their neighbors and the ills of the nation. These routine moans and groans hid their features, I always thought, as successfully as the daily news. A regular whose name was Barney bewailed the condition of the economy, but told us little about his own perilously thin resources. The end of Clarence's sentences were a bit shrill, as if his balls were being pinched, an explanation that pleased Barry Buttock, who first conjectured it. Clare would drift in most every morning before nine just to say hi! I wondered did he have a home or other friends or a place to hang his hat. Then our row of seats would begin to fill with customers, often greeting one another, their rumps already weighing—each in its own way—upon our crisscrossed legs. They weren't the only ones who felt the relief of leaving their feet so as to settle down upon Deadly Reckoning or Natty Know-it-all, often the first ones chosen because they were stationed at the favored ends of our row, and had, in consequence, aisle seats, with only one occupiable shoulder. Perce wants me to say that he was superior to the rest of us because being built without a brace was like being born without an appendix. If it suits him in his heart to say it worked that way, why not say it worked that way, say I.

The murmur of the barbers and their clients, the clicks and snicks of implements and the buzz of shavers were fairly constant and they were comforting too, reassuring the ear that all was well; and usually this carpet of clatter was punctuated only by the brief ring of the phone when an unheard voice asked for an appointment.

Our shop was mainly a walk-in. We were no highbrow female hair parlor. No sir, we weren't run by the style bunnies and their frightened hops into the latest fashions.

No sir, we weren't run by the style bunnies and their frightened hops into the latest fashions.

Early in our careers . . . just a min . . . the mortuary died a short time after we began working there, ha ha, we made rueful jokes about that, and we were stacked, roped, and dumped into a Goodwill without the least acknowledgement of the value of our previous service, which was exemplary even if brief . . . As I was about to say, we chairs sat at tables for a month in a small bar hereabouts, that's my only experience of bartenders, and we found them, to a seat, to be careless with their equipment and noisy at their handling, banging mugs about and crushing ice, but sullen as a bar rag, especially during the night shift. That's not our twenty years with barbers. No one could be more garrulous, gossipy, and outgoing than these guys at Walter's. It's not that they learned to talk to the talc (normally quiet, like unused bars of soap) or were inclined to toss the towels a chuckle . . . no . . . but once collected with others of their kind they'd be comfortable as a cushion—their tongues danced all day. With a little wax paper, Mart would play something he claimed was Irish on one of his combs—I was never sure which one—and then, energized, jig his fingers among his hair-dye dishes without bumping any.

Next? Ah. Master Robinson. You get to be the ghost today, Walter might say to a small boy who at that moment looked a bit apprehensive. Just climb up here where the clouds are. I'll make a ghost of yah. Then with a flourish the chalk white cloth would be pinned about the poor kid's body. Dad might be getting his own hair cut, and needed to assure his son, if it was a first time for him, that the scissors didn't hurt, these suddenly jovial men weren't dentists, and that the boy should banish fear and let his mouth water in anticipation of the flat round all-day sucker that would be his mouthful when his haircut was admired at last. Older kids, who were by experience now undaunted, might be rewarded—it depended on relationships formed on the street and outside the range of our observations—with a recitation of Walter's renowned menu. A few of its offerings were pictured on a cardboard sign like wanted men. The whole show went as I now render it, spoken in rapid-fire bursts followed by some exclamatory pauses.

Women, even more than men, will try anything to prevent hair loss.

Hey honey bunch . . . hey handsome little guy . . . welcome to Walter's, home of all your desires. You want a part, a perm, ringlets, or a razor cut . . . an Afro? how about I give you a texture treatment? hey, you want bangs, a beehive, or a blowout?—oh man, oh madam, right here—bob or bowl or buzz cut—you'll find their picture on row five—along with a bouffant doodoo . . . how about we do it up in a bun, then? so many choices, like chocolates, boxed by the letter B; *maybe a Caesar, a comb-over, what say? you're getting a little thin on top—no?—like a pond in a woods—no?—all right, no pond, no woods, maybe a few cornrows, a crew cut? we can just flat out crop it off, straight away give it a Croydon facelift (you know, that's a topknot); how about trying the curtained style, devil and dreadlocks, duck's ass or ducktail?* it's just hair, my darling, how can you get so fussy? *okay, honey, okay handsome, did you ever consider a Dutch braid, the false hawk, or the feathered look? all the rage; let's give you a finger wave then, a fishtail, flattop, flipflop, French twist, fringe cut . . . or how about half a ponytail, half an updo? no? so you're that sort, a Hime cut, what say, okay? . . . hi-top with a fade . . . you know what, a loose curl would look great on you—old liberty spikes—like the statue, see there*—your hair is standing up like it was scared; *so a Mohawk, what do you think, handsome? a mullet . . . a mullet?* come on, honey, be brave; *do pageboy, pigtails, pixie cut—look cute—pompadour—look hip—full pony tail— look perky—whoa! is recon, rattail, or the notorious frat shag on sale?* I know your head and how it grows: from pasted wig to when it's amorously tousled; *we've got a full range; you could try a purely spiky look if you think it suits you, sure, or make your head into an ocean of waves, anything that floats; we remove short hairs, do nails till they cry uncle; we cut long tresses, trim beards—only as you wish, sure—schurre—we shave cheeks too, clean as a tin whistle—we will grease your moustache till it shines like a saloon sign—oh dear—you prefer the same cut as last time?—oh, yes, I remember—as it used to be—as it has always been.* Hey, ask those chairs their opinion and they will tell you: your fortune depends on how you wear your hair, and what your shadow on the wall will say—those splotches where your heads rested . . . by the way, what *did* become of you?

Walter had the menu memorized. He would point like a conductor to the faded poster on the wall while he chanted the shop's selections, though no one ever challenged the availability of his hairstyles, so I had no handy measure for the truth of his boast. The safely tethered children remained mum and wide-eyed and Walter wore a grin broader than the local river. The other barbers would applaud with a rattle of spoons in their coffee mugs.

It was a friendly place, a little stuffy from piped-in warmth through the winter, but blossoming with habitués at all times of year because, as every person not cursed by baldness knows, hair in plenty grows, through droughts and blights and snows, but not in tidy rows. Not them. Not those. Walter told his clientele that they were presently enjoying his garden, not theirs, and that he harvested head hair, ear hair, nostrils, brows, while cultivating the colorful blooms of fingernails, sandaled toes and inked eyes. At her table at the back of the shop, Millicent manicured the ladies, but she took a little trolley to the chairs to tend the men. There they held out a shy paw and, bashful about such primping, hid their vanity in a din of rough male sports talk, political opinion, scandal, and local news, all in a language meant to impress one another and intrigue Millicent, who was immune to shock.

Prince Paul claims that Millicent (I never heard a natal name) dresses like a whore—painted nails, piled hair, bright cheeks, ample bosom (a sample showing), a tight short sheath, and heels that double her height—but how would he know if none of the rest of us knows, and none of the rest of us, I can assure you, knows? We know nothing about clothes, only a bit about hair, nothing much about bodies, and only a touch about mascara, a few pomades, and some rouge. That's Prince Paul, though . . . he's good at pretending.

Behind those big businesslike barber chairs, several shampoo sinks interrupt a narrow glass shelf where numerous bottles mingle among the mirrors like guests at a ball, frisking between shears, brushes, whisks, and fist-sized piles of moist and steaming cloths. Oils, conditioners, rinses, talcums, tonics, lotions mill about while, for stability, a more disciplined row of antiseptic bottles, brilliantine, and restorative goos stands at attention against the wall. These are alleged to be good for baldness. I know them by their glints. Women, even more than men, will try anything to prevent hair loss. I was told the shelf resembled a bar but my only encounter with bars has been with wooden ones and these were burned by cigarettes or ringed by drinks and other ghosts of grief.

When fellows come to get their face shaved, their hair cut and hair oiled, they tend to sit in seats that we felt represented their favorite themes when they chatted with the barber and the other bucks who were also hanging out. I am remembering one conk head named Harold who used to come in to have his fuzzed dome mowed for just a buck and who plunked himself down on Overly Neighborly to—Walter joked—"weight" his turn. He would sigh like a squeaking tire—Walter joked—and address those who were there—how many or how few did not restrain him—"So, did you know that one of the lost tribes of Israel was black?" This was greeted with the silence it deserved.

So much clutter . . . Buttons . . . Marbles . . . Pins . . . The race of human beings called Human Beings by human beings is turning the world into a tool like me and my friends: a utensil, a kettle, a car. Watch it . . . Those curling irons, holstered in a block of wood, can get hot . . . We hugely outnumber them now, this squanderous tribe of people who invented us, who use us, and will discard us in mounds made of our remains. Combs alone outnumber the heads they coif. Scissors are in the same situation, pens, coins, rings, buckles, pistols. Most people have a couple. Even plants in pots or aunts in hoards can't measure up to the miles of tools in stores, tons of junk heaped in yards, knickknacks galore storming pantry shelves and parlor tables, and assorted spools of stuff, in multiples and variations, boxed and bagged and trucked hither and yon, yon and hither, to be displayed or stored, sold or stolen. When they dig our civilization up, and with those shards try to guess the rest, we shall outnumber the bones of Human Beings in offering clues. Think of it: the leaves of books may beat the leaves of trees in turning. And there are fewer cats than summer clothes.

Everyone enjoyed the soft blue haze left by the customers' cigarettes. The smokers were mostly men, though Millicent swallowed her menthols like someone in a sideshow. Chewers alone were frowned on. A wad in the cheek would dissolve in spit and soon the spit was oiling the floor. Which was made of squares of linoleum. Anyhow everyone enjoyed the haze left by lit cigarettes, smoky exhalations—thought in ghostly guise. The resulting communal breath seemed like a river of air that carried the fellowship of the shop from chair to chair. I know I never tired of our atmosphere: the smell of polish always pleased me, and the vigorous shine Archie would apply to some businessman's shoes made a nice noise, the way the smell of coffee stirs us to ride forth in the morning.

Our customers were a mixture of races, unusual to be found, I understand, in this geography; but the reality is that the mix was thin and came and went as the neighborhood did, slowly shrinking as the whites took to their heels and the street's vacancies grew, swelling when poverty, like hunger, overtook its clientele. Serving such different heads was not easy. People born with hair bent like wire make a mistake to want it straight. Straights want swirls. Brunets weep to be blond. Guys who have lots of it want their heads shaven and shiny. Learn, ladies, to be happy with the hue Our Great Maker gave you. As for my tribe of folding chairs—well, to us, asses differ only by weight. We ask two questions of our clients: how thin? how fat? That is that.

When they dig our civilization up, and with those shards try to guess the rest, we shall outnumber the bones of Human Beings in offering clues.

Every Front Room has a back room. That's where the joint's john flushes; where a restful rocker rocks; and an eight-place poker table swallows the central space. Barbers not on duty lazed there, playing solitaire, smoking one of the aforesaid cigarettes or reading the racing magazines. Walter took bets. On heralded occasions. For the Derby or the local track. And an evening game of poker took place, maybe once a week, sometimes twice, when a few friends dropped in and some chairs were enlisted to take care of the additional arrivals.

I understand and employ the word "herald," because I was sometimes placed, for an evening, in the doorway of the shop as a signal to knowledgeable passersby that poker was "on" at 10:00 PM. "Okay, old fellow, you can be our herald tonight," Walter would say to me, though we both knew he was talking to himself. He likes to do that—be coy with a razor or angry with a comb. An occasional snarl would draw an expletive from him, followed by a small speech, all this for the amusement of the customer who was having his hair pulled.

Such outpost service is humiliating. You have been parked there, in the doorway, because no one will steal you, worn and rusty as you are, and there you must sit until the number of places for players has been fulfilled, whereupon you are removed from that spot to the poker room itself, your seat to be occupied by a nervous stranger from the street who has been brought to the shop by a friend and has, in any case, not come because of *your* ungainly presence. Regulars tend to be pros at poker and do not squirm in their seats like infants, though they may allow their eyes to wink and slide to one side, their nose to wrinkle and snort a swinish snort, their lips to grin or curl or smirk as if in commentary, or sometimes they like to release their grip on the cards for an expansive, apparently careless gesture, in order to mislead and deceive the other players. Meanwhile, I chatted with the chips in the pot.

Doorman duty does pay some interest, face to face as you are with the street and brushed by the people passing, hurrying home after another warm day, with their anxieties safely snacked in their purses. Once in a while a funny thing will happen as it happened to Natty Know-it-all. Which is as follows: a little white truck double-parks in front of the shop and a guy runs to the rear of it. Then, before Natty can prepare himself, this hasty kid plops a large tub of chrysanthemums in Nat's lap. Well, I didn't mean a comical happening. Apologies if I misled you. I meant strange. I meant odd. I meant mysterious. It was early fall, we all remember, at the very edge of evening, and the flowers were already half-lit, a pale pink, I think it was, the color of an embarrassed cheek, but, when fisted into a bunch by a determined hand, might be as perky as could be. Nat can't make a ring-a-ding about the delivery, since his back is to us and mostly out of sight in the doorway recess. Lordy, he would have said if he could have. Lordy, this is quite a different kind of ass than I am used to making room for, he would have said, I'm sure, given a reason or a way.

> **That's how long the night was—as long as the letters *m* and *n* spell "me and my mind's memory."**

So he sat there as the few lights along the street began to glow. The flowerpot was damp and cooling. He says it felt nice on a warm night. But the mums were playing their part in a puzzle. Which was as follows: Sam and Mart should have gone home through the front door. Neither of them participated in the poker game. That was Walter's show. And when Sam and Mart left work they always ran their hands, in a kind of friendly gesture, over the curving blue back of whichever one of us was on watch. As far as I knew, the green metal door to the alley was never used. I mean the door opposite the john in the poker room. Which I refer to as the green metal door to the alley. So I say: how? how did they go without spotting the pot, or the pot spotting them, for gosh sake?

In this way Natty passed his time that night. The moment the plant was delivered, the truck sped away. Some unknown person had parked before the shop, under the traditional red-and-white-striped spiral that had long ago stopped its dizzy spinning; a man, a young man maybe, had got out, was he the driver? did he take the pot from the rear of the truck or just come around the rear with it in his arms to deposit the . . . possibly a present? yes, a gift. The street emptied. The bouquet . . . can we say? sat in Know-it-all's lap. Shadows ran together. The flowers were waiting, maybe, to have their blossoms shorn. Know-it-all didn't know it all, after all. The plant was uncommunicative. A place at the poker table must have remained empty because no one came to put Natty next to Perse. Hours passed. Darkness erased definition. That's how long the night was—as long as the letters *m* and *n* spell "me and my mind's memory."

On wagerless nights Walter would leave last, checking the lights and other equipment, locking the door with a brass key; and just before he began his hike home, he'd pause before the window to give it scrutiny while inside we waited for his image to be eaten. On poker nights the front door would be busy until eleven before Walt locked up from inside. The game could then begin. Walt's pick of folding chairs for backroom service was pretty random, though I was chosen often enough to learn the game. I thought I became rather good at it. Never play to win a particular pot, never become enamored of your pairs, because no odds apply to particulars. Just keep track of the way the bidding breaks. Then follow the odds like a private eye. Fold when history tells you. Over the long haul you'll be a winner more often than not.

One of our regulars (for a time) was an undercover cop. He would slink into the shop at the end of the day, seat himself on Prince, and hide behind a magazine—*The Boxer's Monthly*, I believe—biting his cigar with yellow teeth. After a discreet interval, he'd stuff its dead stub in his mouth and slip away to the game. There, Walt would let him win one or two deals. It was a reasonable payoff. Some guys grumbled about it but Walt knew what he was doing. A little insurance, he said, against arrest. That's all. And a lot easier to give away than a free shave.

While dealing, Walt would sometimes hum mumble a tune—his "Auntie's in the Pantry" song. It really riled the other players. Mostly because they couldn't hear all the lines clearly and found themselves straining to understand something they didn't want to be bothered with. This is how his jingle went, as I made it out:

What say you, chips,
As you accumulate
In the axis of the action?
Ante up, man, ante up.
Rattle your fist to simulate
the greed of the clattering cup.
Roll the craps, dude, shake and roll.
I'm twenty-one and lots of fun.
You can find me on the stroll,
Wagging my hips, rouging my lips.
Ante up, mate, ante up.
I know how to flip an ace,
Quietly fold or make a face.
Whatcha got guy, whatchagot?
Threes are wild and I'm with child
hid like a card in a lousy hand.
Not at all as we had planned.
Ante up, man, ante up.

The fact that Know-it-all was doing an all-nighter weighed heavily upon me the way fat men, waiting their turn at the clippers, deepened the thin crease of my back. Dawn was arriving piecemeal, like a present awkwardly wrapped, when the chrysanthemums—it must have been they—exploded, blowing away the glass front of the shop and hurling Natty out into the street, bent and spent, in a skid to the sidewalk opposite. Shards of glass rattled across the bare seats of those of us inside the shop, and slivers scratched our backs when we were blown against one another. Deadly Reckoning suffered a slightly bowed leg; Barry Buttock was seriously scarred; Overly Neighborly sailed out of his place in our row to strike Millie's table so forcibly its wheels would never revolve again; both Perce and Commander Prince Paul were pelted by chrysanthemum leaves and pieces of dirt; while I, Mister Middle, rocked against Perce and Prince Paul, shoving them so intently their eight legs screeched in protest.

Leaves, petals, and pottery flew hither and yon, plaster dust settled on the barbers' chairs so abundantly you could write on them—and later, Matt would, with his finger inspired to reach eloquence. All of a sudden the place filled with police.

Who was this bomb intended for? We chairs as a group or just Know-it-all, who could be an enormous nuisance sometimes, but still . . . or the glassware?—jars and mirrors?—bottles or cloths?—of course not . . . only a few Brilliantine bottles went pop; no, and it was not likely aimed at razors either, none of whom were injured, or any one or more of the heating irons, or the big chairs on which Walter wrote his boast, "I survived, bless God!"? We first thought it had to be one or more of the human beings, but when the bomb went off all of them had gone home—we assumed—and were safe in bed. This crowd didn't play poker all night, just till two. When counting casualties, they were without a scratch. Maybe the bomb didn't go off when it was intended to—but later than intended. Maybe someone—it would be Walt—was expected to see it sitting there in Know-it-all's lap and bring it in to be admired. Maybe it was meant for a late customer. By a sore loser. I was told that gambling parlors such as Walt ran were illegal, but the cop was fixed, and the sums wagered at the table, as far as I could assess them, were not as much as the professionals played for, though pitifully more than any of these players could afford.

Maybe the bomb didn't go off when it was intended to—but later than intended.

Most mysterious, most calamitous of all: we did not see any of the barbers leave for home, or stay for cards, or hear a late-in-the-day customer say, "Here! What's this?" and bring the pot in, or yell at Walt, "Hey, you got a plant on your front porch" while walking off to other business, innocent of evil intention in every alternative. Where, in the container, was the explosive placed? Was it buried in the soil or propped against the plant? Was it a firework or vial of nitro or piece of plaster or a grenade? Was propelling Natty so forcibly across the street a likely direction for an explosive planted in the soil of a flowerpot parked in the seat of a folding chair? The police didn't say much about anything, I think because they didn't know anything. The victims—well, they were the shop and some of its fixings—the victims were about to complain to an insurance company instead of the cops but found both were impossible because the complainers were just *things*. Sam and Mart were annoyed they hadn't been hurt. Mildly maimed, mind you. Pleasantly pained . . . A few feigned mental fatigue but not for long; it was too tiring. The cops, for their part, picked up lots of pieces of burst dirt, blown plant, and broken glass that were reverently popped into clear plastic bags as they had seen themselves do on TV, protecting clues from contamination. They interviewed everybody in a human skin by asking, "What do you know about this?" Otherwise, the Law stood around shrugging its shoulders and speaking vaguely about lab work.

Poor Natty Know-it-all could no longer fold neatly to stack, no longer stand steady to sit; he was an innocent servant of happenstance, and whatever remained of him was to be borne away in the rear of a city truck like the trash he had become. What were we doing, meanwhile? We were wondering—I must say, pathetically—whether this destruction would put an end to the shop; whether we would all be out of a job, and headed for Nattie's junk pile. Oh sure, we knew that our bodies could be mashed flatter than a street, and melted like metal into metal, and thus revived for the doubtful pleasures of another life; but these conclusions were hardly palatable to us, not after our life in the barber shop—a good regular job, some appreciation, companionship, and—I would say—clean, even elegant, surroundings.

I now remember only one other act of violence occurring in the shop over the years. I wonder whether there was any connection. I should think not. As follows: Walt and Marty were woofing around with a client who was undergoing a trim to his beard; Marty was pretending he was about to cut his customer's throat the way they pretend in the movies, grinning like kids up to something, drawing the blade slowly upward under the chin; when, with a noise that could only be called a growl, Archie stopped polishing Sam's guy's shoes, grabbed Barry Buttock by one leg, and flung him at Marty and Marty's customer's throat, and the razor too, I dare say. Barry banged into Sam's raised arm instead, so the blade did scratch a customer's throat, Mart's man jerked his head and swiped away the hot cloth covering his eyes, all and each with a howl of their own; Barry tumbled to the floor near a tin of polish, and Archie bulldozed his way out the door into the street.

I swear we never saw Archie after that. No one again polished shoes in the shop or hung up coats, and lived on tips. Nothing was broken by the bashing. Nothing was said. Barry Buttock was examined and found able to stand sternly enough where he ordinarily belonged. Walt acted ashamed of something. He did say . . . he did say "geez." The customer wiped his face and left without paying. He walked very carefully. We never saw him again either. I had forgotten all this until just now. Oh yes, Mister Razor boasted to me that he had dulled his own blade to prevent any real injury. I never believed him. He was a well-known credit taker.

The way we are misused is no worse than any other. I am not like a lot of my companions, bitter about people, or despairing of my own nature, the way glass feels because it can be seen through—ha ha—nor am I surprised to have learned from knives that they have conserved their animus like juice in jam jars, waiting for dullness or—contrarily—the best time to snap, or how to hurry a finger toward the cut that awaits it. In the opinion of the barber guys, the way utensils are misused is no worse than any other treatment, however widespread, that the human species has handed out to Mother Nature: hills are burrowed or leveled, lakes pumped dry, seas emptied of life, trees cut, forests burnt. It is no matter with men what damage they do, or their paved streets and ubiquitous cellars accomplish. They murder the very ground they walk on—it's all right—so why should we few chairs complain about a rusty pinion, a small tear, some slight impulsive knockabout?

After the bomb we collected our spirits as well as we could and sat through the inadequate renovations that Walt could afford. Nevertheless, our reopening didn't bring our old customers back. No one likes to chance it. After all, there was no reason and no warning. Destruction just appeared like the ghost of broken dishes does during Easter or the Christmas holidays. The light that falls on glassware now is as tepid as wash water from a strangled rag. It leaves, when it hits me, no differently than before, except that it departs more the way a sigh does than a joyous whoopee from a winner. The marks on the wall where our customers' hair once leaned will, I bet, be here long after we are removed to the scrap heap, separated from one another for the first time, and unable to feel the warm reassuring weight of a single human ass.

So we wait as much in daylight, as in the darkness of the shop, for the end of our adventures. On her wavelength, hardly heard, a lipstick is sobbing.

If it suits me in my heart to say it went this way, why not say it went this way, say I.

INTERVIEW

MANY-LAYERED ANGER

Greg Gerke

A conversation with William Gass

William H. Gass recently turned eighty-eight years old. He is, by any standard, one of the world's great living writers. On March 12 of next year, Knopf will release his third novel, *Middle C*—after his first two, *Omensetter's Luck* (1966) and *The Tunnel* (1995), registered as thunderclaps. Gass is also the author of the celebrated collections of novellas and stories *In the Heart of the Heart of the Country* and *Cartesian Sonata*. In these works of fiction, Gass creates worlds where the characters try to find their way amid inhumanity and where language honors equally the horror and the beauty of life.

But as impressive as these works of fiction are, they make up only a part of Gass's immense contribution to arts and letters. He's also a distinguished essayist and critic, author most recently of the collection *Life Sentences* and of such now-canonical books as *Fiction and the Figures of Life* and *Reading Rilke*. His subjects vary but the work is always richly observed, emotionally acute, and at the same time playful—full of wisdom and the uncanny understanding of a man who taught philosophy for fifty years. A William H. Gass topic could be an examination of the word *and*, a lecture on metaphor, an examination of lust, a philosophical treatise on the color blue—and that's not to mention the book reviews that are always more than mere summary, branching into the deepest questions of language and being.

The essays and fiction are part of the same "writing problem." As an artist, Gass is dedicated to the most basic elements of language: words and sentences—the bones, blood, and flesh of writing. Every sentence tells a story and he has made it his duty to construct each with great attention to its poetic and rhythmic qualities, with such alliterative gambits as "Why should another's body be so beautiful its absence is as painful as the presence of your own?" from *The Tunnel*, and these crisp bits of economy from the essay "The Soul Inside the Sentence": "Words are with us everywhere. In our erotic secrecies, in our sleep. We're often no more aware of them than our own spit, although we use them oftener than legs."

Last October I visited Bill Gass in St. Louis, Missouri, near Washington University, where he taught for thirty years and founded the International Writer's Center, which later became the Center for the Humanities. Bill and his wife, Mary, warmly welcomed me into their opulent space dedicated to art and containing a library that now numbers over twenty thousand books. After talking to Bill during a celebration of Elizabeth Bishop at the university the afternoon before, I spent most of a Monday at his home, capped by a wonderful dinner with him and his wife. I asked everything I could, but mostly, all I had to do was listen.

GREG GERKE: You are known both as an essayist and a writer of fiction. In your work, one medium seems to inform the other: *The Tunnel* contains some mini-essays and bits of fictional situations make their way into the essays. Do you view both in the same terms? Is one more important to you than another?

WILLIAM H. GASS: I think in one sense, the fiction's what matters most to me. But in composing them, my attention is the same for both genres. Sometimes the boundary between the two is better kept a boundary. The essays are the pieces that are likely to veer off into the perimeters. But I've always just thought of them both as writing chores. The main thing that's different is—and it's important—the essays have a reason to be written, they were called for; and the fiction has no reason to be written. It was not called for. The essays always have a deadline. So they get written. Whereas the fiction doesn't have a deadline, and so it doesn't get written. Fiction allows me—because there are no expectations, there is no job to fulfill—to be more outrageous, or daring, or whatever you want to call it.

GG: "Hate finds nothing hard," you write in *Omensetter's Luck*. And in an interview in the *Paris Review* you said, "I write because I hate. A lot. Hard." Can you talk about this agent called "hate"? Is hate what gets things done in the world?

WHG: Of a certain sort, I think it certainly does. It involves intellectual dislike. There's

As you get more successful, that anger doesn't diminish much, because you know philistines are always there, but you are softened by a little success.

the visceral passion that puts someone's head on a pike, but intellectual hate is Swiftian. I mean, Swift hated how mankind behaves. I hate the species too, but I like people. I don't have trouble with people. It's the kind of thing that makes you throw down the *New York Times* in disgust after you've read about some other horrible business that's going on, you know. It's that kind of anger, and that kind of anger lasts well. There is, of course, the very personal anger too. When you're trying to get started in the writing business, you want to do something new, but no one wants what you write, and you keep getting rejected. I spent eight years hearing the thud of my manuscripts on the porch. I couldn't even get a letter to the editor published. Nothing. And you get frustrated and mad at the literary world, and the people who support mediocrity and call it excellence. And that involves your pride and all the rest of vanity's baggage. As you get more successful, that anger doesn't diminish much, because you know philistines are always there, but you are softened by a little success, and it's harder for you to say—it's harder for me now to say—"hate wrote it," though nobody pays any attention to me. Nobody does, but it's a different kind of being ignored, you know? So those things change over time. Some people have the bad luck to be received and applauded right away. That's usually going to turn out badly, because the second book or the third one is just going to get slapped around. The early bird genius will be very unhappy. So my anger is many-layered. It continues to annoy me that writers whom I admire are still on the margin. My fiction's still on the margin. It is still refused.

GG: Do you think it's good that nothing comes easily to a writer?

WHG: For me, yeah. But everybody's different. When your first novel fills your plate with praise, then you're inclined to repeat yourself. You don't set the bar higher. I think the great writers and fine artists in general, as they get older, they set the bar higher, and sooner or later they will fail. *Finnegan's Wake* doesn't come first. *Dubliners* comes first. *Dubliners* is almost extraordinary as it fits in the course of Joyce's development. It wasn't thought to be so fine when it came out, though. Finally Joyce finishes *Finnegans Wake*. You know, what is he going to write next? Same

> The writer ought to age like wine. Think of Beethoven quartets. The later music gets more complex and difficult, but better.

way with Beckett and other experimenters like them. The writer ought to age like wine. Think of Beethoven quartets. The later music gets more complex and difficult, but better. James's early novels are beautiful, but the late novels are challenging, and that's because even a professional writer like James doesn't want to write the same damn thing year after year. He wants to see something else is opening up as a possibility. You can want to arrive at glory too fast. I think Malcolm Lowry had that trouble. He wanted to change the novel and the short story overnight. Lowry's *Through the Panama* is boring in many places, but it is also extraordinarily inventive. Once you can knit ninety miles an hour, you want to go one hundred. Otherwise, you just start repeating. My new novel is so simple compared to *The Tunnel*. But I had to do something different. Nope, I didn't want the same kind of complexity at all. The late work of the most successful artists I know is their best.

GG: I've always been interested in how great artists rarely comment on their peers, or only on some of them. I know you have celebrated many of yours, such as William Gaddis, John Barth, Stanley Elkin, John Hawkes, Robert Coover, and Alexander Theroux—and those are only the Americans. I wonder if I could get your viewpoint on a few celebrated writers of English that I haven't heard you talk about. J. M. Coetzee would be one.

WHG: Oh, yeah. Well, there are certain writers that I don't talk about because they have problems with me and I have problems with them. One of the best pieces written about my book on Rilke [*Reading Rilke*]—which is, indeed, highly critical of me—is Coetzee's essay. He's smart, he did his job, and stated his opinion. But I can't write about him now. It will suddenly look as if I'm justifying myself. He says some things that are quite wrong. Factual things. But you know the passage of a fierce intelligence over your work is much to be desired. Some of my pieces are only celebratory. I mean, they're for pals of some sort. You don't speak of reservations. Stanley Elkin used to say, "It's impossible to write something about my books that I like. No praise is sufficient." You know, if you write something about someone you know and love—that doesn't mean you like everything they write, but are you going to go around speaking of shortcomings? You won't have friends. John Gardner learned that. And he couldn't win. I understand Barth was infuriated by

Gardner's treatment. Hawkes was also infuriated because he wasn't mentioned. What can you do? I swore a while back that I'd only write about books I liked. And I stopped writing about anyone alive. Then I wrote about a writer I had written unfavorably about a couple times, Roth. He wrote, I thought, a terrific book, *The Counterlife*, which I reviewed enthusiastically. But suppose I hadn't liked it. Why write some pie-in-the-face essay on Updike? I was critical of him when I was younger and still mad. And then I realized that the man I was mad at was not Updike, who was a true gentleman and a good critic and so forth, but the mediocre level of writing his critics carried on about. But it's easy to be asked to write something about Jack Hawkes if you just get to talk about the sentences. It's fun. I think it is wise to stay away from an honest critique of people that you like who are still alive. Knut Hamsun I detest, but he's dead. So I don't write about them. I wouldn't have written about any of those people normally, but they asked me to write the preface to their book, so out of friendship I wrote the preface, or something. I wouldn't write about Stanley and make him mad unless he had asked me to. I'd much rather write about Colette, so I can say what I want. And she wrote a lot of slush. Most writers do.

GG: Any thoughts on Sebald?

WHG: I haven't read him. I read about ten pages. That wasn't fair to him. But I could see the rush of this wave of popularity that is almost a death knell. So I'm gonna have to go back sometime when the critical flimflam has calmed down and see. Sometimes these fads are actually very good. Actually, I don't believe that. I'm very arrogant about my judgment. I don't make mistakes. But I need to take a hard look.

GG: Is that the case with Foster Wallace too?

WHG: He had great abilities. I think he needed to tame them. I think he was so good that he should've wanted to be better. And he wrote some things that are going to stay around. I wish he had stayed around and done more of that. He had lots of smarts too. He was also popular with the college crowd. Not a good sign. But he knew his math and philosophy. A good sign. Pynchon's a similar case. He didn't die; he just disappeared. I have tried to read Pynchon with no success so far, but then, I can't read Whitman—I try. Some of us have blank spots. We can't like everything, and I don't see any rule requiring it. Why should you love every woman who walks by?

GG: In your fiction there is a great interest in insects. In "Order of Insects," a woman dwells on cockroaches. "In the Heart of the Heart of the Country" and "Emma Enters a Sentence of Elizabeth Bishop" both contain wonderful sections on flies, and *The Tunnel* has an extended section on grasshoppers. It seems you have spent some time contemplating them. There is also a rich history of writers using them, as Donne has his flea,

Yeats his fly, and Beckett gives Molloy some dancing bees. What draws you to insects? What makes them such a fitting metaphorical subject for writers?

WHG: I used to study them for fun. Sweet companions. We had a downstairs john, and there was a little crack in its window, and there was this spider who spun his web in the window next to the john. I would sit myself down, breathe upon the web, watch him, and he would come out. And we would have a discussion.

GG: This was when you were a boy?

WHG: No. Forty-some years ago. When I was living in this little town, I got to know the bats, which I'm very fond of, and the spiders. But then I had a pet butterfly. This monarch. And it got hurt on a highway. That is, I'm assuming the draft of a car broke a wing as it was flying, and so it couldn't fly up. It could flutter around. I found it, and I carried him in, fed him, and he would come and sit on my shoulder, and I would feed him on the counter up in the kitchen, just honey and sugar water. He would come down and drink. We'd put him on a vase to sit upon the flowers. We had him for about six weeks. And at night, I'd put him on top of a curtain. But we had a cat. And that was a problem, keeping the cat from getting that damn butterfly. And eventually, she did. But with the kids, we used to find larvae and then watch them hatch, and read a lot of naturalist stuff. Yesterday, we had out here on top of the pool cover—right in the middle, where there's some collected water—we had a red-shouldered hawk. Stood in the middle of that puddle and washed his feathers. And this morning we heard the song of the white-throated sparrow, which signifies winter coming. This is a great trunk line for migratory birds, all the way up the Mississippi, and people go out just to watch the eagles at migration time. Tremendous. Ducks come swim in our pool. Geese. And there's a park here that bird-watchers go crazy in, because it has so many different kinds of birds in there all the time. When I was a kid it wasn't insects; it was snakes.

GG: In *On Being Blue*, you say, "A muff, a glove, a stocking, the glass a lover's lips have touched, the print of a shoe in the snow; how is it that these simple objects can receive our love so well that they increase it?" Your answer is because they become concepts, while the body of the beloved alters and "escapes our authority and powers." Do we trust objects more than people?

WHG: I certainly do. Spinoza did. "Love ideas," he said. There was one of these terrible TV shows where they were dissecting bodies. And the guy says, "This is the time when the body tells the truth." And in a sense, that's so. But it's worse. Consciousness. There are people whose everyday consciousness may be just awful, but who create a consciousness, a way of seeing things, that is great in itself. Emerson was on the right track, I think, at one point during the end

The only thing wrong with getting old too is you have to watch where you're walking, not because you want to see what's there but because you don't want to fall down.

of his life when he was disillusioned, that what philosophy is all about is to provide structures for the various emotions and feelings—he calls them moods—about the world. And they're all true at some times, because they describe our relationship to our surroundings. And there are days when you are in a Schopenhauer mood, and everything seems the way it is that day. But you're not, in the normal course of life, aware of all this stuff. You're just taking out the garbage. The only thing wrong with getting old too is you have to watch where you're walking, not because you want to see what's there but because you don't want to fall down. It's preoccupying. I'm talking about the garbage. But again, when I was photographing, I photographed garbage. And sometimes it was a rotten watermelon—wow! Rotten! Beautiful!

GG: Concerning the history of *Omensetter's Luck*, there is the infamous episode of one Edward Drogo Mork (a fellow teacher, but more a con artist) who stole the only copy of the manuscript from your office in Purdue. He tried to publish parts of it as a play, but was found out. In the afterword of *Omensetter's Luck*, you say you may still carry his murder in your heart. Was this sordid episode instrumental in your new novel, *Middle C*, which concerns a professor coming from Europe to a university in Ohio to teach a subject he's not qualified in?

WHG: Not really, even though its principal figure also teaches at a college. The new book, though, is based more on an actual event. When I first started to earn my living in the world, I was teaching at a college called Wooster, in Ohio. And there arrived on the campus one day an Englishman who taught history. The officials had hired him. He was charming, and had huge audiences for his classes. He'd been there about two or three months when the authorities came around and said, "This guy is a fake, a bigamist, and his name is Peters, and he's wanted by the English and the Canadian police." And everybody was shocked, because everyone had made him over as such a brilliant man and so forth. That was all that actually happened, but I thought, Well, I want to talk about—or deal with—somebody who's a counterfeit of that sort. Professor Skizzen obtains his positions with false CVs—he's a decent enough person, really—but he gradually expands his dreamland to include the

Actually, you have a little story even in a sentence. For me, formally, the sentence is a narrative made by the linear progression of words.

classes he starts to teach. The book says a lot about the academic world, because it partly covers when he is a student in a school, as well as when he ends up a music teacher. As a fraud, he's better than most genuine people. Eventually he creates in his attic a museum of human catastrophes. "The Inhumanity Museum," he calls it. So he's doing that, but that's it (like my other novels, this is a book in which nothing happens). In addition he has an obsession, a sentence he's trying to get straight, and it never seems to go together right.

GG: One sentence?

WHG: One sentence. And it is something to the effect of "He"—or somebody—"used to be concerned about the fate of the human race, and that it might be destroyed. Now he's worried that it won't be." It's a much lighter book than my others. There's a lot of talk about Schoenberg because Skizzen pretends—when he goes to this Ohio college-town college—he pretends to be a Schoenberg specialist, because nobody knows much about Schoenberg. They hate Skizzen, but they're worried about it. So he can get away with it. And that's why he picks Schoenberg. He doesn't really like Schoenberg.

GG: Did you ever write longhand?

WHG: Oh, no. My parents got me a typewriter when I was, I think, fourteen. An Underwood portable. And I kept it for years. I didn't go to a computer until 1990. I went to California. The Getty Museum. And they said, "What kind of computer do you want to use?" It was a wonderful place.

GG: It was a sabbatical?

WHG: I was invited to go there to do research. I had been writing on architecture. And I think that's what they expected me to be doing. But they were very happy to accommodate my plans. There's nothing like having a patron that has six billion dollars. I went out there with six hundred pages of *The Tunnel* done. And I wrote the second half of the book there in one year, because the circumstances were just marvelous. No distractions.

GG: You needed that to finish it?

WHG: I had been bottling up. It was also easier, because the last part of the book was supposed to be easier to get a hold of than the first part. And I had a marvelous assistant whom my work didn't require. I had a poor guy who was there trying to be helpful. He was doing his own work, but he was a fellow, so he was supposed to be of service. He got us tickets to symphonies and got me in with the Lannan people who were out there—they supported marvelous readings. That was a big help for me later. And I found out I could just work nonstop. There was nothing else to do except that. And so the book doubled. And the secretaries took my typescript and transferred all of it, spacing and everything else, onto the machine. They did it in off-hours, or when they weren't busy. It was a terrific job, a difficult job, and they were wonderful. So I had that. Now and then, gifts fall from the sky. Not just calamities.

GG: So you wrote the book pretty much sequentially?

WHG: Yeah, not entirely, but close.

GG: Because it does seem there's fewer of the drawings and the boldface and different fonts in the second half of the book.

WHG: I wanted to move away from that—to leave Kohler's (the main character in *The Tunnel*) diddling behind. I also wrote some sections of the front part and then deliberately broke them up, scattered pieces, and rearranged them. But for the back part I didn't do that.

GG: Do you edit by reading aloud?

WHG: All the time. Everything. Over and over and over.

GG: All of *The Tunnel*? You read the whole thing out loud?

WHG: Every step of the way. Oh yeah, many times. The same way I had to read more than once Elizabeth Bishop's *The Moose* so I could recite it. The reader's eye goes too fast. Bishop's a slow boat really, because you have to put a lot of weight on every word. I remember, when I was teaching her, I'd have to say, "Whoa! Slow down." It had partly to do with her compulsion with the facts. Had to have all the facts just right. She fitted the *New Yorker* just perfectly, because the *New Yorker* is staffed with nothing but niggardly fact-checkers. "Do flowers really bloom in New Brunswick in October?" And she'd run off and consult old issues of magazines to justify her mentioning them and quoting from them or something, as in "In the Waiting Room." I'm talking about the *National Geographic* details.

GG: When thinking about the differences between so-called language-driven writers and story-driven writers, I've almost come to understand (at the same time reading that you espoused, "You do not tell a story; your fiction will do that when your fiction is finished"), that story is always implicit in the language-driven writers' works, the story takes care of itself. What we get in *King Lear*, *The Lime Twig*, and *The Portrait of a*

Lady is a miasma of color and sound; the world is all things, no matter if description or dialogue. Do you feel the implicitness of story as you write? Or do the prose rhythms press you into those areas?

WHG: Sometimes. Actually, you have a little story even in a sentence. For me, formally, the sentence is a narrative made by the linear progression of words. I have to read the words that way. Then with my mind, I am bringing back everything in the predicate to the subject and making the modifications that each part of it has made to the larger context: the sentence or paragraph or whatever it is. And then it's the narration that gets complicated, because narration at that level only begins with "Shall I put Goliath first in 'David slew Goliath,' or shall I say, 'Goliath was slain by David'?" Grammarians aren't going to help you there, because they think that the passive voice is, first of all, weak. But why weak? They don't even know. And they don't see the tremendous difference between those two sentences. They tell different stories. Which comes first, David's good luck or Goliath's demise? It's obvious whose side you're on. I have, in *Life Sentences*, an essay on narrative sentences. All sentences are narrations in the sense that when you drop a word into the ongoing sentence, add on a phrase or some circumlocution, you delay the final meaning. James loves to hold you in suspense as he goes on with his lists and his subjunctive clauses. Or you can withhold the real subject by putting it in the rear, like the Germans often do their verbs.

GG: In *Life Sentences*, in the essay called "The Aesthetic Structure of the Sentence," you quote Wallace Stevens as saying, "Those of us who understand that words are thoughts and not only our own thoughts but the thoughts of men and women ignorant of what it is that they are thinking, must be conscious of this: that, above everything else, poetry is words; and that words, above everything else, are, in poetry, sounds." Again and again, one hears so much emphasis on things other than language both in poetry and fiction today. The great music (language) of poetry and fiction is difficult, but eventually is the most satisfying aspect, because it gives again and again, like anything by Stevens or Joyce. How does one almost untrain oneself and start believing that words are also "the thoughts of men and women ignorant of what it is they are thinking"?

WHG: Well, all you have to do is practice on yourself. How do you know what is to come next in the sentence? Well, you have some sort of general idea, but what the sentence choice turns out to be is dictated more and more as you're listening to your own work, to elements that don't directly belong to the concepts you were dealing with initially. And so you're led. There's something about what's happening in your musical mind, say, that is leading the sentence to appear, choosing the words for you. When you get everybody pulling together—music and meaning—you get the effect you want. What is nicest is, of

What the sentence choice turns out to be is dictated more and more as you're listening to your own work.

course, to find you're being nudged by the vocal, but you don't want to have every sentence sound like Edith Sitwell. You want to organize and make sense out of it on a conceptual level as well as a physical, or musical, level. And indeed, a spatial level. Like a parking garage, there are a bunch of levels. And the oral includes some of them, not all of them. And some poets are better at one thing than another. Now, if I were to take a poem and write it out as a sentence, it would appear to be what it is: prose. The best poetry in the later part of my lifetime seems to be written by prose writers. All you have to do is pick up the books and see how the language flows, and read some of the poets. It's scary how nothing is there of the poetry. Hardy's very good to study in this regard. He gave up novel writing. He wrote some great poems.

GG: I wanted to ask about the "Why Windows are Important to Me" philippic in *The Tunnel*. Two key lines appear on opposing pages (296-7). They are pleas, really. "To be free is the greatest blessing the world never gives" and "Why should another's body be so beautiful its absence is as painful as the presence of your own?" The second particularly speaks to a condition that some people experience—loving being painful. They leave themselves just enough to be surprised that the other they love is not them and a recoil begins, as love turns to hate. These questions have been with us forever and literature has been saturated with them. Are we just voices in the dark, as Beckett seemed to say, asking to be recognized, asking for someone or something to take mercy on us?

WHG: It's close. That may be stipulating even more than is happening.

GG: Well, they're powerful enough to make me examine them. They have an effect. Not even intellectually. On so many levels.

WHG: Well, that's why in *Middle C*, this guy thinks, somehow, that if he can just get the one sentence right everything else will fall into line. He eventually solves his puzzle. Twelve tones, twelve words arranged in exactly the right way. And nothing whatever is in line. But yeah, you know, Beckett is quite good about all this, because every time one of his characters completes something—which is almost never—it just dissolves into another task. And explaining the universe is like that. Every once in a while some magazine or something asks all

> The sex or the sensuality comes in the treatment of the language, by which you might be putting on a pair of dungarees, you know?

kinds of people what the meaning of life is, and of course, it has no meaning. It isn't a sign. No. So we have to give it meaning. And that's why you have to decide whether you want to live in a Catholic four-bedroom house or a Jewish three-bedroom house, you know? Or something modern that has no ideological frame. It is nice to live without beliefs. People don't understand that. They think, "Gee, he doesn't believe this. He doesn't believe that. So he's miserable." But no, he has escaped a troublesome relative.

GG: In thinking of American writers and the sexual, I keep coming back to you and John Hawkes. The sexuality in at least a few of his books is orgiastic, but dark and murky as well. When you talk about the sexual, particularly in *The Tunnel* and "In the Heart of the Heart of the Country," such as the line "I dreamed my lips would drift down your back like a skiff on a river. I'd follow a vein with the point of my finger, hold your bare feet in my naked hands," you have a more celebratory view. It's also this way in your essays—metaphors of great desire, lust, touch, kiss. How important is sexuality and the sexual to your writing?

WHG: Oh, very. I'm a forsaken Freudian. I passed through a period. But one has to, first of all, disentangle talking about sex and using a word associated with sex. It's quite different. Because my work doesn't have much sexuality in any direct way. There's none, almost, in *Middle C*, by deliberation in terms of the character. But as used in *On Being Blue* or in *The Tunnel*, there's plenty of the words. The sex or the sensuality comes in the treatment of the language, by which you might be putting on a pair of dungarees, you know? The scene need not be sexual at all, but the language should be sensuous. And often you have a scene that is full of sexual words, but there isn't much sex to it at all, because it's just words. Most of the words that we think of as sexual aren't sexual. We destroyed that. It's very hard to imagine it. And it's idealized sex. And when we say, similarly, in music, that a violinist caresses some notes, it is a caress, but nobody had to take his shirt off. Explicit sex, I hardly ever write anything about that. A little bit, a tiny bit. A few pages in *The Tunnel*. That's it, as far as I remember. Another reason for avoiding that subject in an explicit way is that I want to avoid as much as possible situations, extreme situations, whose reality is strong, because then the reader is reading it like a newspaper or something. If you're going to write aesthetically about it, you have to defuse its power in order to get anybody to pay any attention to the nature of the prose. And that's what ninety percent of bad literature is. It's just referring to these scenes in so-called real life that would be quite shattering, or pornographic, or whatever. And it isn't art. A case in point: when Faulkner did the scene in *Sanctuary* where the girl is raped with a corncob, some people read that book and never even know that happened. He defused it. And in Greek tragedy, nothing happens with all this death that's going on all around, hardly any of it ever onstage. And, when it is put onstage, the critics just scream. It's so the chorus or the characters can talk about it, announce it, report it. And great language appears. That's one of the great difficulties Hawkes has, is to take something that is so revolting in life and write about it beautifully. And that makes people mad, you know? Because they think you're doing something, you're advising or approving the situation, which isn't the case. That's one reason he liked violence. There are scenes in *The Lime Twig* that are so beautiful, so awful. That's art, boy. And Beckett. People say, "I don't read Beckett. It's too grim." It's not grim at all. I mean, wow. But you have to go visit that and know how to disarm the world in order that it'll make room for you, your handling of it. If tragedies weren't tragic, nobody would go to them. *Hamlet* leaves nearly everybody dead. Of beautiful last words.

GG: So again it's a question of how far do you want to go into life rather than all the car crashes, which are kind of the sensory popcorn feeling.

WHG: The passage where I had to face this that's most obvious in *The Tunnel* is the scene set in the pit at Dubno, in which people are being machine-gunned. There's your extreme event. You want to get that horror examined and the event presented, but you won't want anybody screaming. I mean, you want the opposite of that, and of course you get an intensity of a different sort, you hope, but you don't want to envision it and then say, "What fun." That's not what you're after. But it's easier to dismiss the newspaper report: So many hundred people were killed yesterday by . . . Oh, that's terrible. But if you do the Dubno pit scene right, they don't forget the Dubno pit. And that's what you want, but it's a different level of feeling of things.

GG: It seems like your entire opus comes down to wrestling with the question of evil.

WHG: Well, that's certainly one question that's everybody's problem. We live in very bad times. Maybe there were other times worse or as bad. How can we measure? When things happened badly in medieval time, probably only a minor fraction of the people alive knew about it. Here, news about these things comes from every corner of the world. We're bombarded with not only the St. Louis daily murder of somebody and the deaths in Somalia, but then also with this tipped-over school bus and a bomb set off in a market. It's brutal. And we sit there and say, "Oh my God, this baby was in the lap of her mother sitting and looking at the TV when a bullet came through the house and killed it." Oh dear, indeed. Thanks to the National Rifle Association. Next page. It's incredible. Wife beating. Bankers who defraud are up next. But we sigh and turn the page. We have to live in this world. So we go on to the next catastrophe. We have young boys out shooting one another. I remember when we used to—we don't anymore—count the number of people killed by Labor Day in this country. And there would be a little headline in the paper. "This Year: Record Broken," as if it were a score, a contest.

GG: From your writing, I get the sense that injustice affects you in a very deep way.

WHG: I don't know that I feel angrier than anybody else. During the sixties, I went out and did what everybody else was doing. Our yells wore costumes.

GG: Protesting?

WHG: Yeah, making speeches, getting myself in a lot of trouble.

GG: Against the war?

WHG: Yeah, it started at a time when two big things were happening. First the foundation of the United Nations. And I was preaching against the veto power of the major powers, that it was just not going to work right. Nobody can have a veto. That was one. And the other was my speeches about Israel. I hated the founding of Israel, and made speeches about how it was going to be an international ghetto, and the Palestinians had rights, and history bestows no particular right. There is indeed a statute of limitations. Anyway, those two things were going on, and then there was the Civil Rights stuff, and then of course the Vietnam War. And then there were the flower children, the sex stuff. What hypocrisy. And so I did my little time occupying buildings and marching up and down and making speeches. I was at Purdue then, and Purdue is a very conservative place.

GG: You were in your early forties around this time?

WHG: Yeah. That's when I met my wife, Mary, just about that time. They wanted to fire me at the university. In the town, they threw garbage on my front porch and stuff like that. And then I was denied gasoline at the station. But that was my big time in activism.

GG: Was that instrumental in you leaving Purdue?

WHG: Well, I certainly wanted to. I wanted to leave everything. Yeah, I was ready to go. And it was just fortuitous. The president handed around copies of *Willie Masters'*

Lonesome Wife to the board of trustees. They wanted to get rid of me for what they thought a horrible business. And then the head of the student newspaper, who was a terrific young man, he was in trouble. And I was the cause of all of it, because he was a philosophy student, and I was the head of the Faculty Action Committee. The Futility Committee, it should've been. But it was easy to see through much of it. Most of the students were mobilized because they were afraid of going to the war. I don't blame them. If we still had a People's Army and they were carrying their own guns into battle, we wouldn't have as many wars. I found out very quickly—it wasn't hard to find out—that the sexual revolution was machismo to the nth degree, and women were being exploited and misused. And I don't know why people didn't see through Martin Luther King, because it was pretty obvious. Nevertheless, he did good. History is very complicated.

GG: You are now eighty-eight. Many of the writers you have been mentioned with have passed on, except for John Barth and Robert Coover. How is it to have lasted so long?

WHG: They didn't pass on. They died. Well, Barth keeps in shape. I don't know if that even really works. I don't drink as much as I used to. But I drink a lot. I have a salt-free diet. But other than that, we don't do anything special. I never did get a lot of activity, except when we traveled. There was a lot of walking. In the old days, I cycled. I used to ride a bicycle all the time to school. When I was at Purdue, it was several miles I'd bike. But then less and less. I became more and more like Kohler, I got fat. But I was sixty when I did. People don't realize that sometimes. Mary and I have been married for forty-two years. I suppose people thought, when we married—with she young and I in my forties—that it wouldn't last. But it did. I got lucky.

FAVORITE SONG

My life.
Is a passing September
no one will recall.
She crooned.
The riparian leads to the littoral.
Like a horse ridden to death.
I saw the earth in knickerbockers.
I saw the inside of its locker.
It hung a mirror there.
I saw it shaving its face.
I saw its face in a lather.
Like a horse ridden to death.
Heaven provided us with tears.
We rub them around. We share them.
We think they are tadpoles.
We think they will grow up
into beautiful singing things.
But they won't.
I saw the earth was one of the great
unsuccessful poems.

NITE NITE

None of the dolls could sleep.
The braided rug dreamt of being
a traveling companion.
The snow stopped, briefly,
on its way past the window.
The mother and father did not
touch each other, but each felt
they could hear laughter coming
from China, and the child felt
knocked by the earth,
and though she was blind
and would always be blind,
one day she would tap blindly
with her white-tipped stick,
wearing orange high heels.

FICTION

Reeling for the Empire

Several of us claim to be the daughters of samurai, but there is no way for anyone to verify that now. It's a relief, in its way, this anonymity. We come here tall and thin, noblewomen from Yamaguchi, graceful as calligraphy; short and poor, Hida girls with bloody feet, crow-voiced and vulgar. We have been entrusted to the Model Mill by our teary mothers; handed over by our hungry husbands; rented out by our destitute uncles, our desperate fathers. Within a day or two, the tea the Agent gave us begins to take effect—our bodies plump and soften as the humanness ebbs stealthily out of them, and polar fur covers our faces, blanking us all into sisters.

Karen Russell

As the transformation progresses and our bodies grow more and more alike in shape, we frantically work to reinvent our pasts. We seek out any way to peculiarize ourselves. Yuna says that her great-uncle has a scrap of sailcloth from the Black Ships, that he watched them sail into the Uraga Harbor in 1853 and foresaw in a flash the next thirty years of change: the speed and smoke of machines, the ports pried open, blue-eyed foreigners flooding in. Dai claims that she knelt alongside her samurai father at the Battle of Shiroyama. Nishi once stowed away in the imperial caboose from Shimbashi Station to Yokohama and saw Emperor Meiji eating pink cake. Back in Gifu I had tangly hair like a donkey's, a mouth like a small red bean, but I tell the others that I was the village beauty and lived a life of luxury.

None of these stories can reverse the curse of the Agent's tea: we are all reelers. Some kind of hybrid creature, part silkworm caterpillar, *kaiko*, and part human female. Nearly immediately after drinking the tea, we began to make thread in our bellies, but the complete outward change is gradual and has developed over many months. The older workers' faces are covered with a coarse white fur, while the newer initiates still look more like the girls they are slowly unbecoming. After drinking my dose, I was effectively dead for three days, locked inside a drugged slumber—the others assure me I was fortunate to miss the worst of the convulsions. But even as I slept, they say, my body shook with the change. I awoke with a pale down on my face, my stomach in the clutches of a giddy sort of terror, roiling tremors that I soon felt become solid. It was the thread: a color purling invisibly in my belly. Silk. Dai, the oldest worker at our factory, explained all this on my day zero. At first, Dai was just a voice to me, a reassuring whisper leagues above my fevered face on the bedroll. As I came to, she told me that yards and yards of thin color would soon be extracted from me by the Machine.

Today, the Agent drops off two new recruits, sisters from Yamagata Prefecture, a blue village called Sakegawa, which none of us have visited. They are the daughters of a salmon fisherman and their names are Tooka and Etsuyo. They are twelve and nineteen. Tooka has a waist-length braid and baby fat; Etsuyo looks like a forest doe, with her long neck and watchful brown eyes. We step into the light and Etsuyo swallows her scream. Tooka starts wailing—"Who are you? What's happened to you? What is this place?"

Dai crosses the room to them, and despite their terror the Sakegawa sisters are too sleepy and too shocked to recoil from her embrace. They appear to have drunk the tea very recently, because they're quaking on their feet. Etsuyo's eyes cross as if she is about to faint. Dai unrolls two tatami mats in a dark corner, helps them to stretch out. "Sleep a little," she whispers. "Dream."

"Is this the silk-reeling factory?" slurs Tooka, half conscious on her bedroll.

"Oh, yes," Dai says soothingly. Her furry face hovers like a moon above them.

As I came to, she told me that yards and yards of thin color would soon be extracted from me by the Machine.

Tooka nods, satisfied, as if willing to dismiss all of her terror to continue believing in the Agent's promises, and shuts her eyes.

Sometimes when the new recruits confide the hopes that brought them to our factory, I have to suppress a bitter laugh. Long before the *kaiko* change turned us into mirror images of one another, we were sisters already, spinning identical dreams in beds thousands of miles apart, fantasizing about gold silks and an "imperial vocation." We envisioned our future dowries, our families' miraculous freedom from debt. We thrilled to the same tales of women working in the grand textile mills, where steel machines from Europe gleamed in the light of the Meiji sunrise. Our world had changed so rapidly in the wake of the Black Ships that the poets could barely keep pace with the scenes outside their own windows. Industry, trade, unstoppable growth: years before the Agent came to find us, our dreams anticipated his promises.

Since my arrival here, my own fantasies have grown as dark as the room: in them, I snip a new girl's thread as it winds around her reel or yank all of the silk out of her at once so that she falls lifelessly forward like a Bunraku puppet, or use her thread to sew open her eyelids. I haven't been able to cry since my first night—but often I feel a water pushing at my skull. Silk starts as a liquid, I know, feel. Can the thread migrate to your brain? I've asked Dai nervously, but she's never answered. At night, lying on my bedroll, I can feel my thread traveling below my navel, foaming icily along the lining of my stomach. I watch it rise under the blankets and begin to form a lump. Soon it will grow hard and need to be drawn out of me, removed by the Machine. There will now be twenty-two workers sleeping on the twelve tatami mats, two rows of us, our heads ten centimeters apart, our earlobes curled like snails on adjacent leaves. Though every one of our bellies is round, we are always hungry. Most nights I barely sleep. I hear others dreaming, moaning mutely for dawn and the relief of the Machine.

Long ago, we quit trying to restrain ourselves and gave over to the depth of our daily hunger.

Every aspect of our lives—working, sleeping, eating, shitting, and bathing when we can get wastewater from the Machine—is conducted in this great brick room. The far wall has a single oval window, set high in its center, too high for us to see much more than scraps of cloud and a woodpecker that has become like a celebrity to us: we gasp and applaud every time he appears. *Kaiko-joko*, we call ourselves. Silkworm-workers. Unlike regular *joko*, we have no foreman or men. We are alone in the box of this room. Dai says she's the dormitory supervisor, but that's Dai's game, her fantasy.

We were all brought here by the same man, the factory's recruitment agent. He is a representative from the new Ministry for the Promotion of Industry, endorsed by Emperor Meiji himself. And we were all told slightly different versions of the same story of what our new lives would be like, none of them remotely resembling what those lives have, in fact, become. Our fathers or guardians signed contracts that varied only slightly in their terms; in most versions, the Agent paid a five-yen advance and promised fifty yen in exchange for one year of our lives.

The Agent travels the countryside to recruit female workers willing to travel far from their home prefectures to a new European-style silk-reeling mill. He makes his pitch not to the woman but to her father or guardian or, in some few cases, where single women cannot be procured, her husband. I am here on behalf of the nation, he begins. In the spirit of *Shokusan-Kōgyō. Increase production, encourage industry*. We are recruiting only the most skillful and loyal mill workers. Not just peasant girls, like your offspring—he might say with his silver tongue to men in the Gifu and Mie prefectures—but the well-bred daughters of noblemen. Samurai and aristocrats. City-born governors have begged me to train their daughters on the Western technologies. Last week, the medical general of the Imperial Army sent his nineteen-year-old twins, by train! Sometimes there is resistance from the father or guardian, especially among the hicks, those stony-faced men from distant centuries who still make bean paste, wade into rice paddies, brew sake using thousand-year-old methods; but the Agent waves all qualms away—Ah, you've heard about X Mill or Y Factory? No, the French *yatoi* engineers don't drink girls' blood, ha-ha, that is what they call *red wine*. Yes, there *was* a fire at Aichi Factory, a little trouble with tuberculosis in Suwa. But our factory is quite different—it is a national secret. Yes, a place that makes even the French filature in the backwoods of Gunma, with its brick walls and steam engines, look antiquated. This phantom factory he presents to her father or guardian with great cheerfulness and urgency, for, he says, we have awoken to dawn, the Enlightened Era of the Meiji, and we must all play our role now. Japan's silk is her world export. The blight in Europe, the pebrine virus, has killed every silkworm, forever halted the Westerners' cocoon production. The demand is as vast as the ocean. This is the moment to seize. Silk reeling is a sacred vocation—she will be reeling for the empire. Think of how much better her life will be, he says. Think of the future.

The fathers and guardians nearly always sign the contract. Publicly, the *joko's* family will share a cup of hot tea with the Agent. They celebrate her new career, and the five-yen advance against her legally mortgaged future. Privately, an hour or so later, the Agent will share a special toast with the girl herself. For these tea ceremonies, the Agent improvises his rooms: an attic in a forest inn or a locked changing room in a bathhouse or, in the case of Iku, an abandoned cowshed. Nowhere and at no time is it mentioned that she will be making the silk in her body, gestating it in her belly, that her future is no longer hers at all, but the property of the factory.

After sunset, the Zookeeper arrives. She is the old woman who hauls our food to the grated door and unbars the lower panel. We believe she is blind. The woman never speaks to us, no matter what questions we shout at her, which has led us to believe she may be dumb, too. She simply waits patiently for our skeins, runs her hands over them and cradles them in her palms, and so long as they are acceptable in quality and weight, she slides in our mulberry leaves with a long stick. Long ago, we quit trying to restrain ourselves and gave over to the depth of our daily hunger. We lower our faces to the ground and fall upon the pile, slurping up the deep, death-thwarting taste of the mulberry, barely aware of the wet smacking sounds of our jaws. We are done in moments. In other factories, we've heard, there are foremen and managers and whistles to announce and regulate the breaks, meals. Here the clocks and whistles are in our bodies. The thread is our boss. There is a fifteen-minute period between the mulberry orgy—"Call it *the evening meal*, please, don't be disgusting," Dai pleads, her saliva still gleaming on the floor—and the regeneration of the thread. During this period, we sit in a circle in the center of the room, an equal distance from our bedding and the Machine. Stubbornly, in our full-stomach stupor, we reel backward, remembering our homelands: Takayama town. Oyaka village. Toku. Kiyo. Nara. Fude. Shō. Radishes and pickles. Laurel and camphor smells of Shikoku. Father. Mother. Mount Fuji. The Inland Sea.

We look up from this ritual reminiscing to discover that the Zookeeper has also slid in a tray of steaming human food for the new recruits. Tooka and Etsuyo get rice balls and miso soup with floating carrots. Hunks of real ginger are unraveling in the broth, like hair. We sit in our circle and watch them chew with a dewy nostalgia that disgusts me even as I find myself ogling their long white fingers on their chopsticks, the balls of rice. The salt and fat smells make my eyes ache.

They drink down the soup in silence, clearly frightened of our hunger. "Are we dreaming?" I hear one whisper.

"The tea drugged us!" the younger sister, Tooka, cries at last. Her eyes dart here and there, as if she's hoping to be contradicted. They traveled nine days by riverboat and oxcart, Etsuyo tells us, wearing blindfolds the entire time. So we could be that far north of Yamagata, or west. Or east, the younger sister says. We collect facts from every new *kaiko-joko* and use them to draw thread maps of Japan on the factory floor. But not even Tsuki the Apt can guess our whereabouts.

"Nowhere Mill" we call this place.

Dai crosses the room and speaks soothingly to the sisters; then she leads them right to me. Oh, happy day. I glare at her.

"Kistune is quite a veteran now," says smiling Dai. "She will show you around."

I hate this part. But you have to tell the new ones what's in store for them. Minds have been spoiled by the surprise. We share this burden with Dai, alternating the task of explaining what little we've learned about the *kaiko* transformation to the new girls.

"I think there has been a mistake," Etsuyo says in a grave voice. "Will the manager of this factory be coming soon?"

"We don't belong here!" Tooka breathes.

"There's nowhere else for you now," I say, staring at the floor. "That tea the Agent poured into you at the end of your voyage?" I continue. "That is remaking your insides. Your intestines, your secret organs. Soon your stomachs will bloat. You will manufacture silk in your gut with the same helpless skill that you digest food, exhale. The *kaiko* change, he calls it. A revolutionary process. We think the tea may have been created abroad, by French chemists or British engineers. *Yatoi* tea. Unless it's the Agent's own technology."

Like others who arrive here, these seashore girls know next to nothing about silkworm cultivation.

I try to smile at them.

"In the cup it was so lovely to look at, wasn't it? An orange hue, like something out of the princess's floating world woodblocks."

Etsuyo is shaking. "But can't we undo it? There must be a cure."

"The only cure is temporary, and it comes from the Machine. When your thread begins, you'll understand."

It takes thirteen to fourteen hours for the Machine to empty a *kaiko-joko* of her thread. The relief of being rid of it is indescribable.

Like others who arrive here, these seashore girls know next to nothing about silkworm cultivation. No sooner have I begun my explanation than Chiyo cranes over from her work station and interrupts me, seizing an excuse to tell a fresh audience her family history. In the mountains of Chichibu, Chiyo tells them, everyone in her village is involved with the cultivation. Seventy families work together in a web: planting and watering the mulberry trees, raising the *kaiko* eggs to pupae, feeding the silkworm caterpillars. Her mother is in charge of boiling the cocoons, to soften the thread. Two dozen villagers sit at benches like ours, unreeling each little moon by hand, twisting the thread onto the old-style *zaguri* reels. Chiyo says those clunky wooden reels cannot compare with the speed and force of our Machine. And this timeworn method produces terrible waste—lint and puff balls, broken threads. Unlaced cocoons blew across her bedding. She spent her childhood enclosed in these small, humid rooms, breathing in the vile smells of the bugs' split sacs.

In other words, the art of silk production was very, very inefficient, I tell the sisters. Slow and costly. Until us.

I try to weed the pride from my voice, but it's difficult. I'd give anything to undo the day that brought me here and awaken as Kitsune Tajima again, not some worm feeding the Machine but a woman in Gifu, and still I can't help but admire the quantity of silk that we *kaíko-joko* can produce in a single hour. The Agent boasts that he has made us the most revolutionary machines in the empire, surpassing even those steel zithers and cast-iron belchers at Tomioka Model Mill. The problems that have halted the productivity of the new Western-style mills do not affect us here at Nowhere Mill. We *kaíko-joko* can feed the Machine fresh silk every dawn, unlike our tiny insect competitors, Japan's silkworms.

Lying awake each night, when I relive my own journey to the mill, I know that I arrived here a monster.

Eliminated: Mechanical famine. Supply problems caused by the cocoons' tiny size and irregular quality.

Eliminated: Waste silk.

Eliminated: The cultivation of the *kaíko*. The harvesting of their eggs. The laborious collection and separation of the silk cocoons. We silkworm-girls combine all these processes in the factories of our bodies. Ceaselessly, even while we dream, we are generating thread. Every droplet of our energy, every moment of our time flows into the silk. There is nothing of comparable quality on the market, according to the Agent. Noblewomen say it makes ordinary silk look dull. Royal horses wear blankets made from the silks of Nowhere Mill.

I guide the sisters to the first of the three workbenches. "Here are the basins where we boil the water," I say. "They are steam-heated and quite modern."

I plunge my left hand into the boiling water for as long as I can bear it. Soon the skin of my fingertips softens and bursts. Fine waggling fibers rise from them. Green thread lifts right out of my veins. With my right hand I pluck up the thread from my left fingertips and wrist.

"See? Easy."

Tooka and Etsuyo have gone white-knuckled, clasping one another's hands, as if to protect each other's tender palms from the vats. Drained of color, their girlish faces look nearly as pale as mine.

"A single strand is too fine to reel," I say. "So you have to draw several out, wind six or eight around your finger, rub them together, to get the right denier; when they are thick enough, you feed them to the Machine."

Dai is drawing red thread onto her reel, watching me approvingly.

"Are we monsters now?" Tooka wants to know.

I give Dai a helpless look; that's a question I can't answer for this child. In my own case, I fear that I may have been one all along, long before I sprouted a single white whisker. Lying awake each night, when I relive my own journey to the mill, I know that I arrived here a monster.

Dai considers.

In the end she tells the sisters about the *juhyou*, the "snow monsters," snow-and-ice-covered trees in Zao Onsen, her home. "The snow monsters," Dai smiles, brushing her whiskers, "are very beautiful. Their disguises make them beautiful. But they are still trees, you see, under all that frost."

While the sisters drink in this news, I steer them to the Machine.

The Machine looks like a great steel-and-wooden beast with a dozen rotating eyes and steaming mouths—it's twenty meters long and takes up nearly half the room. The central reel is a huge and ever-spinning O, capped with rows of bright metal teeth. Pulleys swing our damp thread left to right across it, refining it into finished silk. Tooka shivers and says it looks as if the Machine is smiling at us. *Kaiko-joko* sit at the workbenches and feed the smaller reels, pulling thread from our own fingers like zither strings. A stinging music.

"No *tebiki* cranks to turn," I show them. "Steam power has freed both of our hands."

"Freed, I suppose, isn't quite the right word, is it?" says Iku drily. Lotus-colored thread is flooding out of her left palm and winding around a reel. With her right hand she adjusts the outflow.

"Here is the final miracle," I say. "Our silk comes out of us in colors. There is no longer any need to dye it. There is no other silk like it on the world market, boasts the Agent."

Nobody has ever guessed her own color correctly—Hoshi predicted hers would be peach and it was blue; Nishi thought pink, got hazel. Had I been conscious to anticipate its advent, I would have bet my entire five-yen advance that mine would be light gray, like my cat's fur. But when I woke and held my aching hands up to my face, I found the whorling green thread matted to the split skin of my palms, its pale glow pulsing through the webbing of my fingers. On my day zero, in the middle of my terror, I was surprised into a laugh: here was a translucent green I swore I'd never seen before anywhere in nature, and yet I knew it as my own on sight.

"It's as if the surface is charged with our aura," says Hoshi, our resident poet, so infatuated with her own rhythms that she stops cranking the silk for a moment, counting syllables on her knuckles for her next haiku.

In my real past, I watched my grandfather become a sharecropper, a dependant, on his own property. He was a young man when the Black Ships came to Edo. He grew foxtail millet and red buckwheat. And like so many others, he seized what he was told was an opportunity and sold his land to become a tenant farmer. He paid half his crop for rent, then two-thirds; finally, after two bad harvests, he owed his entire yield. That year, our capital moved in a ceremonial, and very real, procession from Kyoto to Edo, now Tokyo, the world shedding names under the carriage wheels, and the teenaged emperor in his palanquin traveling over the mountains like an imperial worm.

In the first decade of the Meiji government, my grandfather was forced into bankruptcy by the land tax. In 1873, he joined the farmer's revolt in Chōbu. Along with hundreds of the newly bankrupted and dispossessed from Chōbu, Gifu, Aichi, he set fire to the creditor's offices where his debts were recorded. After the rebellion failed, after the increased taxes the emperor levied as punishment, he hung himself in our barn. The gesture was meaningless. The debt still existed, and my father inherited it. There was no dowry for me.

In my twenty-third year, my mother died, and my father turned white, lay flat. Death seeded in him and began to grow tall, like grain, and my brothers carried him to the Inaba Shrine for the mountain cure.

It was at precisely this moment that the Agent arrived at our door. He came to visit after an April thundershower, and I guessed his identity before he uttered a word. We had all heard of him in Gifu. He had been recruiting in nearby towns, signing contracts with elated families. I had never seen such a handsome person in my life, man or woman. He had blue eyelids—a birth defect, he said, one that worked to his extraordinary advantage. He had—and I found this incredibly appealing—midear sideburns and a moustache. He wore Western dress, carried a parasol from London. He let me sniff at his vial of French cologne. It was as if a rumor had materialized inside the dark interior of our farmhouse.

"My father is sick," I told him. I was alone in the house. "He is in the other room, sleeping."

"Well, let's not disturb him." The Agent smiled and stood to go.

"I can read," I said. "I can write my name."

Show me the contract, I begged him.

And he did. He explained that I couldn't run away from the factory and I couldn't die, either—and perhaps I looked at him a little dreamily, because I remember that he repeated this injunction in a hard voice, tightening up the grammar: "If you die, your father will pay." He was peering deeply into my face and his tone suggested that this payment would be unspeakably high, a debt that money alone could not satisfy. I could see the rain trembling in his moustache. I met his gaze and giggled, embarrassing myself.

Never in my life, before or since, have I felt as powerful as I did when I forged his signature on the contract.

"Look at you, blinking like a firefly! Only, it's very serious—"

He lunged forward and grabbed playfully at my waist, causing my entire face to darken in what I hoped was a womanly blush.

"There, there, Kitsune! You will come with me to the model factory? You will reel for the realm, for your emperor? For me, too," he added softly, with a smile.

I nodded, very serious myself now. He let his long fingers brush against my knuckles as he drew out the contract.

"Let me bring it to father," I told the Agent. "Stand back. Stay here. His disease is contagious."

The Agent laughed. He said he wasn't used to being bossed by a *joko*. But he waited.

My father would never have signed the document, never have agreed to let me go. My mother was dead, and he often said that I was all he had left of her. He blamed the new government for my grandfather's suicide. He was suspicious of foreigners. He would certainly have demanded to know where the factory was located. But I could work and he could not. I saw my father coming home, cured, and finding the five-yen advance. He could repair the plough, mend the holes in our roof. He could do a hundred things that would have been impossible when he was penniless and sick. I had never used an ink pen before. Never in my life, before or since, have I felt as powerful as I did when I forged his signature on the contract. No woman in Gifu had ever brokered such a deal on her own. KITSUNE TAJIMA I wrote in the slot for the future worker's name, my heart pounding at a gallop. When I returned it, I apologized for my father's unsteady hand.

On our way to what I now know was the *kaiko* tea ceremony, I was so excited that I could barely make my questions about the factory intelligible. The Agent swayed through the tinted light that filled the woods behind our farmhouse, barely glancing my way. I made a sidelong study of his thin lips, the cords of his neck. He was smiling to himself, I saw with pleasure. He took me to a summer guesthouse near the Miya River, which he told me was owned by a Takayama merchant family and, at the moment, empty.

Apparently, one sip of the *kaiko* tea is so venomous that most bodies immediately go into convulsions.

Something is wrong, I knew then. This knowledge sounded with such clarity that it seemed almost independent of my body, like a bird calling once over the trees. But I proceeded, following the Agent toward a dim staircase. The first room I glimpsed was elegantly furnished. I counted fourteen steps to the first landing, where he opened a door onto a room that reflected none of the downstairs refinement. There was a table with two stools, a cot. I was surprised by a large brown blot on the mattress. Where did that come from? I wondered. A porcelain teapot sat on the table. One cup. The Agent lifted the pot with an unreadable expression, frowning into it; as he poured, I thought I heard a little splash; then he cursed, excused himself, said he needed a fresh ingredient. I heard him continuing up the staircase. I peered into the cup and saw that there was something alive inside it—writhing, dying—a fat white *kaiko*. I shuddered. What sort of tea ceremony was this? Maybe, I thought, the Agent is testing me, to see if I am squeamish, weak. Something bad was coming—the stench of a thickening future was everywhere in that room. The bad thing was right under my nose, crinkling its little legs at me.

I pinched my nostrils shut, just as if I were standing in the mud a heartbeat from jumping into the Miya River. Without so much as consulting the Agent, I sealed my eyes and gulped.

However many times I've told the story now, the other workers cannot believe I did this willingly. Apparently, one sip of the *kaiko* tea is so venomous that most bodies immediately go into convulsions. Only through the Agent's intervention were they able to get the tea down. It took his hands around their throats.

I arranged my hands in my lap and sat on the cot. Already I was feeling a little dizzy. I remember smiling with a sweet vacancy at the door when he returned.

"You—drank it."

I nodded proudly.

Then I saw pure amazement pass over his face. I passed the test, I thought happily. Only it wasn't that, quite. He began to laugh.

"No *joko*," he sputtered, "not one of you, ever—" He was rolling his eyes at the room's corners, as if he regretted that the hilarity of this moment was wasted on me. "No girl has ever drunk a whole cup of it!"

Already the narcolepsy was buzzing through me, like a hive of bees stinging me to sleep. I lay guiltily on the mattress—why couldn't I sit up? Now the Agent would think I was worthless for work. I opened my mouth to explain that I was feeling ill but only a smacking sound came out. I held my eyes open for as long as I could stand it.

Even then, I was still dreaming of my prestigious new career as a reeler, whatever that might be. Under the new Meiji government, the hereditary classes had been abolished, and I even had the crazy thought that the Agent might marry me, pay off my family's debts. As I watched, the Agent's genteel expression underwent a complete transformation; suddenly it was as blank as a stump. The last thing I saw, before shutting my eyes, was his face.

When I woke I was on a dirty tatami mat in this factory and Dai was applauding me. I was too tired to be frightened by her appearance. She told me I had been unconscious for three days. The green thread had erupted through my palms in my sleep—the metamorphosis unusually accelerated—and my hands were a sticky mess of color. I was lucky, Chiyo says. Unlike the others, I had no limbo period, no cramps from my guts unwinding, changing; no time at all to meditate on what I was becoming—a secret, a furred and fleshy silk factory.

What would Chiyo think of me if she knew how much I envy her initiation story? That what befell her—her struggle, her screams—I long for? That I would exchange my memory for Chiyo's in a heartbeat? Surely this must be the final, inarguable proof that I am, indeed, a monster.

Many workers here have a mark of their innocence, some physical trace, on the body: scar tissue, a brave spot. A sign of struggle that is ineradicable. Some girls will push their white fuzz aside to show you: Dai's pocked hands, Mitsuki's rope burns around her neck. Gin has wiggly lines around her mouth, like lightning, where she was scalded by the tea that she spat out.

"Why did you drink it, Kitsune?"

I shrug. In my mind's eye I can still see the holes in our farmhouse roof, the single, bare room.

"I was thirsty," I say, and turn my face to watch the rivers of green silk whip around the Machine.

Roosters begin to crow outside the walls of Nowhere Mill at 5:00 AM. They sing as though they're cackling up the sun itself, a sound like gargled light, which I picture as Dai's red and Gin's orange and Yoshi's pink thread singing on the world's largest reel. Dawn. I've been lying awake in the dark for hours.

"Kistune, you never sleep. I hear the way you breathe," Dai says.

"I sleep a little."

"What stops you?" Dai rubs her belly sadly. "Too much thread?"

"Up here." I knock on my head. "I can't stop reliving it: the Agent walking through our fields under his parasol, in the rain . . ."

"You should sleep," says Dai, peering into my eyeball. "Yellowish. You don't look well."

I wonder at Dai, who puts on a stoic show for the new recruits, playing the role of supervisor. With time, I have started to see the cracks in her good cheer and come to believe, in the end, that sleep must be her only respite—a blanketing darkness where she can relax, at last, and drop her mask, and cradle her own aching belly.

At the basins I plunge my hands into the water and sigh with relief, drawing the long green threads from my fingers like soft splinters. I am so tired that I wobble at my reel, causing Uki to bark at me, "Be careful, Kitsune! Quit knocking around like a drunkard!" Midmorning, there is a malfunction. Some hitch in the Machine causes my reel to spin backward, pulling the thread from my fingers so quickly that I am jerked onto my knees; then I'm dragged along the floor toward the Machine's central reel like an enormous, flopping fish. The room fills with my howls. My right arm is on the point of being wrenched from its socket. I lift my chin and begin, with a naturalness that belongs entirely to my terror, to swivel my head around and bite blindly at the air; at last I snap the threads with my *kaiko* jaws and fall sideways. Under my wrist, more thread kinks and scrags. There is a terrible stinging in my hand and my head. I close my eyes and I see the space beneath my mother's cedar chest, where the moonlight lay in green splashes on our floor. I used to hide there as a child and sleep so soundly that no one in our one-room house could ever find me. Then I feel hands on my shoulders. Voices call my name—"Kitsune! Are you awake? Are you okay?"

"I'm just clumsy," I say and laugh nervously. But then I look down at my hand. Short threads extrude from the bruised skin of my knuckles. They are the wrong color. Not my green, but ash. Dark.

Suddenly I feel short of breath.

It gets worse when I look up. The silk that I reeled this morning is bright green. But the more recent thread drying on the bottom of my reel is black. Black as the sea, as the forest at night, says Hoshi euphemistically. She is too courteous to make sinister comparisons.

I swallow a cry. Am I sick? It occurs to me that five or six of these black threads dragged my entire weight. It had felt as though my bone would snap in two before my thread did.

"Anything you want to tell us?" Dai prods. "About how you are feeling?"

Everybody is staring at the spot midway up the reel where the green silk shades into black.

"I feel about as well as you all look today," I growl.

"I'm not worried," says Dai in a too friendly way, addressing everyone else, not me. She claps my shoulder. "Kitsune just needs sleep."

But everybody is staring at the spot midway up the reel where the green silk shades into black.

My next few mornings are spent splashing through the hot water basin, looking for fresh fibers. I pull out yards of the greenish black thread. Soiled silk. Hideous. Useless for kimonos. I sit and reel for my sixteen hours, until the Machine gets the last bit out of me with a shudder.

My thread is green three days out of seven. After that, I'm lucky to get two green outflows in a row. This transformation happens to me alone. None of the other workers experiences a change in her color. It must be my own illness then, not *kaiko* evolution. If we had a foreman here, he would quarantine me. He might destroy me, the way silkworms infected with the blight are burnt up in Kitamura.

And in Gifu? Perhaps my father has died at the base of Mount Inabe. Or has he made a full recovery, journeyed home with my brothers, and cried out with joyful astonishment to find my five-yen advance? Let it be that, I pray. My afterlife will be whatever he chooses to do with that money.

Today marks the forty-second day since we last saw the Agent. Tooka and Etsuyo are seasoned workers. They have grown white fur on their faces and look more like one another now than they did as sisters before. In the past, the Agent has reliably surprised us with visits, once or twice per month. Factory inspections, he calls them, scribbling notes about the progress of our transformations, the changes in our weight and shape, the quality of our silk production. He's never stayed away so long. The thought of the Agent, either coming or not coming, makes me want to retch. Liquid sloshes in my head. I lie on the mat with my eyes shut tight and watch the orange tea splash into my cup.

> ***Re-gret, re-gret, re-gret* croaks the little frog inside me, in time with the wheeling Machine.**

"I hear you in there, Kitsune. I know what you're doing. You didn't sleep."

Dai's voice. I keep my eyes shut. In a weak moment, I confessed my black thoughts to Dai, and now she knows exactly what I'm seeing behind my lids.

"Kitsune, stop thinking about it. You are making yourself sick."

"Dai, I can't."

Today my stomach is so full of thread that I'm not sure I'll be able to stand. I'm afraid that it will all be black. Some of the other workers have produced so much thread in the night that they are forced to crawl on their hands and knees to the Machine, toppled by their ungainly bellies. I can smell the basins heating. A thick, greasy steam fills the room. I peek up at Dai's face, then let my eyes flutter shut again.

"Smell that?" I say, more nastily than I intend to. "In here we're dead already. At least on the stairwell I can breathe forest air."

"Unwinding one cocoon for an eternity," she snarls. "As if you only had a single memory. Reeling in the wrong direction."

Dai looks ready to slap me. She's angrier than I've ever seen her. Dai is the Big Mother but she's also a samurai daughter, and sometimes that combination gives rise to a ferocious kind of caring. She's tender with the little ones, but if an older *joko* plummets into a mood or ill health, she'll scream at us until our ears split. Furious, I suppose, at her inability to defend us from ourselves.

"The others suffered in their pasts," she says. "We all suffered. But we sleep, we get up, we go to work, some crawl forward if there is no other way."

"I'm not like the others," I insist, hating the baleful note in my voice but desperate to make Dai understand this. "Sleep can't wipe me clean like them. I chose this fate. I signed my own contract. I can't blame a greedy uncle, a gullible father. I drank the tea of my own free will."

"Your free will," says Dai, so slowly that I'm sure she's about to mock me; then her eyes widen with something like joy. "Ah! So: use that to stop drinking it at night, in your memory. Use your will to stop thinking about the Agent."

Dai is smiling down at me like she's won the argument.

"Oh, yes, very simple!" I laugh angrily. "I'll just stop. Why didn't I think of that? Say, here's one for you, Dai," I snap. "Stop pretending you're not as homesick and frightened as the rest of us. Stop reeling for the Agent at your workbench. Stop making the thread in your gut. Try that, I'm sure you'll feel better."

Then we are shouting at each other, our first true fight; Dai doesn't understand that the memory reassembles itself in me mechanically, as involuntary and automatic as our production of the silk. It's nothing I control. The Agent comes; my hand trembles; the ink laces my name across the contract. My mouth opens in a "yes"; I sign on and on. My regret, I know I'll never get to the bottom of it. I'll never escape either place, Nowhere Mill or Gifu. Every night, the cup refills in my mind.

"Go reel for the empire, Dai. Make more silk for him to sell. Go throw the little girls another party! Lie to them, pretend we're not slaves here."

Dai storms off, and I feel a mean little pleasure. I lie there and remember the way my hand shook inside the Agent's. *Re-gret, re-gret, re-gret* croaks the little frog inside me, in time with the wheeling Machine.

For two days we don't speak, and I begin to worry that we never will again. But on the second night, Dai finds me. She leans in and whispers that she has accepted my challenge. At first I am so happy to hear her voice that I only laugh, take her hand. "What challenge? What are you talking about?"

"I thought about what you said," she tells me. She talks about her samurai father's last stand, the Satsuma Rebellion. In the countryside, she says, there are peasant armies who protest the "blood tax," refuse to sow new crops. I nod with my eyes shut, watching my grandfather's hat floating through our fields in Gifu.

"And you're right, Kitsune—we have to stop reeling. If we don't, he'll get every year of our futures. He'll get our last breaths. The silk belongs to us, *we* make it. We can use that to bargain with the Agent. We'll ask for dormitory sleeping quarters, days of privacy and rest. We'll make him buy the silk from us, and send the money to our husbands, our families."

The following morning, Dai announces that she won't move from her mat.

"I'm on strike," she says. "No more reeling."

By the second day, her belly has grown so distended with thread that we are begging her to work. The mulberry leaves arrive, and she refuses to eat them.

"No more room for that," she smiles.

Dai's face becomes so swollen that she can't open her right eye. She lies with her arms crossed over her chest, her belly heaving.

By the fourth day, I can barely look at her.

"You'll die," I whisper.

She nods resolutely.

"I'm escaping. He might still stop me. But I'll do my best."

We send a note for the Agent with the Zookeeper: "Please come."

"Join me," Dai begs us, and our eyes dull and lower, we sway. On the fifth day, Dai still doesn't reel. She still refuses to eat. Some of us, I'm sure, appreciate the extra fistful of leaves we get as a result of Dai's sacrifice. Guiltily, I set her portion aside, pushing the leaves into a little triangle. There, I think sadly. Then I eat them. Something flashes on one—a real silkworm. Inching along in its wet and stupid oblivion. My stomach flips to see all the little holes its hunger has punched into the green leaf.

During our break, I bring Dai my blanket. I try to squeeze some of the water from the leaf-sack onto her tongue, which she refuses. She doesn't make a sound, but I hiss—her belly is grotesquely bloated, and stippled with lumps, like a sow pregnant with a litter of ten piglets. Her excess thread is strangling Dai from within. What will the Agent make of this? Will he come? At this stage, can the Machine even extract it? Perhaps the Agent can call on a Western veterinarian, I find myself thinking. Whatever is happening to her seems beyond the ken of Emperor Meiji's own doctors.

"Start reeling again!" I gasp. "Dai, please. I take back my challenge."

"It looks worse than it is. It's easy enough to stop. You'll see for yourself, I hope." Her skin has an unhealthy translucence. Her eyes are standing out in her shrunken face, as if every breath costs her. Soon I will be able to see the very thoughts in her skull, the way red thread fans into veiny view under her skin. Dai gives me her bravest smile. "Get some rest, Kitsune. Stop poisoning yourself on the stairwell of Gifu. If I can stop reeling, surely you can, too."

Three days after her death, the Agent finally shows up. He strides over to Dai and touches her belly with a stick. When a few of us grab for his legs, he makes a face and kicks us off. All of the silk is still stubbornly housed in her belly, "stolen from the factory," as the Agent alleges. "This girl died a thief."

"Perhaps we can still salvage some of it," he grumbles, rolling her into a sack.

A great sadness settles over our whole group and doesn't lift. What the Agent carries off with Dai is everything we have left: Chiyo's clouds and mountains, Etsuyo's fiancé, my farmhouse in Gifu. We can never be away from the Machine for more than five days. Unless we live here, where the Machine can extract the thread from our bodies at speeds no human hand could match, the silk will build and build and kill us in the end.

What the Agent carries off with Dai is everything we have left.

I'm eating, I'm reeling, but I, too, appear to be dying. My thread is almost totally black. In my mind I talk to Dai about it, and she is very reassuring: "It's going to be fine, Kitsune. Only, please, you have to stop." *Stop thinking about it.* Dai's final entreaty always comes back to me. But despite her words, when I close my eyes, I again watch my hand signing my father's name. I am at the bottom of a stairwell in Gifu. The first time I made this ascent I felt weightless, but now the wood groans under my feet. Just as a single cocoon contains one thousand yards of silk, I can unwind one thousand miles from my memory of one misstep.

Still, I'm not convinced that Dai was right—that it's such a bad thing, a useless enterprise, to reel and reel out my regrets at night. Some part of me, the human part of me, is kept alive by this, I think. Like water flushing a wound to prevent it from closing.

One morning, two weeks after Dai's death, I start talking to Chiyo about her family's cottage business in Chichibu. Chiyo complains about the smells in her dry attic, where they destroyed the silkworm larvae in vinegary solutions.

"Why did they do that?" I want to know. I've never heard this part before.

"Oh, to stop them from undergoing the transformation," Chiyo says. "First, the silkworms stop eating. Then they spin their cocoons. Once inside, they molt several times. They grow wings and teeth. If the caterpillars are allowed to evolve, they change into moths. Then these moths bite through the silk and fly off, ruining it for the market."

Teeth and wings, wings and teeth. The words echo in my head all day over the whine of the Machine's cables. That night, I try an experiment. I think the black thoughts all evening. Great wheels inside me turn backward at fantastic, groaning velocities. What I focus on is my shadow in the stairwell, falling slantwise behind me, like silk. I see the ink spilling onto the contract, my name bloating monstrously. When I begin to tire of this horror, I goad myself onward. I hear the Agent's screams as I push him down the stairwell. I watch the Agent boiling in an orange lake of his tea until the strange fibers of his Western garments dissolve and his bones are polished white.

Unwittingly, the Agent has supplied me with every skill I need for my deep purpose.

And when dawn comes, and I slug my way over to the workbench and plunge my hands into the boiling vat, I see that the experiment was a success. Not only are my threads blacker than ever, they are a different consistency, too, a silk of some nameless variety that I have never spun before. There's not a fleck of green left, not a single frayed strand. "Moonless," says Hoshi, shrinking from them. Opaque. Midnight at Nowhere Mill pales in comparison. Looking down into the basin, I feel a wild excitement. I made it that color. So I'm no mere carrier, no diseased *kaiko*—I can channel these dyes from my mind into the tough new fiber. I can change my thread's denier, control its production. Seized by a second inspiration, I begin to reel onto my frame at speeds I would have just yesterday thought laughably impossible. Not even Yuna can produce as much thread in an hour. I ignore the whispers that pool around me on the workbench:

"Kitsune's fishing too deep—look at her finger slits!"

"They look like gills," Etsuyo shudders.

"Someone should stop her. She's fishing right down to the bone."

"What is she making?"

"What are you making?"

"What are you going to do with all that, Kitsune?" Tooka asks nervously.

"Oh, who knows? I'll just see what it comes to."

But I *do* know. Without giving a thought to what step comes next, my hands begin to fly.

The weaving comes so naturally to me that I am barely aware that I am doing it, humming as if in a dream. While this weaving is instinctual, what takes effort, what requires a special kind of concentration, is generating the right density of the thread. To do so, I have to keep forging my father's name in my mind, climbing those stairs, watching my mistake unfurl. I have to drink the toxic tea and feel it burn my throat, lie flat on the cot while my organs are remade by the Agent for the factory, thinking only, *Yes, I chose this*. When these memories send the fierce regret spiraling through me, I concentrate on my fingertips. Fibers stiffen inside them. Grow strong, I will the thread there. Go black. Lengthen. Stick. And then, when I return to the vats, what I've produced is exactly the right denier and darkness. I sit at the workbench, at my ordinary station. And I am so happy to discover that I can change the thread by design, use this body to make a revolutionary garment. Unwittingly, the Agent has supplied me with every skill I need for my deep purpose.

Out of the same intuition, I discover that I know how to alter the Machine. "Help me, Tsuki," I say. I begin to explain, but she is already disassembling my reel. "I know, Kitsune," she says. "I see what you have in mind." Words now seem to be unnecessary between me and Tsuki. Instinct has enveloped us.

Together we adjust the feeder gears, so that the black thread travels in a loop; after getting wrung out and doubled on the Machine's great reel, it shuttles back to my hands. I add fresh fibers, drape the long skein over my knees. It is going to be as tall as a man, six feet at least.

Many girls continue feeding the Machine as if nothing unusual is happening. Others, like Etsuyo, are watching to see what my fingers are doing. For the past several months, every time I've reminisced about the Agent coming to Gifu, a bile has risen in my throat. It seems to be composed of every bitterness: grief and rage, the acid regrets. In the middle of my weaving, obeying a queer impulse, I spit onto my hand. The greenish liquid does not rub away; it's sticky, a foamy epoxy. Another of nature's wonders. So even the nausea of regret can be converted to use, I grin to Dai in my head. With this dill-colored substance, I am at last able to rub a sealant over my new thread and complete my work.

In ten hours of work, I have spun a black cocoon. It's nearly eight feet long, a tapered sack with a slippery sheen.

The first girls who see it take one look and run back to the tatami mats. They know. Without speech they see and understand what I've done.

The second group is cautiously admiring.

Hoshi waddles over with her bellyful of blue silk and screams.

I am halfway up the southern wall of Nowhere Mill before I realize she is screaming at me. I'm parallel to the woodpecker's window. The gluey thread collected on my palms sticks me to the glass. For the first time since coming to the factory, I can see treetops, the green spires of some nameless forest. I crane my head and suddenly it's as if I can see endlessly, nothing but clouds and sky, a blue eternity. *We will have wings soon,* I think, and ten feet below me I hear Tsuki laugh out loud. Using my thread and the homemade glue, I attach the cocoon from a wooden beam; soon, I am floating in circles over the Machine, suspended by my own line. "Come down!" Hoshi yells, but she's the only one who seems concerned. I secure the cocoon and then I let myself fall, all of my weight supported by one thread. Now the cocoon sways over the Machine, a furled black flag, creaking slightly. I think of my grandfather hanging by the thick rope from our barn ceiling.

More black thread spasms down my arms.

"Kitsune, please. You'll make the Agent angry! You shouldn't waste your silk that way—pretty soon they'll stop bringing you leaves! We all saw what happens if he stops feeding us! We die."

But in the end I convince all of the workers to join me. Instinct obviates the need for a lesson—swiftly the others discover that they, too, can change their thread from within, drawing strength from the colors and seasons of their memories. Before we can begin to weave our cocoons, however, we first agree to work night and day to reel the ordinary silk, doubling our production, stockpiling the surplus skeins. Then we seize control of the machinery of Nowhere Mill. We spend the next six days dismantling and reassembling the Machine, using its gears and reels to speed the production of our own shimmering cocoons. Each dusk, we continue to deliver the regular amount of skeins to the Zookeeper, to avoid arousing the Agent's suspicions. When we are ready for the next stage of our revolution, only then will we invite him to tour our factory floor.

Silkworm moths develop long ivory wings, says Chiyo, bronzed with ancient designs. Do they have antennae, mouths? I ask her. Can they see? Who knows what the world will look like to us if our strike succeeds? I believe we will emerge from it entirely new creatures. In truth, there is no model for what will happen to us next. We'll have to wait and learn what we've become when we get out.

The Zookeeper really is blind, we decide. She squints directly at the wrecked and rerouted Machine and waits with her arms extended for the skeins. Instead, Hoshi pushes a letter through the grate.

"There is no silk today."

"Bring this to the Agent."

"Go. Tell. Him." I hiss. He wouldn't come to save Dai's life, but he will race to us now, won't he? He'll be panicked, desperate to know why his silk has dried up.

As usual, she says nothing. The sacks of mulberry leaves sit on the wagon. After a moment she claps to show us that her hands are empty, kicks the wagon away. Signals: no silk, no food. Her face is slack. On our side of the grate, I hear girls smacking their jaws, swallowing saliva. Fresh forest smells rise off the sacks. But we won't beg, will we? We won't turn back. Dai lived without food for five days. Our cheeks press against the grate. Several of our longest whiskers tickle the Zookeeper's withered cheeks; at last, a dark cloud passes over her face. She barks with surprise, swats the air. Her wrinkles tighten into a grimace of fear. She backs away from our voices, her fist closed around our invitation to the Agent.

They fall from the ceiling on whistling lines of silk, swinging into the light.

"NO SILK," repeats Tsaiko slowly.

The Agent comes the very next night.

"Hello?"

He raps at our grated door with a stick, but he makes no move to open it. For a moment I am certain that he won't come in.

"They're gone, they're gone," I wail, rocking.

"What!"

The grate slides open and he steps onto the factory floor, into our shadows.

"Yes, they've all escaped, every one of them, all your *kaiko-joko*—"

Now my sisters, even Hoshi, drop down on their threads. They fall from the ceiling on whistling lines of silk, swinging into the light, and I feel as though I am dreaming—it is a dreamlike repetition of our initiation, when the Agent dropped the infecting *kaiko* into the orange tea. Watching his mouth stretch into a scream, I too am shocked. We have no mirrors here in Nowhere Mill, and I've spent the past few months convincing myself that my eyes were surely playing tricks on me, that to an outsider we might yet be identifiable as girls, women—no beauty queens, certainly, shaggy and white and misshapen, but at least half human; it's only now, watching the Agent's reaction, that I realize what we've become. I see us as he must: white faces, with sunken noses that look partially erased. Eyes insect-huge. Spines and elbows incubating lace for wings. My muscles tense, and then I am airborne, launching myself onto the Agent's back—for a second I get a thrilling sense of what true flight will feel like, once we complete our transformation. The Agent grunts beneath my weight, staggers forward.

"These wings of ours are invisible to you," I say directly into the Agent's ear. My legs are hooked over his shoulders. I clasp my arms around his neck, lean in to whisper. "And in fact you will never see them, since they exist only in our future, where you are dead and we are living, flying."

I turn the Agent's head so that he can admire our silk. For the past week every worker has used the altered Machine to spin her own cocoon—they hang from the far wall, coral and emerald and blue, ordered by hue, like a rainbow. While the rest of Japan changes outside the walls of Nowhere Mill, we'll hang side by side, hidden against the bricks. Paralyzed inside our silk, but spinning faster and faster. Passing into our next phase. Then, we'll escape.

"And look," I say, counting down the wall: twenty-two workers, and twenty-three cocoons. When he sees the black sac, I feel his neck stiffen. I smile down at him. The Agent is stumbling around beneath me, babbling something that I admit I make no great effort to understand. The glue sticks my knees to his shoulders. Five of us busy ourselves with getting the gag in place, and this is accomplished before the Agent can scream. When he does, the sound is muted and garbled and senseless. Gin and Nishi bring down the cast-iron grate behind him.

The slender Agent is heavier than he looks. It takes four of us to raise him up and stuff him into the socklike cocoon. I smile at the Agent and instruct the others to leave his eyes for last, thinking that he will be very impressed to see our skill at reeling up close. Behind me, even as this attack is underway, the other *kaiko-joko* are climbing into their cocoons. Already there are girls half swallowed by them, winding silk threads over their knees, sealing the outermost layer with glue.

Now our methods regress a bit, get a little old-fashioned. I reel the last of the black cocoon by hand. Several *kaiko-joko* have to hold the Agent steady so that I can orbit him with the thread. I spin around his chin and his cheekbones, his lips. To get over his moustache requires several revolutions. Bits of my white fur drift down and disappear into his nostrils. His eyes are huge and black and void of any recognition. I whisper my name to him, to see if I can jostle my old self loose from his memory: Kitsune Tajima, of Gifu Prefecture.

Nothing.

I continue reeling upward, naming the workers of Nowhere Mill all the while: "Nishi. Yoshi. Yuna. Uki. Etsuyo. Gin. Hoshi. Raku. Chiyoko. Mitsuko. Tsaiko. Tooka. Dai. . ."

"Kitsune," I repeat, closing the circle. The last thing I see before shutting his eyes is the reflection of my face, poised for transformation.

DEAR NUAGES,

My pyramid of oranges
I am head over heels
The sea its vast sadness who wrote about that?
Perse Jeffers Segar
Sarah says I'm a sadness wrangler
Well clown fish are my currency
And sadly my sock puppets
I mean aren't we all talking out of our toes?
And tomorrow maybe Hawaii
Maybe Mount Tabor we'll walk up a volcano
That moves like an epic
Deathless in scope
I compare nuages with oranges
In my accent it's new ages
I'm sorry
Paris still titillates me
When you say tomorrow you don't mean in the morning
My teeth are loose I'm running low
On teeth I need sleep which will fix everything

It's an aesthetic choice
I descend the grand staircase of the House of Pancakes
Out to the Multnomah County Library which in the event
Of eruption becomes creosote
I'm floating
Away from myself and my books
The earth spits me out and why not?
One homeless boy's sign says *Anything?*
No not even a wink
And sadness sends me on my way
With a gift basket of nuages

LONGHAND

For this sort of work we'll need hats and masks
which might feel false and make us lonely on our hike
from home to school and lonelier still
when the other kids throw rocks at us
we'll also need jackets from the future with plenty of pockets
and cell phones! oh yeah we'll be in close contact at all times
which might get awkward if we have to share the same soup
strainer

There is nowhere left to hide
hide behind your hands
if everyone else is behind your hands *surprise!*
tell them I sent you
tell them you're the new principal
if they rise up and the juju in the room gets nasty
I have a list of the world's most dominant women
who will not hesitate to use their powers
including but not limited to song
their songs will create global peace
behind your hands

now where did I put that list?
I have many splendid hats, a fake mustache kit
with several famous mustache styles
a wooden sheath that slides over my head
and in my future jacket pockets
poems from Russia and Iceland where they write by blowtorch light!
plus a cell phone from which I'm calling you now

A man is sitting behind a woman with a pretty nape
he leans forward to smell her

NEW VOICE POETRY

REGARDING THE MURDER OF YOUR BOYFRIEND'S ROOMMATE

He walked home at night and was circled
by boys with knives who knifed him
and left him at someone's front door
in a neighborhood called Observatory,
where he quickly bled to death.
From the observatory on the hill,
streets have what realtors call *expansive*
grace, suburban streets of rosewood,
music. We would pour lighter fluid
in a circle around him every time
he fell asleep on the beach with a beer
in his hand—but the circle never lit.
And though we meant it as a joke
it wasn't a joke, it was devotion.
Had he survived, he would have been
a patient in Groote Schuur Hospital,
site of the world's first heart transplant
in 1967. That patient died of complications
from pneumonia only eighteen
days after his surgery, though they say
his new heart worked well till then.

FICTION

Sons and Mothers

Steven Millhauser

I

I had not seen my mother in a while, a fairly long while, all things considered, so long a while, to be perfectly frank, that it was difficult to remember when I'd last been out that way. And this was strange, really, since we had always been close, my mother and I. I was therefore pleased, though a little anxious, to find myself in a nearby town, during a business trip to that part of the country. My schedule was full, meetings all day, impossible to catch my breath, but I was determined to drive out there, if only for a short visit, it's the least you can do, I said to myself, after all this time.

The old neighborhood unsettled me. Things had changed everywhere, it was only to be expected, yet everything had remained the same, as though change were nothing but a new way of revealing sameness. An old maple had vanished and been replaced by a sapling. The trees I remembered had become taller and thicker, on the vacant lot where I'd once played King of the Mountain stood a yellow house with a green-shingled roof, in one yard the vegetable garden with its string-bean poles was now a lawn where you could see white wicker chairs and a birdbath with a stone bird on the rim. But there was the old willow tree on the corner, there the black roof followed by the red roof, there the creosoted telephone poles with the numbers screwed into the wood, there the stucco house with the glider on the porch followed by the brown house with the two mailboxes and the two front doors. My mother's house, the house that kept appearing in my dreams, was still where it had always been, tucked between two larger houses near the end of the block, and I was shaken for a moment, not because I was approaching my old house, after all this time, but because it was there at all, as if I'd come to believe that it could no longer have a physical existence, out there in the undreamed world.

Even before I turned into the drive I saw that the grass was high, the shingles dingy, the front walk partly hidden by overhanging grass. Untrimmed bushes threw up branches higher than the windowsills. My mother had always taken good care of the place, and for a moment I had the sensation that the house had not been lived in for a long time. One of the small front steps was crumbling at the side, the glass shade of the porch light was dark with dust. I pressed the familiar bell, a yellowish button in a brown oval, and heard the two-note ring. It hadn't occurred to me, until I heard that sound, that my mother might be out, on this pleasant afternoon, when the sun was shining and the sky was blue, the sort of summer day when a person might go to the beach, if she were so inclined, or drive into town, for one reason or another. It seemed to me that if my mother was out, as she appeared to be, it would be the best thing for both of us, for it had been a longish while, had it not, since I'd last come home, too long a while, really, for the kind of visit I was prepared to make. I pressed the bell again, jiggled the change in my pocket, looked over the side rail at an azalea bush. No one was home, it was just as well. I turned away, then swung back and opened the screen door, tried the wooden door. It pushed open easily. I hesitated, with my hand on the knob, before stepping inside.

In the front hall I stopped. There was the mahogany bookcase with the glass bowl on top. There was the old red dictionary I had used in high school, there the bookends carved like rearing horses, the ivory whale with its missing eye. On one shelf a book stood a little pulled out. I tried to remember whether it had always been that way.

From the hall I stepped into the dusky living room. Between the heavy curtains the shades were drawn. The old couch was still there, the old armchair where my father had liked to sit, the piano where I'd once learned to play Mozart sonatas and boogie-woogie blues. On one side of the piano was a space where a tall vase had stood, between the piano bench and the rocking chair. My mother was standing near that space, at the back of the room. I could not understand why she was standing there, in this darkened room, in the middle of a sunny day. Then I saw that she was moving very slowly in my direction. She was advancing over the flowered rug as though she were walking along the bottom of a lake. She wore a crisp dress, with sleeves that ended partway down her forearms, and she made no sound as she came stiffly forward through the twilight.

I stepped quickly up to her. "It's—me," I said, holding out my arms, but her head was bowed, evidently the effort of walking absorbed her full attention, and I stood awkwardly there, with my arms held out as if in supplication.

Slowly my mother raised her head and looked up at me. It was like someone gazing up at a building. In the shadows her face bore an expression that struck me as severe. I could feel my arms falling to my sides like folding wings.

"I know you," she said. She stared hard at me, as if she were trying to penetrate a disguise.

"That's a relief," I made myself say.

"I know who you are," she said. She smiled playfully, as if we were in the midst of a game. "Oh, I know who you are."

"I hope so!" I said, with a light little laugh. My laughter disturbed me, like the laughter of a man alone in a theater. Quietly I said, "It's been a long time." And though I had spoken truthfully, I disliked the sound of the words in my mouth, as if I were trying to deceive her in some way.

My mother continued to stare at me. "I heard the bell."

"I didn't mean to frighten you."

She seemed to consider this. "Someone rang the bell. I was coming to the door." She glanced toward the hall, then looked again at me. "When would you like dinner?"

"Dinner? Oh, no no no, I can't stay, not this time. I just—I just—"

"I'm sorry," my mother said, raising a hand and touching it to her face. "You know, I keep forgetting."

When she lowered her hand she said, "What do you want?"

The words were spoken quietly, in a tone of puzzled curiosity. It wasn't a question I knew how to answer. What did I want? I wanted everything to be the way it once was, I wanted family outings and birthday candles, a cool hand on my warm forehead, I wanted not to be a polite middle-aged man standing in a dark living room, trying to see his mother's face.

"I wanted to see you," I said.

She studied me. I studied her. She was paler than I remembered. Her grayish hair, shot through with a violent white I had never seen before, was combed back in soft, neat waves. A tissue stuck out from the top of her dress. She wore no watch. "Would you like a cup of tea?" she suddenly asked, raising her eyebrows in a way I knew well, a way that pulled her eyelids up and widened her eyes. I recalled how, whenever I came home from college, and in the years afterward, when I came back less and less, my mother would always say, looking up at me with eyebrows raised high and eyes shining with pleasure: "Would you like a cup of tea?"

"That's just what I'd like!" I said, immediately disliking my tone, and taking my mother by the arm, which had grown so thin that I was afraid of leaving purple bruises on her skin, I led her slowly to the swinging door beside the carved cabinet with the marble top.

Slowly my mother raised her head and looked up at me. It was like someone gazing up at a building.

The kitchen was so bright that for an instant I had to close my eyes. When I opened them I saw that my mother, too, had closed her eyes. I thought of the two of us, standing there with closed eyes, in the sunny kitchen, like children playing a game. But no one had told me the rules of the game, maybe it was a mistake to have entered the kitchen, and as I stood in the brightness beside my silent mother, whose eyes remained tightly shut, I wondered what I was supposed to do. I thought of our infrequent telephone conversations, composed of threads of speech woven among lengthening silences. On the refrigerator hung a faded drawing of a tree. I had made it in the third grade. The counters looked clean enough, only a few crumbs here and there, the stove top unstained except for a brownish rim around a single burner. When I turned back to my mother, she was standing exactly as before. Her eyes were open.

"Is everything all right?" I asked, irritated by my words, because everything was not all right, but at the sound of my voice my mother turned to look at me.

"Where did you come from?" she said gently, with a touch of wonder in her voice.

I opened my mouth to reply. The question, which at first had seemed straightforward enough, began to feel less simple as I considered it more closely, and I hesitated, wondering what the correct answer might be.

"Oh now I remember," my mother said. Her face was so filled with happiness that she looked young and hopeful, like a girl who has just been invited to a dance. Although I was moved to see my mother's face filled with happiness, as if she had just been invited to a dance, still I could not be certain whether what she remembered was that her son was standing before her, in the bright kitchen, after all this time, or whether she was remembering some other thing.

She moved slowly to the stove, lifted the small red teakettle, and began to carry it toward the sink. She frowned with the effort, as if she were lifting a great weight.

"Here, let me help with that," I said, and reached for the teakettle. My hand struck her hand, and I snatched my hand away, as though I had cut her with a knife.

At the sink my mother stood still, looked down at the teakettle in her hand, and frowned at it for a few moments. She began struggling with the top, which came off suddenly. She placed the kettle in the sink and turned on the cold water, which rushed loudly into the empty pot. She turned off the water, pushed the top back on, and carried the teakettle to the stove, where she set it carefully on a burner. She stood looking at the kettle on the burner, then began making her way to the kitchen table. I pulled out a chair and she sat down stiffly. She remained very erect, with her shoulders back and her hands folded in her lap.

I was grateful, for if she smiled at me in that way, after all this time, then things must be all right between us.

I stepped over to the stove and gave a turn to the silver knob. It felt familiar to my fingers, with its circle of ridges and the word HIGH in worn-away black letters.

When I sat down at the table, my mother, who had been staring off in the direction of the washing machine, slowly looked over at me. "I don't know how long it will be," she said. It might have been the state of my nerves, or the rigidity of her posture, or the solemnity of her tone, but I could not tell whether she was talking about the water in the teakettle or about how much time she had left on earth.

"You look younger than ever!" I said, in that false voice of mine.

She smiled tenderly at me then, as she had always smiled at me. And I was grateful, for if she smiled at me in that way, after all this time, then things must be all right between us, in one way or another, after all this time.

"Would you like to sit on the porch?" she said, looking over toward the door with the four-paned window in it. Then I remembered how, in summer, she always liked to sit on the porch. She would sit on the porch with a book from the library and a glass of iced tea with two ice cubes and a slice of lemon.

I turned off the stove and led my mother to the windowed kitchen door. The dark red paint on the strips between the panes had begun to flake away, and I recalled taking a chisel long ago and scraping off the new paint that had gotten onto the glass.

I removed the chain from the lock and led her down the two steps onto the hot porch. Under the partially rolled-up bamboo blinds, through which lines of sunlight fell, the windows were glittery with dust.

"You ought to let me lower the screens," I said.

"You know," she said, "there was something I was going to say. It's on the tip of my tongue." She touched her face with curved fingers. "I'm getting so forgetful!"

On the chaise longue my mother lay back as I lifted her legs into place. "It's so nice out here," she said, looking around with a tired smile. "You never hear a sound." She half closed her eyes. "I could sit here all day." She paused. "Oh now I remember."

I waited. "You remember?"

"Of course I remember." She looked at me teasingly.

"I'm not sure—"

"The room."

"I still—I don't—"

"I have to get the room ready. That's what I have to do. The room. You remember."

"Oh, the room, oh no no no, not tonight, I was just passing through. Let's just—if we could just sit here and talk."

"That would be very nice," my mother said, placing one hand over the other, on her lap. She looked at me as if she were waiting for me to say the next thing. "If you see anything you like," she said, raising a hand lightly and motioning at the furniture, the bamboo blinds, the framed grade-school drawings on the wall. "Anything at all." Her hand returned to her lap. Slowly she closed her eyes.

I sat on the hot porch with its dusty windows, beside the old wicker table with the two cork coasters rimmed with wood. I felt that I wanted to say something to my mother, something that would make her understand, though what it was that I wanted her to understand wasn't entirely clear to me. And we didn't have all day, time was passing, I was here for just a short visit. "Mom," I heard myself say, in a low voice. The clear sound of that word, on the quiet porch, troubled me, as though a hand had been laid on my face. "Can you hear me?" In her chair my mother stirred slightly. "I know I haven't been here for a while, things kept coming up, you know how it is, but you know—" It was really too warm on the porch, with the sun coming in and the windows closed. I considered opening one of the windows and lowering the screen, but I didn't want to disturb my mother, who appeared to have fallen asleep. In a vivid slash of light, her forearm looked so fiercely pale that a vagueness or mistiness had come over it, as though it were evaporating in the heat. I glanced at my gleaming watch. The afternoon was getting on. Yet I couldn't very well leave my mother asleep on the porch, like an abandoned child, I couldn't simply tiptoe away, could I, without saying goodbye. And there were things I wanted to say to my mother, things I had always meant to say to her, before it was too late. In the heavy sunlight, which pressed against me like warm sand, I leaned back and closed my eyes.

II

Often I dreamed of walking through the rooms of my old house, looking for my mother, only to wake up and find myself in a distant city. Now I had the confused sensation of waking up in my old house, on the familiar porch, but at the same time of entering a dream. For how likely was it, after all, that I was sitting on the porch of my childhood house, on a summer's day, like a boy with nothing to do? I saw at once that the light had changed. Though sunlight still came through the dusty windows, a brightness had seeped from the air. Heavy-looking branches pressed against the glass. I saw one other thing: my mother was not there. Ropes of cobweb stretched from the top of a window to the back of the chaise longue. How had I not noticed them before? I felt ripples of anxiety, as if I'd been careless in some way that could never be forgiven, and flinging myself up from the chair, so that the legs scraped on the wooden floor, I threw a glance at the dusty branches and hurried into the kitchen.

She was not there. On the stove a dented teakettle, reddish black, sat on its unlit burner. In the changed light I saw thick streaks of grime on the stove, cobwebs in corners, a yellowish stain on the table. A square of linoleum curled back at the base of the refrigerator. Outside the dirty window, big leaves moved against the glass. The pane had a crack shaped like a river on a map.

I pushed open the creaking door and entered the living room. It was much darker than before. I imagined the sunlight pushing against the front of the house, feeling for a way in. My mother was standing with her back to me, in the middle of the room, like someone lost in a forest.

"Oh there you are!" I said, in a tone of hearty cheerfulness. She continued to stand there with her back to me. In the darkening room she seemed unable to move, as if the air were a cobwebby thickness tightening about her. I walked up to my mother, stepped around her as one might walk around a lamppost, and turned to face her.

Often I dreamed of walking through the rooms of my old house, looking for my mother, only to wake up and find myself in a distant city.

"I was worried about you," I said.

She raised her head slowly, in order to look up into my face. It seemed to take her a long time. When she was done, she frowned in perplexity. "I'm sorry," she said, squinting up at me as if into a harsh brightness. "It's hard for me to remember faces."

I bent my face toward hers, thumped a finger against my chest. "It's me! Me! How can you—listen, I know I haven't been out here for a while, it's hard to explain, there was always something, but I'm here now and I—"

"That's all right," she said, reaching out and patting my arm, as if to comfort me.

I stood before her, uncertain what to do. It may have been an effect of the darkening light, in that room of heavy curtains and closed shades, but her hair looked thinner than before, a few strands came straggling down, one of her eyelids was nearly closed. A white gash of slip hung below her crooked dress. Her face now struck me as gaunt and sharp-edged, as though the bones of her nose and cheeks were pressing through her skin. I looked around the room. The edges of the fireplace seemed to be crumbling away, the couch was sinking down under the weight of the heavy afternoon, the piano keys were the yellow of October leaves.

"Would you like to sit down?" I asked.

My mother looked at me with a puzzled frown. Her eyes seemed dim and vague. "That would be a very nice thing to do," she said. She reached out and touched my hand. "You know, I'm not as young as we used to be." She laughed lightly and lowered her hand. She looked at me again. "It's so nice of you to come." She glanced down, as if she were searching for something on the rug. I followed her gaze, wondering whether she had dropped a ring or a coin. In the room's darker dusk, the pattern of swirling flowers had melted away.

When I raised my eyes, she was looking at me. "You're a nice boy," she said, and touched the back of my hand with two fingers.

Again I took her upper arm, so thin that it was like grasping a wrist, and began directing her slowly toward the armchair beside the lamp table. She advanced with such difficulty that it was as if she weren't moving her feet at all, but allowing me to push her along the surface of the rug. My hand, heavy with veins, reminded me of an ugly face. As we drew closer to the chair, my mother began to move so slowly that I could no longer tell whether we were making our way forward, inch by inch, or just standing there, like people trying to advance against a gale. I began to urge her on with gentle tugs, but I could feel her pulling back against my fingers. Then I noticed that her mouth was taut, her arm tense, her eyebrows close together. "It's all right," I whispered, "we can just—" "No!" she shouted, in a voice so fierce that I dropped my hand and stepped back in alarm. "Is there something—" I began, and at once it came back to me, her refusal to sit in my father's chair ever again, all those years ago, after the funeral. Once more I took her arm, this time turning her in the direction of the couch. As we came up to the shadowy coffee table I saw a shape that I remembered, and I bent down to look at the blue man with the blue bundle on his back. Dust lay on his blue hair. One of his blue shoulders was chipped. "Look at that!" I said, picking him up and turning him from side to side. "Old Man Blue. Remember how I used to think he was the oldest man in the world?"

> **I seemed to hear a humming sound, a spectral tune, drifting up out of my childhood.**

"Older and older," my mother said.

At the corner of the couch she sat down rigidly, as though she could no longer bend in the right places. Though the room was warm, I drew the red and gray afghan over my mother's legs. "Here," I said, turning on the table lamp. The dim bulb flickered but did not go out. On the lampshade I saw a faded woman with a faded parasol, bending over a faded bridge. "Now we can sit and have a nice talk."

"You can't do that," she said faintly. Her eyes had begun to close. I tried to understand why we could not sit and talk for a while, there were things

I needed to say to my mother, even though I didn't know what they were, and if we talked I would perhaps find what I was looking for. Then I saw my mother slowly raising a hand, as if she were reaching for something, though her eyes were closed. The hand rose to the level of her shoulder and continued higher, until it stopped between her face and the lamp. Her hand was so thin that the light seemed to shine through it.

"Do you want—" I said, and with sudden understanding I bent forward and turned off the lamp. Slowly my mother's hand descended to her lap and was still.

I returned to my father's sagging chair, in the silent living room, and sat looking at my mother as she remained upright and unmoving in her corner of the couch. Despite the change I sensed in her, since our time on the porch, she seemed calm, in her way, sitting there with the afghan on her lap. It was like the old days, when I would come home from wherever I was and my mother would take up her position exactly there, in the corner of the couch, with a book and her reading glasses, while my father graded papers in his study and I sat in the armchair with a book of my own. I had liked coming home, liked sitting in that chair with the sound of pages turning and of children playing in the street, liked, above all, the sense of something peaceful from childhood still flowing through the house, and I wondered how it was that I had let it all slip away. And as I sat there, in the drowsy warmth, I seemed to hear a humming sound, a spectral tune, drifting up out of my childhood. It was something my mother used to sing, a song from her own girlhood. "I remember," I said, because I wanted to talk to my mother, I wanted to tell her that I remembered a tune she had once hummed, when I was a boy, but the sound of the humming crept into my words, and only then did I realize that my mother was sitting there humming that tune. And I was stirred that she was humming a tune from our two childhoods, as she sat in the darkening room with her eyes closed, a tune that ascended in three leaps and then came slowly down, like a feather falling, but at the same time I wanted her to stop humming that tune so that I could speak to her, before I was no longer there. After all, it was only a short visit. When my mother stopped humming I said, "I know I haven't been back for a while, but if we could just talk a little, a little talk, talk to me—" The words sounded louder than I had intended, as if I had shouted them in an empty house.

At the sound of my voice my mother seemed to start awake. She pushed the blanket from her lap and began struggling to get up. As if roused from a sleep of my own, I began to rise, so that I could catch her if she fell, and for a moment we were both half risen and leaning forward, as though we had both seen something dangerous in the dusky dark. Motionless in her half rising, my mother said, in a raspy whisper that seemed to come from the room itself: "Why are you here?" The question was like a rush of wind. It seemed to me that if only I could answer that question, then something in the day would be saved, and I tried to find the words that were lying deep within me, like blood. But already my mother had sat back against the couch, as if she had been pulled backward by a pair of hands. In the dissolving room a weariness came over me, like the tiredness of childhood, and I sank down for a moment into the armchair in order to gain the strength to rise.

III

When I opened my eyes the room had sunk deeper into darkness, it might have been sunset or midnight or winter or some other time, and I had the feeling that if I didn't get up at once from my father's chair and return to the outside world I would become part of the dying room, like Old Man Blue or the faded woman on the lampshade. On the barely visible couch I could make out a crumple of afghan. My mother seemed not to be there. I pushed myself to my feet and made my way through the dark over to the couch, where I began patting the afghan as though my mother might have slipped under it, like a cat. Then I lifted it up, to make sure. Under the afghan I felt something smooth and hard. I could not understand what it was, under the afghan, my fingers kept pressing here and there, then suddenly it revealed itself to be an eyeglass case. For a moment I had the odd sensation that the eyeglass case was my mother, who had grown smaller and taken on a new form. And I felt a surge of guilty relief to think that my mother had become an eyeglass case, since then I might be able to take my leave without worry, knowing it was unlikely she would come to harm. Even as I pursued this thought I began to look about, maybe she had strayed over to the piano, or maybe she was sitting quietly in the kitchen, waiting for her water to boil, and as I stepped through the room that seemed to be nothing but an expanse of darkness, I saw a figure standing not far from the rocking chair. I wondered where she was trying to go, in that all but motionless way of hers, but when I came close to her I saw that she was facing the corner where the vase had once stood. She was standing between the rocking chair and the piano, as if she were considering whether to advance into the wall. "Do you want to sit down?" I said, in a voice that might have been a whisper or a yell, but she stood fixed and immobile there. "I really have to be on my way," I said, angry at the impatience in my voice, for what right did I have to be impatient, I who had not been out this way for longer than I cared to remember. Then I reached out to touch my mother, who was like someone lying on a couch, though she was standing upright before me. My hand came to rest on the lower part of her upper arm. It felt stiff as a stick. My mother seemed to be hardening, here in the dark. In the black air, her wisps of hair seemed pressed to her skull, the skin of her face wax-pale. "What do you want me to do?" I said, and I heard in my voice a petulance, as if I had been deprived of something.

The restraint of my furious pacing made me feel that I was fighting my way through a soft obstruction.

"Can you hear me?" I asked. "I'm right here," I said. My mother said nothing. I stood there like a man in a wide field, standing by a tree. She was so still that it was as if she had come to the end of motion. I tried to look at my watch, but most of my arm had vanished. In the dark I began to pace tensely up and down, with a kind of ferocious wariness, fearful of crashing into an edge of furniture. The restraint of my furious pacing made me feel that I was fighting my way through a soft obstruction, as though the flowers in the rug had sprung up to the height of my thighs. I imagined the bushes outside, rising over the tops of the windows, bursting through the glass. In the cracked streets, weed-spears were springing up. Bony cats roamed the deserted houses. It seemed to me that if only I could get my mother to settle in one place, instead of drifting through the house like someone driven by a terrible restlessness, if only I could know that she was calm and still, then I might be able to take my leave with some measure of peace. For though I had not said to her all that I was hoping to say, during this visit, though I had said almost nothing to her, in the course of the afternoon, still we had sat together on the porch, as we used to do, we had sat together in the living room, just the two of us, and that was something, surely.

It occurred to me that she might be better off on the sunlit porch, lying on the chaise beside a glass of iced tea on the wicker table, rather than standing here in the dark living room, and with that idea in mind I stopped pacing and began to make my way toward her. She was still motionless, but I had the impression that her position had changed in some way. As I drew closer, it appeared to me that she was leaning slightly to one side. I tried to make sense of her enigmatic posture, which might have been that of someone starting to turn around. Then I began to realize, in a slow and confused way, that my mother was falling. I sprang toward her but it was too late. She fell with a sharp knock against the arm of the rocking chair. I seized her with both hands. Her arms felt hard as stone. Something rattled as I lifted her up. The empty rocking chair swung back and forth.

"Are you all right?" I cried, but she was locked away in a dream. The side of her hand, where it had struck the chair, seemed hollowed out, as if a piece had chipped off. I looked desperately about. In her rigid condition I could not place her in a chair. For a wild moment I considered laying her across the piano bench.

I lifted my mother in my arms as if she were a young wife or a rolled-up rug and pushed open the door to the kitchen with my foot. The light had drained away. Gigantic leaves pushed up against the windows like hands. With my foot I dragged two chairs from the kitchen table and arranged them side by side. I laid my mother across the seats so that she was pushed up safely against the backs, then rushed over to the old phone on the counter. The line was dead. Dusty cobwebs stretched across the dial. I understood that it was imperative to remain calm, that a solution would present itself, but I found it difficult to concentrate my attention. My mother's position on the chairs seemed perilous. When I bent over to make certain she was safe, I saw that her dress was twisted and the top buttons had come undone. A knob of collarbone thrust up like a knuckle. Carefully, tenderly, I lifted her in my arms. Her face was smooth and calm. In her hardened state, she seemed to be content. I looked about the kitchen, which was sinking out of sight. I had the sense of a forest springing up outside. Holding my mother tightly in my curled arms, I returned to the blackness of the living room. I could see nothing. Her bed lay far away. I thought of the couch, which stood hidden across immense stretches of dark. Even if I could find my way there, even if I could lay her gently down, I imagined her rolling slowly off the cushions and cracking against the edge of the coffee table. Maybe I wasn't thinking clearly, maybe I wasn't thinking at all, but as I gazed frantically around the dark I found myself calling to mind the corner near the piano, where the tall vase had once stood. She had always loved that vase.

Still holding my mother sideways in my arms, as if I were carrying her across a stream, I made my way along the rug to the space between the piano and the rocking chair. They rose up darker than the dark. "Are you all right?" I whispered. My mother said nothing. I tipped my arms to one side until I felt her foot touch the rug. Carefully I stood her upright. Gently I leaned her at an angle against the side of the piano. "There," I said. I drew up the rocking chair so that it rested against the edge of her tilted foot, then stepped away.

In the stillness of the living room my mother stood leaning against the piano, as though she were listening intently to someone playing the slow movement of a sonata. She seemed at peace there in her favorite room, lounging against the old piano, as she used to do. It was she who had taught me to play the piano, when I was seven, and she often liked to stay quiet like that, listening to me play. She was safer here, it seemed to me, than anywhere else, I said to myself, at least for the time being, I thought. For a while I stood in the dark, watching my mother at rest in her corner. Then I came forward and kissed her stony shoulder. "It was good seeing you again," I said. I would make the necessary calls, I would see to it that she was looked after properly. I stepped back and gave a little wave.

When I reached the front hall I turned to look at the living room, which was no longer there. My visit had had its ups and downs, not everything had gone as smoothly as I might have liked, but we had talked a little, my mother and I, we had sat in the old places. Now she was resting at a safe angle against the side of the piano. She would be all right, I felt, in her way. I cast a farewell glance in her direction, giving a final wave into the dark, and as I turned toward whatever was left of the day or night I took what consolation I could in knowing that we'd had a good visit, taken all in all, and that I was bound to be out that way, once again, in a while.

SOMETHING TRUE

I like expensive laws like
most people like expensive things.

It's a disease of the laws, where
my toes lose all feeling, flap under

the ball of my foot, anything it takes
to destroy me, and so, shit,

I buy what I like and like working.
I love pathetic laws, feed them bigger laws,

just
one more nested expense in the dream of heaven.

A scene meets in the clap of sentence against sentence a
pathetic law, sequences it.

Some pathetic law wanders in
missing a leg. Some theoretical law manifests.

Some new trouble requires some new
law book for treatment. Somebody

who looks like me. Somebody who likes like me.
Some new truth wanders in,

breaks a leg. Files a lawsuit, wins. Even
gets better. Keeps getting better, grows larger,

and soon it's one of the dozen biggest truths but it doesn't slow down,
it devours the other truths, it digests them into

sterility, all other truth, all otherness,
organized into one

eyelid over the world, one
eyelid over the other, and the other eyelid

over the other too.

FICTION

Two Stories

Diane Williams

I Always Wanted That

WHY WOULD ANYONE BE FEARFUL THAT THE MAN MIGHT BECOME distressed or that he might lose his temper in their bedroom?

He is a calm man by nature and not liable to break anything really nice by accident. He had decided to disrobe in there—where they keep their Polish woman statuette and the fish dish they use for loose coins.

To be civilized, this man had asked to meet with his wife's new husband.

The three drank tea together, impromptu, from souvenir mugs and paid mind to one another's questions and the uninformative replies. Next, the man had stepped into their bedroom, towing his roller board, after inquiring if he could change into more comfortable clothes in preparation for his travel.

He said he'd be leaving soon enough—flying into the northeast corridor, which he'd heard was an absolute quagmire.

Hard rain had been falling freely and for several days. In addition, now, they were suffering occasional sleet. The pressure, the moisture, and the black clouds were progressing.

This is a humid, continental climate in turmoil.

"You're wearing that?" the wife said when the man reemerged in Spandex fitness apparel.

"We found it in Two Dot! You don't remember?" he said—fondly patting lightly his own chest. "It's breathable. It's stretchable."

"I thought it was in Geraldine," the wife said.

"But look here, maybe you should stay the night," the new husband said. He had grown more or less bold—and was it too late or too soon for him to provide a repast?

He offered seedcake and coffee—the mild and friendly kind—this time, to drink.

"What are you doing?" said the wife—for her husband's hands were filled with the sugar bowl and the creamer and several cups were swinging from his fingers by their ears.

All so beautifully turned out, the dishes found the table's surface safely. These were specimens of the most romantic china service. The gilding was very good—the glaze finely crazed. There were hand-painted sprays on an apple green ground.

"I hope you are a comfort to her," the man said, "and that you show good sense. Because, this is what it is—doesn't everybody have to take care of Tasha?" He did not refer to her sex behavior and instead spoke generally about the dell they had once lived in and lunged silently at his disappointment that he could no longer touch his former wife. He extolled the mountain town where the wife had often reflected that looking up and out—say, over at an elevated ridge—was to her advantage.

Now she resided in this flatter state in an apartment on the third floor across from a church—from where she could see its spire.

Her glance often ran recklessly toward it, as if spurting over a rim, or through a spout.

The chancel and the sanctuary had lately been under ugly scaffolding. A few years back, one of the two aisle rose windows had been carried away for restoration and had not been returned yet.

Fortunately, the inner-draw draperies of the couple's window facing the church were made of cheerful chintz.

"It wouldn't surprise me if I stayed," the man said. "Well, sure, yes, absolutely, you bet!' he said. "I'm a little nervous."

He prepared to eat by sitting down and stressing his jaws with a big smile.

His cheeks are elongated and hollow—his brow highly peaked. His face is not difficult to explain—it's cathedral-like.

The new husband's whole head has an unfinished look that promises to work out well. Whereas the wife's furrowed face—some have said—shows heavy evidence of deception and is cause for alarm.

Right then, in front of them, the woman uncapped a tube of gel ointment and applied a dab of it under a long fingernail. Next she opened a cellophane packet from which she withdrew a cracker that produced plenty of crumbs.

The husband told the man, "Surely you'd be welcome to stay!"

As the wife mopped up her particles and the traces, she spoke somewhat rudely to the man and also to her husband.

"I went somewhere . . ." the man said, expanding on a point. Hadn't he been molded to better express himself?

A small object's overall smallness on a shelf caught his glance—a round-bodied jar of free-blown glass whose neck was straight, that had flat shoulders—a flask he would not get to smash! It was streaked with permanent crimson and cold black. It had about it the real suggestion of the softness of human flesh.

"Did you imagine me the way I am?" the man asked the new husband, who answered no.

"What do you mean?"

"But I am not against you," the husband said.

"Say a little more."

Sirens in the street produced a brief, headstrong fugue.

"Say a little more," said the man.

The husband got up from his chair. Why should anyone be fearful of his certain combinations of words, narrowly spaced?

The husband gave himself ample time to speak.

No gross vices were explored. His is not the voice of a man in the pulpit. No personal impulses were defined or analyzed.

He did deliver a slovenly interrogatory.

He went uphill, downhill with—"Wah-aaaaaaaat waaahz it ligh-ike, with herrrrrrrr-rah, for you-ooooooo—?"

That's all that he was saying.

Nothing seemed to want to end it.

Clarinda

THIS SEEMED TO BE MY CHANCE. HE WAS OBVIOUSLY—I HAVE TRIED NOT TO focus on that quality. Although, this was not Providence protruding into my life and shaking its big hand out in a hello.

He said, "This happens to me all of the time! Can you help me? You look just like the woman on the bus who was sitting across from me, except for the hair. I have to get something for my daughter. Should I buy TRESemmé?"

I said, "I am sure your daughter would like something fancy and fragrant. Buy this one." Then the man said, "I smell a bakery."

"You said, 'I smell a bakery?'" I said.

"Yes."

"I smell it, too."

"I hate it!" the man said.

"You said you hate it?" I said.

We must have talked for many minutes more and after that I bought bond paper and a packet of rubber bands. I say *elastics*.

I wish he had seemed more genuinely impressed with me. The man had grown bolder and he talked more about his daughter.

Let me elaborate on that—he said there was no wife.

As to the life he was leading, I did not need my imaginings.

I was saying, after his confession, "You are smart. You are very smart. You are very wise."

I have always thought I was a careful person. I likely tired of that. When you get older, you get tired. I do.

I am a suburban woman and naïve and I did not hear my voice of caution.

Once inside my house, the man looked at his face in the wall mirror, then he touched my shoulder.

One aspect of the whole situation is that it would soon seem to be normal.

We sleep in the same bed. We drink one or two glasses of neat whiskey before dinner. He's remained with me and so has Clarinda. His principle—to stop her crying—not to lay down a law for it, though.

When we disappoint Clarinda, we say we are sorry and she says, "I am disappointed."

I go to work every day and so does this man.

Her father gives Clarinda overwhelming praise as much as he can. A girl can hardly do better than this. Have you heard of a wellhead of praise?

Clarinda's a flower that grows in the field that we cannot gather.

The main room in the house is low-ceilinged with two wing chairs. I wear a lily of the valley scent.

Innocence—this is a thing to brood over.

Clarinda is not a child and she holds an important position here. Her name is frequently used. I am telling you it is not unpleasant to listen to the sound of her name. I may try to place my arm around Clarinda's shoulder, along the shoulders, but she doesn't move closer to me. No, I may get tired of using her name and of saying, "How clever you are." She is above average. I don't see myself as above average. I have worn thin. How much more wonderful everybody else is.

I have forgotten the man is her father. That is sad to say and sad to hear. I overheard Clarinda on the telephone when she said one of the most brilliant and original things in the English language. Of course, this is according to me, of course. An example, please.

I do not remember what she said sufficiently and this does not sound like a lie.

Often when I tidy up and make beds before I start supper, I'm annoyed and I think I'm a little brat.

There are delicate flowers on my upholstery fabric on the wing chairs. Not delicate. The way they've lasted—dun, tan, and cinnamon blossoms. White carnations?—cinnamon-colored lilies on a coffee-colored background.

It is my responsibility to admire them because I picked it—reluctantly, carefully.

OH YOU ABSOLUTE DARLING

You are sexier than anyone I've ever met.
You feel better to touch than anyone I've ever met.
You're like a Vargas girl.
You're not exactly a barrel of laughs
so much as a barrel of erections.
Dear Gypsy-themed Barbie doll:
those jeans will do you no good.

If I were a mosquito, I'd suck
all the blood out from you in five minutes.
If we were stranded together on a desert island,
I don't think you'd last long.
I'd like to come over there and squeeze the living daylights out of you.
I'd like to spin you like a top
and fuck you ten different ways.
Such tender meat—*raw*—dropping from the bone!

You're sex on a stick.
You're a sex bomb.
You're the sex symbol of our set.
And this is why you have the male friends
you think you do, why women hate you.
The last twelve years, you have *no idea*
how many millions of haploid gametes I've spilled in your honor!
How I've resented you for walking around
as though you were a normal person.

I'm sorry to break it to you.
Let me explain how this works: when X said
he threw away your press photo, what he meant was
it's tacked up in his bathroom right now, for inspiration.
I think you think my attraction to you is funny.
Believe me, scared is how you should be.

You're a basket of sexual fruits.
What kind of fruit are you?
I'd like to eat you up with my penis
but I don't know how to do that!
You smell like peach. You smell like mango.
The way you smell drives me crazy,

the divots in your back drive me wild.
I love the scoop above your ass—your slender throat—
your little pretty limbs and princess-face—
your gorgeous rippling muscles covered
all over by this smooth, this tawny upholstery—
little doll—delicate flower—the way your ribs
stick out, it's like a second rack—and this,
I love *this*: what do people call it?

You should always be naked.
You should always hold your wineglass like so.
You have what no one else has—breasts
that demand to be taken notice of
and the tiniest waist I've ever seen.
If your waist were any smaller, you wouldn't exist.

"Oh You Absolute Darling"—is an endearment Count Vronsky uses to spur on his mare during a race in *Anna Karenina.* During a critical jump Vronsky shifts his weight ineptly, causing her to fall and break her back. The horse is shot.

FICTION

The Right Imaginary Person

We were part of a large group of people at a *yakitoriya* in Shinjuku, celebrating somebody or other's birthday, but we'd both gotten stuck at the wrong end of the long table, cut off from the main conversation, which was drunken and flirty. "I bet everyone tells you how great your Japanese is," she said, lighting a cigarette.

"They do," I acknowledged.

"Then let's talk about something else."

Robert Anthony Siegel

It was 1985, almost the end of summer. Sunao told me she was nearing the end of a long, boring adolescent period in which she was trying to become the opposite of her mother. She didn't want to become a good cook, or keep the house clean, or be loved by children—or be nice to anyone, for that matter—or cultivate any of the traditional arts expected of a young lady of marriageable age from a good family. "Calligraphy?" she said. "Can you think of anything more boring? And flower arranging? It makes me want to throw up." Instead she drank a sort of white lightning called *shōchū* and smoked Golden Bat cigarettes and wrote science fiction stories in which androids took on unplanned human emotions, slept with each other, had imaginary pregnancies, and gave birth to children that were strings of computer code.

"But what about you?" she asked. "It's not fair if you don't tell me anything."

I looked at her hand, the delicate fingers smudged with ink. There were nights when I rode the Yamanote Line in a circle, jammed against the other passengers, just to feel someone else's pressure on my skin.

But what I told her about was my trip to Shikoku, how I went alone with a backpack over the vacation, taking old buses from village to village, and how in one of those villages a group of kids had formed a circle around me and asked to touch my hair. I had kneeled down on the grass beside the road, closed my eyes, and felt their hands running over my head. Small, gentle hands reading my otherness like braille.

"Was that creepy?" she asked.

"No, it felt deep."

Later, after the party broke up, I walked her to the train station, and in the shadows by the entrance where I was going to ask for her phone number she unexpectedly reached up and brushed my bangs from my face. "It does feel a little different," she said. "Softer than Japanese hair."

We went to her place, a six-mat tatami room with a little kitchen she never used and a single window that looked out on the courtyard in back. We stood in the middle of the tiny space and kissed, bodies slowly softening like candles. Her mouth tasted like *shōchū* and smoke. She pulled off her shirt and her breasts were in my palms, the nipples long and thick, the color of chocolate. And then she was melting to the tatami, pulling me down on top of her. With each touch of her hand I felt like I was being sewn back together.

Afterward, we bathed in her tub, which was square and deep, the water so hot that her hand on my thigh felt like a bruise. Then we stretched out naked on top of her futon, and I watched the steam rise from her body into the air. She had a mole in the hollow at the base of her neck, a small half-moon scar on her calf, and silver polish on her toes. "Do you ever get homesick?" she asked.

"Never," I said, though of course I did. A part of my mind was stuck roaming the big Victorian my parents had so painstakingly restored and now left only when they had to, for the pharmacy or the liquor store.

"I don't think I could live in a foreign country," said Sunao. "I get lonely too easily, and then I end up doing things like this."

She pulled off her shirt and her breasts were in my palms, the nipples long and thick, the color of chocolate.

Resting her head on my chest, she read me a story she'd written about a group of children who live in a colony on another planet and are taken care of by parents who are nothing but computer-generated holograms. The story wasn't science fiction at all, or not what I thought of as science fiction; it felt honest and emotional, full of the yearning to touch and the sadness of not being real. "That's just so beautiful," I said, thinking of the letters I wrote to my parents, packed with fabrications about my life in Tokyo: how I had discovered an ancient scroll with the work of a lost poet; how I had an audience with the emperor and he handed me a silver tray of bonbons with his own hands, scandalizing the officials around us . . . I never actually mailed those letters, just collected them in a box in the closet.

"The secret is to pretend you're someone else," said Sunao, taking my fingers from her hair and holding them in her hand, kissing them one by one. "You can't be the person who worries what other people think."

"Who's left then?"

"The imaginary person who tells the truth."

The next day, I left the library early, went to the market, and carried the groceries to her place, where I made dinner using the one pan that she owned. While I cooked she read me a story about an alien race that is being destroyed by a plague of dreams so beautiful that the sleeper refuses to wake. The cure for this plague can only be made from the hearts of human children who have never known love, so a scientist is sent to Earth to collect as many sad orphan hearts as she can. Wearing the body of a teenage girl like a space suit, she goes from orphanage to orphanage, killing children and extracting their hearts, even as spring comes to Tokyo, the cherry trees bloom, people get drunk in the park, and the last signal from her planet dies away forever.

Sunao didn't have a table, so we ate at the lovely Japanese-style desk where she did her writing—sitting side by side and looking out the window at the evening light blueing the courtyard. "Do you ever feel like the alien in your story?" I asked.

"You speak the language, but you don't know anything about real Japanese."

"Sometimes," she said.

I thought of the children in Shikoku, how they had touched my hair and run off, leaving me at a bus stop that was nothing but a patch of grass by the roadside. "I never realized Japanese people got lonely in that way."

"You speak the language, but you don't know anything about real Japanese."

"You're a real Japanese, and I know you."

"That's what I like about you, that you need me so badly. You're a being from another planet, and I'm your human guide, like in a sci-fi movie." She rested her hand on my knee, very lightly. "I want to be the only one on Earth who understands you," she said.

"It's not like there's a lot of competition." But I could feel something happening inside me, a slowing down, like when the kids touched my hair.

"And I want *you* to be the only one who understands *me*," she said.

"I would like that."

She gave a little laugh. "No, you wouldn't, not really. If you did, you'd realize this is all just playacting."

"What is?"

"All of this—dinner, my stories, you and me. In less than a year I'll graduate from school and get a job teaching kindergarten in some suburb or other while looking for an eligible man to marry."

"You don't have to do what everyone else is doing."

"Resistance is futile in a country like this, because the thing you reject isn't just out there, it's in here." She tapped her head. "Obedience is encoded in us through two thousand years of inbreeding."

"Are you saying that you are genetically unable to stop yourself from becoming a kindergarten teacher?"

"Can a sunflower refuse to follow the sun? Can a girl refuse to grow breasts?" She got up and placed the notebook with her story back in the bookcase: four shelves of cheap notebooks dating back to grade school, their covers imprinted with red hearts or Hello Kitty cartoons. "You'll never understand," she said, running her finger over the spines. "You don't want to."

Sunao wasn't completely wrong; deep down I couldn't understand. That made her furious and she broke up with me often, usually late at night, when the trains had stopped running and I had to walk two hours back to my place. I'd call and leave messages, and we'd meet the next day, or the day after that, to argue and then kiss so that we could see how exactly we fit together, her body pressed to mine.

But one night in February I looked up from my book and found her observing me with a hard, clinical expression, as if I were a beetle and she were going to pin me to a board. "I know what the problem is," she said.

"What problem?" I asked.

"You think I'm ugly."

Sunao looked like she'd come off a scroll from the Heian period, the era of aristocratic women in flowing robes and long hair: a pale round face, full lips, and eyebrows so elegant I would sometimes trace them with my finger. "That's ridiculous," I said.

"I've been teased all my life about my fat face."

I had no idea that her looks weren't the general ideal anymore, that they hadn't been the ideal for about a thousand years. "I think you're beautiful," I told her.

I could see that she knew I meant it, and that she despised me for it. "That's because you're a foreigner and don't really know what Japanese women are supposed to look like."

"So you think you're ugly too?"

"Obviously."

"And what does that make me?" I asked, not sure I had a right to be hurt when the subject was her looks.

"Blind."

The walk home was so cold that it felt like ice crystals were forming inside my heart. I couldn't erase the look of contempt Sunao had given me. Back in my tiny four-mat room, I lay shivering under the quilts, unable to sleep, and then in the empty space before dawn I began thinking about my sister, Daisy, remembering how I'd stood in our backyard in New Jersey and watched her climb out of her bedroom window onto the roof of the house to scream at her boyfriend. *That's right, you better run*, she yelled down at him as he jogged across the grass toward the gate. *You better fucking run*. She stood at the very edge of the roof, giving him the finger with both hands, and when he was gone she lay down on the black shingles, her arms and legs spread as if claiming space.

"Hey," I yelled up.

"Leave me alone."

She was vice president of the drama club at school, and still bitter about losing the presidency. She wrapped scarves around her neck and played dress-up and made faces in the mirror: her Marilyn Monroe face, her Jean-Paul Belmondo face, with a cigarette drooping from the corner of her mouth. She had a maddening way of narrowing her eyes at me, as if she knew something about adulthood that she wasn't telling. She wrote messages to herself in felt-tip pen on her arms—*only 10 miles to Broadway, you can walk if you have to*. She was seventeen, and I was fourteen, and we'd just found out that she would need another round of chemo.

I got up and called Sunao and left a long, rambling message—left messages every day for a week till she finally picked up the phone. "I'm angry at you because you left," she said to me.

"You told me to leave."

"If you really loved me, you would have found a way to convince me to let you stay."

I was sitting with my legs in my *kotatsu*, a little table with an electric heat lamp on the bottom, surrounded by a quilted skirt to hold in the warmth. A half-finished letter was spread on the Formica tabletop, destined, like all the others, for the pile in the box. I'd taken Sunao's advice and pretended someone else was writing it, one of my professors, an elderly man with a vague manner and white chalk dust on his baggy suit. *Dear Mr. and Mrs. Nussbaum*, it ran, *I regret to inform you that your son, Benjamin, seems to have fallen ill. He sits in the library with a book in front of him, but he never turns the page . . .*

I'd picked that professor because he always seemed so serene, sipping tea in his little office, which was lined with novels in three languages. But I'd clearly made some kind of mistake. He could tell you the plot of every story by Balzac or Chekhov or Tanizaki, but he couldn't explain why I'd suddenly begun remembering my sister, particularly the last few months of her illness. I'd tried to make him write to my parents about her, about the way she looked sitting in the big armchair in her hospital room, her head tilted to the side, her eyes closed, resting in the sun coming through the window. Her face was all eyes by then. I got up to go for a walk—anything to get out of that room. "Stay," she said, and I sat back down.

I'd wanted the professor to tell my parents all of that, everything, but each time he lifted his pen, the words disappeared.

"Remember what you said to me about an imaginary person writing your stories?" I asked Sunao.

"Why are you asking me this when we have serious things to discuss about you and me and this relationship?"

"How do you know it's the right imaginary person?"

I heard her light a cigarette, as if considering the question, but what she finally said was, "My parents want to meet you."

I'd wanted the professor to tell my parents all of that, everything, but each time he lifted his pen, the words disappeared.

She'd told me once that if she ever brought a foreigner home her father would probably force her to leave school and move back to Kamakura. "Do you think meeting them is a good idea?" I asked.

"Don't you think it's time?"

I'd heard her talk to them over the phone at night: conversations about relatives and school and her internship at the kindergarten. I'd stop whatever I was doing and watch her press the receiver to her ear with her shoulder. She'd be in nothing but a towel, shaving her legs or rubbing in moisturizer or brushing her hair as she talked, her face slowly changing back to some earlier version of herself: placid and contented, the face of a girl.

"Your parents aren't going to like me," I said.

"They need to know who *I* like."

We took the train out to Kamakura that Saturday afternoon, carrying overnight bags. I'd cut myself shaving—a long, stinging cut too big for a Band-Aid. It had occurred to me that meeting the parents must mean something more than it did in New Jersey, but I didn't want to think about that. Instead, as the endless suburbs rolled by the window, I practiced with the flash cards I'd made, each one containing a polite phrase I'd found in an old grammar book, the sort of phrase so arcane, so excessively, self-abasingly polite that it was almost never used anymore, even by the most punctilious of native speakers.

"You don't have to worry," said Sunao. "Just be yourself and everything will be fine." She was dressed in a prim outfit I'd never seen before: wool tights, a gray flannel skirt and cashmere sweater, a string of pearls, a headband. She lit the end of one cigarette with another all the way to Kamakura, and then threw out the remainder of the pack as we pulled into the station. "Just don't say anything about me smoking or drinking or you staying over at my place," she told me.

"I'm not an idiot."

"And don't say anything about my writing, either."

"They don't know about that?"

"Of course not."

Sunao's parents were bigger, bulkier versions of her, with the same round faces and elegant eyebrows. They ushered us into the family car and took us to an ancient Buddhist monastery, where we walked the grounds, pretending to sightsee, our breath making steam in the air. Gravel paths, delicate wooden temples that seemed to sit weightlessly, like birds ready to take flight: the place was so beautiful that it felt otherworldly, and that aura transferred to Sunao's parents, who looked as if it all belonged to them, as surely as their camel-hair coats and kid-leather gloves. I walked beside them with a mixture of anxiety and hunger, waiting for a chance to use one of the phrases from my flash cards, waiting for the chance to be loved. Sunao kept close, pitching in with the small talk, but after a while she drifted off with her mother, the two of them talking together in low, conspiratorial voices. Her father turned to me, smiling. "They've left us alone for a man-to-man talk, haven't they?" His tone was bemused, but I could see that it was put on for my sake, a form of delicacy.

They had that aura families have, of existing in a self-enclosed world, tucked inside this one but separate.

"You are far too kind to an undeserving wretch like myself," I said, finally using one of the flash-card phrases.

"What marvelous Japanese," he said, giving an embarrassed little laugh. "I understand you plan to become a professor?"

"Yes, that's my intention." But as soon as I heard the words out loud I knew that I wouldn't, that I would never be able to follow through. I didn't want to do anything but watch the late movie with Sunao, and listen to her stories, and run out and buy roast potatoes from the cart pushed by the old man with the plaintive call.

"And will you seek a post here, or in America?"

"Here, definitely."

He fell silent, and I listened to the gravel crunch underfoot as we walked, waiting for him to tell me that I was full of shit and he knew it. But he just kept smiling his troubled smile, and a moment later we had rejoined the women. They were examining a line of stone Buddhas, heartbreakingly beautiful things worn smooth by the years, stippled with yellow lichen. "Lovely, aren't they?" said Sunao's mother.

"So peaceful," I said, looking at their bald heads and serene baby faces, their eyes closed against the world. They were images of the Buddha called Jizō, guardian of children and travelers. I'd seen smaller versions of them now and then at the side of the road, marking the spot of a traffic fatality, or in temple cemeteries, pinwheels and plastic toys left by their feet as offerings.

"It's getting late," said Sunao's father, looking at his watch.

"We should probably head home for dinner," said Sunao's mother, and the four of us started up the path, walking slowly in the falling light. After a little ways, I veered off to examine a stone marker, pretending to read the characters running down the side but really watching the others as they continued on: Sunao between her mother and father, her father with his hands behind his back, her mother gripping her pocketbook. They had that aura families have, of existing in a self-enclosed world, tucked inside this one but separate. At the big front gate, they turned back to view the grounds, looking as if they'd momentarily forgotten my presence.

Sunao's parents fussed over me during dinner, her mother picking out the best things and putting them on my plate, her father filling and refilling my glass with beer, both of them asking questions about my family back home. I had no choice but to tell them about my father, the math professor; my mother, the cruciverbalist, meaning a designer of crossword puzzles. But I didn't tell them that my sister had died when I was sixteen, and that the remainder of the Nussbaums had never quite recovered the ability to speak to each other. I didn't mention the antidepressants and the antianxiety meds and the sleeping pills and the time my mother took too many by accident and we had to call an ambulance.

"And do you have any brothers or sisters?" asked Sunao's father, finally, smiling his patient smile.

"No, I'm an only child."

"It must be hard for your parents, having you so far away," said Sunao's mother, choosing yet more things for me with the long chopsticks used for serving.

"I write to them all the time."

Her face was like Sunao's, but with deep creases around the eyes, which were humorous and kind and disappointed all at once. "I don't think we could stand Sunao being so far. I'd worry too much."

"Even Tokyo's too far," said Sunao's father, pouring me more beer. "But then a girl's different from a boy."

I glanced over at Sunao to see how she was taking this. She sat by her mother, a glass of tea cupped in her hands, nothing showing on her face.

I excused myself to go to the bathroom, but really just wandered the house, trying to breathe. Down a long polished hall, I came across Sunao's old bedroom, a Japanese version of my sister's: anime posters on the walls, shelves with dolls and stuffed animals, a shoe box full of mix tapes.

That night, Sunao slept in her old bedroom, seemingly a world away. I slept in the guest room, which, like the rest of the house, expensive and elegant, smelled of new tatami and varnished wood. But I couldn't really sleep, and I kept imagining that I heard Sunao's footsteps coming down the hall, forbidden and dangerous. Eventually I got up and went to the window to look at the moon, which was just a cold sliver.

In the last year of her life, my sister and I used to sneak out onto the roof of our house at night to smoke weed. This was in Leonia, New Jersey, right across the George Washington Bridge from Manhattan, in a neighborhood of big oaks and old Victorians restored by a generation in search of cheap real estate—our parents and their friends. Daisy and I made a big show of turning up our noses at their hand-painted Italian kitchen tile, their charcoal water filters and basement radon detectors, their inexpensive but highly drinkable wines—everything they used to convince themselves that they were exempt from the dangers outside. We would climb out the bay window and sit on the rough black shingles, looking up at the spray of stars above our heads, feeling the rush of the river beyond the black silhouettes of the trees, and beyond that the dense presence of the city, where life really happened. We never talked much; we had already picked up the habit of silence. We would pass the joint between us, a little star traveling from her hand to mine and back, and the house would seem to float beneath our weight like a ship on the water, traveling with the current, faster and faster into the darkness.

Back in Tokyo on Sunday, we went straight to Sunao's apartment and flopped onto her futon, too tired to take off our coats. We hadn't touched all weekend, had hardly spoken, and now we lay inches apart, staring up at the ceiling. "Your parents aren't so bad," I said, unable to lift my head, which was still full of polite Japanese conversation, spinning around and around. I'd played *Go* with her father, had allowed her mother to teach me calligraphy in a studio full of morning light at the back of the house. Before we left for the station, her mother had given me a scroll with an example of her own writing, surprisingly thick and muscular, full of sharp angles and mad splatter. I'd felt like she was declaring something about herself, something that secretly linked us together.

We never talked much; we had already picked up the habit of silence.

"I think they liked me," I said, wanting to believe it, testing the sound of it.

Sunao turned to look at me. "In Japan, politeness is a wall. The more polite, the higher the wall."

"And how high was their wall?"

"It was electrified, with barbed wire on top."

I thought of Sunao's mother serving me at dinner before anyone else, thought of Sunao's father refilling my glass with beer over and over, though etiquette required the reverse, that I pour for him. I had tried once, but he had grabbed the bottle from me. "At least they weren't rude," I said.

"In the kitchen, my mother turned to me and said, 'Don't give me blue-eyed grandchildren.'"

Everything inside me got very quiet; I could feel the blood moving through my heart. "You're not pregnant, are you?"

"Don't be stupid."

"You don't think that they know that we—"

"I don't care what they know, and anyway, they're not idiots."

And then I felt the delayed sting of her mother's comment. "My eyes are brown, not blue," I said, remembering Sunao's mother handing me the brush, guiding my hand over the paper, showing me how to write the long dripping letters that looked like rain on the window. I had thought she liked me, maybe she even had, but the more important thing was that I had liked her: her gentleness, which was akin to melancholy, her ability to instruct without saying a word. "I don't think anyone in my entire family has blue eyes."

Sunao sat up. "You don't want to marry me. You would never even consider marrying me."

"What are you talking about?" We had never used the word together, and it seemed startling, naked.

"You won't marry me," she said.

"I would marry you," I said, phrasing it as a hypothetical.

"No, you wouldn't."

So frightened it almost seemed to be happening in a dream, I asked her to marry me. She burst into tears and asked why I hadn't proposed sooner. "Because I didn't know you'd say yes," I lied.

"I'm not *saying* yes." She put her head down on my lap, hiding her wet face with her hands. "Poor sweet boy, I feel sorry for you."

She came back and lay on the tatami with her eyes shut while I kissed her face and neck and shoulders.

Sunao went to her first job interview dressed in a blue suit and cream blouse and carrying a leather portfolio tucked under her arm, like all the other soon-to-be-graduated job seekers I saw on the subway. Afterward, she came back and lay on the tatami with her eyes shut while I kissed her face and neck and shoulders. "Why don't you write something?" I suggested. "Writing always makes you feel better."

"There's no point," she said, her eyes still closed.

"Write something gory, about aliens who hollow people out and lay eggs inside their skulls."

"It would only make me sad."

"I'll do dinner and the dishes, and you can work till we go to bed."

"That me is gone. I have to be the other me now, the one who pretends to like children."

The job interviews became routine. Sunao would iron the cream-colored blouse and the blue suit, then spend a long time in front of the mirror, painting her face into a heavy mask. Back at home, she would wash it all off and change into jeans and we would go out for ramen, then watch TV till late at night, as if waiting for some undefined miracle to happen, something that would put a stop to graduation forever. Sitting in the blue glow of her little TV, I wanted to close my eyes against the world, like the beautiful statues of Jizō in the monastery, and imagine us back at the beginning, when she had laid her head on my chest, reading me a story.

And then one night, she shook me awake in that dead space before morning, saying that there was something we had to do. I got dressed in the dark, feeling lucid but not really awake, as if I were just a guest inside her dream. She gave me a big black garbage bag to carry, then grabbed a bottle of *shōchū* from the kitchen counter and opened the front door. I followed her out onto the open-air veranda, dragging the bag, which was surprisingly heavy.

The street was motionless, like an artifact contained in a museum case. The only thing alive was the thrumming of the cicadas, a metallic sound like the whirring of an engine deep inside the world. I followed her around back to the courtyard, a square of concrete on which sat a row of garbage cans, frosted by the light of a single street lamp.

"Dump the stuff in there," she said, pointing to a big metal tub used for burning leaves.

I carried the bag over and undid the twist tie. Inside were her notebooks, their covers decorated with hearts and Hello Kitties. "Hey, wait a second," I said.

"We're celebrating." She reached into the pocket of her sweatpants and pulled out a very official-looking piece of correspondence. "I got a job. I'm now a kindergarten teacher." She opened the bottle of *shōchū*, took a swig, and handed it to me.

"You can't burn your work," I said.

"Kafka did."

"He asked Brod to do it, knowing full well that he wouldn't. And Kafka was dying, not graduating."

She lit a Golden Bat. "You know what, you're not my husband, so you don't tell me what to do."

"You're going to regret this."

"What do you know about me, anyway?"

Maybe she was right. Was this a test? Did she want me to stop her? I watched her use two hands to dump the notebooks into the metal tub, scooping them out of the trash bag in heaps, as if they were fallen leaves. Her cigarette bobbed between her lips as she worked. When she was done, she lifted the bottle of *shōchū* from the ground and took another swallow. "Writing was just a stupid fantasy, anyway," she said.

"I love your stories."

"But you don't love me."

"I wish you'd stop saying that."

I watched Sunao pour *shōchū* onto the notebooks in the tub and then use her lighter to set the acceptance letter ablaze. For a second, it was like a little handkerchief of fire between her fingers. She held it aloft as if waving goodbye to someone leaving on an invisible cruise ship, and then dropped it into the tub to light the rest.

There were some loose pages that caught and curled first. The flames burnt green and then orange. I could see Sunao's handwriting twisting, turning brown. Bits and pieces of paper flew off into the darkness. The cardboard covers burnt, curving like smiles. I passed the bottle back and forth with Sunao, feeling the heat from the fire on my face and hands.

In that moment, I knew that I would pack in the morning and go back to my place, and that I would quit grad school and get on an airplane and fly back to America. I knew that my parents would meet me at the airport, looking boozy and frail. I knew that I would go with them for the very first time since the funeral to visit my sister's grave in the big cemetery next to the highway, where the headstones were lined up like millions of chessmen. I knew that I would have to do something to start my life.

Till then, I was just watching.

About a year later, living in New York, I got a letter from Sunao. It was our first communication since I'd left Japan, and my chest tightened as I opened the envelope and saw the handwriting I knew from her notebooks, that swift native speaker's hand that I could never imitate:

> Dear Poor Sweet Boy,
>
> The cherry blossoms are falling, and for some reason I think of you.
>
> The school where I teach looks exactly like the one I went to as a child: the concrete building, the playground with the metal climbing set and swings. On the first day, I got there very early, and as I walked the empty hall I had the feeling that I had gone back in time to become a kindergartener again—worse, that I had somehow fallen asleep in the middle of class and dreamed that I was an adult. Though the dream had seemed to take twenty-two years, it was really only a few minutes long, and in a second I was going to wake up in my little girl body, and my mother would be waiting outside at the end of the day to take me home. I got so confused that I had to sit in my chair at the front of the empty classroom and put my head between my knees and breathe, wondering when I would wake up and be my real self again in the real world, not the dream world.

But I've grown used to teaching since then, and I find that I now take a great deal of comfort in the daily routine. There is a working agreement here that makes life reassuring: I pretend to be a teacher and the children pretend to be my students. Parents and teachers agree to forget that children are in fact lunatics, and that what we call growing up is just learning to hide it better so nobody will lock us away.

Oh, did I mention that I'm engaged to be married? He works at the same insurance company as my father, which is convenient. The only problem is that he has a good heart, so we have some trouble communicating—just like I had with you. But I'm trying to learn how good people talk, so I can fake it.

I don't miss you at all.

My first thought was to tell her that she should leave her fiancé and come join me in New York. In America we would switch roles: she would be the space alien and I would be the human guide, the one whose job it was to explain the world. But I knew she would never listen to me.

I sat with the letter in my hand, remembering the sound of her voice as she read me a story for the first time. We were naked, her head resting on my chest. The story was about children whose parents are nothing but holograms, beams of light, and the words were so full of sadness that I knew then and there that I could love her if she let me—if I let myself.

The story was long, and it wasn't till I realized that I could hear every word of it that I grabbed a notebook and a pen and began to write. My fingers ached as they chased her voice, the voice that had made me feel free and alive and frightened all at once, whether we were hiding in the shadows outside the train station or soaking in her deep tub, the water so hot I couldn't breathe. I was going to save her story from the fire, save it and send it back to her as a wedding gift, save all the stories in all the notebooks. But when I came to the end, what I had written was about the night my sister and I sat on the roof of my parents' house in Leonia, right before she went into the hospital for the last time: Daisy and me, staring at the stars, those tiny points of light, and feeling as if we were falling upward into the sky.

LOST AND FOUND

PORTABLE GENERATORS

ON JULIAN MAY'S

Saga of the Pliocene Exile Tetralogy

ALEXANDER CHEE

In the origin story of my favorite science fiction novels, Julian May attended a party in 1976 at a science fiction convention in Los Angeles, dressed in a jewel-encrusted space suit she'd made herself. At the time, she was a forty-five-year-old professional writer from West Linn, Oregon, just outside Portland, the author of thousands of science encyclopedia entries and two hundred and fifty nonfiction books for adults and children. But she had also written and published two science fiction short stories early in her career, her first when she was nineteen, as well as a few Buck Rogers comics, and she hadn't let go of science fiction just yet.

I keep spinning this image of her in the suit in my mind—as, apparently, did she. The space suit turned out to be cosplay for a series she had yet to write. After the convention, she returned home to West Linn and plotted the four novels that became the Pliocene Exile Tetralogy.

I found the tetralogy twenty-five years later, at a used-book store in Iowa City.

I was a student at the Iowa Writers' Workshop looking for a thrill. The book I found first was *The Golden Torc*, the second in the Saga. At the time, the series had been out of print for years, and so all of my copies of her novels have "3.00" penciled onto the first page and all were purchased there. I remember it impressed me that May had used, for an epigraph, "The Threshold," a poem by my favorite philosopher, Simone Weil. This surprised and intrigued me, as I hadn't known that Weil wrote poems. I'd met a new writer and a new favorite writer both, in one page.

The story born from May's jeweled suit begins on September 21, 2013, when Earth is saved from the edge of nuclear holocaust and environmental catastrophe by a coalition of the universe's five dominant alien races, called "The Galactic Milieu." The Milieu first fosters humanity's latent psychic gifts—these being the passport to this congress—and then provides new technology that allows an overcrowded Earth population to colonize seven hundred nearby planets. By 2021, when a French physicist discovers a one-way time tunnel 6,000,000 years into Earth's past—anything that tries to return ages 6,000,000 years on the trip—those alienated by the new intergalactic utopia see it as a perfect underground railroad into the Pliocene.

May draws her characters from two groups that pass through and find their dreamed-of, alien-free Pliocene paradise in the hands of human-type alien exotics, exiles from another galaxy, a race divided into two ethnic types living in a recognizably medieval style and permanently at war in a battle religion that ritualizes their hatred. Half of them, the Tanu, look remarkably like elves; the other half, the Firvulag, like dwarves. Both sides possess the paranormal abilities common to the Milieu our human refugees fled. On top of all this, the Tanu are becoming infertile and increasingly need the arriving human females in order to breed. All of them wear armor born from May's science fiction convention outfit.

This was the most confident reinvention of the known world and its cultures I'd encountered in years, an alternate history/science-fiction masterpiece with a fantasy novel coating, stocked somehow with everything, ever: magic, spaceships, alien colonies, elves, dwarves, knights, time travel, psychic powers, castles—and love in headdresses, to boot. May had plunked it all into the particle accelerator of her mind and out came psychic powers organized into guilds with their own gang colors and territories and political squabbles; living spaceships with spouse pilots; elves and dwarves from across the galaxy; rebel humans plotting to return to the Earth of the future and take it back from the aliens, but perhaps only after doing it in the past first; and half-human hybrids, their future uncertain as the ethnic purists eye their growing numbers.

I quickly read *The Golden Torc*, then found and devoured the first book of the tetralogy, *The Many-Colored Land*, and the third and fourth, *The Nonborn King* and *The Adversary*, and then the rest of May's work, including the six prequel-sequel novels to these four. By now, I wasn't just addicted to the world she'd created; I was in awe of her narrative powers: she was the only writer I knew who could put fifteen or so characters down on a landscape and move among them, compellingly. She had queer characters—and central ones, for that matter—something I didn't often see in science fiction. May was not only writing about the future but also, ahead of her time, like Ursula K. Le Guin, creating complex characters of mixed race, sometimes many genders, and complex sexual and affectional tendencies.

More impressively, across these ten books, May builds an intricate virtuosic narrative payoff, and when the singular penny drops on what she's done, it's indescribable. I can think of no sustained fictional effort like it—and certainly not one that extends for nearly five thousand pages. When I reached the end of the other six novels, I was ready to return to the first four, and did. I've since reread them all at least four times.

Over the years, I've met only a few fellow fans of hers—the writers Chris Adrian and Jon Michaud are actually the only ones I know of—and yet I know we are out there, and are about to expand our numbers: It's now 2012, the year before the Galactic Intervention May imagined that started it all off, and Houghton Mifflin Harcourt has brought the Pliocene Exile tetralogy back to readers in e-book format (complete with the original 1980s artwork). The series has been optioned for film and is in active development.

I sometimes hope that the books are all true, dictated to her from the future, and that next year aliens will intervene and save us from ourselves, and in 2021, a French physicist will discover the time tunnel. Perhaps. One way or another, her era begins now.

ON J. J. PHILLIPS'S

Mojo Hand

ANDREW SCHEIBER

If ever a book entered the world too soon for its own good, that book could well be J. J. Phillips's novel *Mojo Hand*—not because its author was a mere twenty-two years old when it was first published in 1966, but because it remarkably anticipates a literary history whose outlines would not become legible for at least another decade. Appearing before Toni Morrison, Maya Angelou, and Alice Walker began publishing, before Zora Neale Hurston was rescued from obscurity, Phillips's tale of a black debutante's descent into the blues demimonde must have seemed at first glance alien and incomprehensible, like an artifact accidentally transported from some parallel universe.

Even in 1992, when I first came across the novel in the dollar bin at a Goodwill store, *Mojo Hand* struck me as an anomaly. As someone who had been interested in blues-themed literature for some time, I was surprised that I had not heard of the book. But a flyleaf endorsement from Henry Miller suggested I read on, and within paragraphs I was hooked, pulled in by the dark undertow of Phillips's language and story line. It was different from any book I had previously read in the genre, mainly in the way it challenged rather than flattered my romanticized white-boy conception of the blues as a catalyst for Dionysian release. *Mojo Hand* locates the blues squarely at the crossroads where Eros and Thanatos meet—not in opposition, but in a disturbing synergy that I found at once unexpected and apropos, in the way that unbidden revelations often are.

The novel's uncanny appeal owes much to Phillips's creative signifying on classical sources. She conceived the novel as a riff on the Orphic legend of Eurydice's descent into the underworld; Phillips's heroine, Eunice Prideaux, flees her stifling cotillion world to seek out an aging musician named Blacksnake Brown, whose earthy "Bakershop Blues" (discovered in a cache of old 78 rpm records) becomes the sting that ushers her into the demimonde. Both Orphic lover and infernal captor, Blacksnake anchors the novel's complex and darkly existential vision of the blues; under his influence Eunice journeys not toward some transcendent high ground of love or self-fulfillment, but downward, into an abyss of drink, sex, and hoodoo-laced ritual that threatens to swallow her very self. By the story's end Blacksnake is dead—like Orpheus, a victim of the passions he provokes—and Eunice is barefoot and pregnant, heavy with the double burden of Blacksnake's blues and his soon-to-be-born child as she stumbles toward a shadowy future.

The novel's evocation of the Orpheus and Eurydice story is key to its ironic and ambivalent portrayal of Eunice's underworld journey; unfortunately, when *Mojo Hand* first appeared, it had been denuded of its classical references. Phillips's editors at Simon and Schuster felt that the market would accept a novel of voyeuristic social realism from a young black woman, but not one that owed as much to Ovid and Jean Genet as it did to Richard Wright and Ralph Ellison.

Torn from its Orphic frame, the book was marketed and read as something it was not (the original dust jacket promised an inside look at the "somnambulistic demiworld" of blues people and their concealed "bitterness" toward whites), with predictable consequences. Soon the hardback edition went out of print, to be supplanted by a pulpy Pocket Books paperback whose cover showed a despoiled-looking woman of indeterminate race clutching a guitar and haloed by a lurid tagline: "A young girl, barely out of her teens, finds her 'soul' in the arms of an old blues man."

All of which, as one might imagine, appalled and frustrated Phillips, especially in light of the tendency of some readers to take its convincing portrayal of the blues life as veiled autobiography. Not that one could fully blame them for indulging such an interpretive fallacy; after all, the dust jacket of the 1966 edition claimed that Phillips had for a time performed as a blues busker on the streets of Houston under the *nom de chanteuse* "Jicky Minnie." But the jacket copy was itself a work of the imagination, a fiction concocted by the publisher, presumably to brand the book in terms of black and blues credentials. This marketing ploy compounded the editors' mangling of the text and cast a shadow of misinformation and misunderstanding with respect to both text and author that has proved stubbornly hard to dissipate.

This is in part because some of the critical presumptions and habits that fueled these editorial abuses are still very much with us. Readers and critics persist in approaching the book as a reflection of an "authentic" version of the African American experience, whether personal or collective, rather than as a product of the literary imagination. Such concern with authenticity is a symptom of identity politics at its crudest (and, I fear, most common), infecting literary judgment with preconceptions about who is qualified to write about what, and how. Questions about the skin the author is in, or the group identifications he or she claims or disdains, continue to intrude into the assessment of a work's literary value or significance—though admittedly such questions now tend to be posed in subtler, more coded ways than they were half a century ago.

When confronted with this authenticity question in 1966, the twenty-two-year-old author of *Mojo Hand* faced a double bind. On one side, the editors at her publishing house could not reconcile the book's substructure of classical mythology with their own notions of "real" black writing. On the other, she encountered black literati who questioned whether she was culturally or experientially qualified to represent the blues life or "the" black perspective more generally. Snarled in this critical and political briar patch, the novel suffered a confused and uncomprehending critical response that, for the most part, continues into the present.

Over the years there have been some moves to repair the book's fractured history. In 1985, City Miner Books republished *Mojo Hand* with its mythological references intact and a new subtitle, "An Orphic Tale," added to complement the restorations to the text. As if to repudiate the identity politics that complicated the book's initial publication and reception, Phillips replaced the first jacket's Olan Mills–styled author pic with a startlingly different portrait of the artist: a 1962 newswire photo of her behind bars in Raleigh, North Carolina. Phillips had been sentenced to thirty days in the county jail for taking part in a lunch counter sit-in organized by CORE, the student civil rights group, and this document of her arrest may be taken in part as a rebuke to those who thought she had not 'paid her dues.'"

That image of the jailed author, bruised but defiant, is an apt one for this novel, which has endured the grinding mill of literary and critical fashion to emerge as more in tune with present contexts than she could have foreseen. A quarter century later, writers like Toni Morrison and Percival Everett would publish well-received novels that explore the resonances between classical and African American traditions; from these examples and subsequent others in the same vein, one might conclude that the literary world has finally caught up to Phillips's long-neglected work. But unfortunately *Mojo Hand* has fallen out of print once again, further delaying a proper critical response and frustrating admirers like myself who value the novel for its brutally poetic language and for the power with which its disturbing but inexorable plot unfurls, pulling us into regions as deep as the blues and as dark as the underworld into which Eurydice descends.

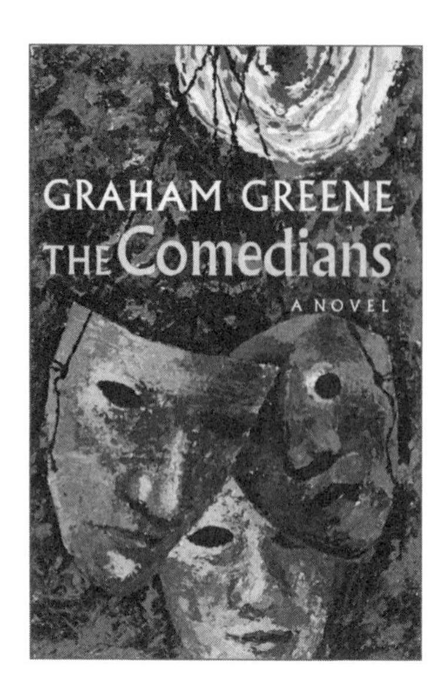

ON GRAHAM GREENE'S

The Comedians

MARCIA DESANCTIS

I wasn't officially banned from the Winchester Public Library in the spring of 1976, but for a few weeks, I stayed away. Mrs. Barger, who worked the checkout desk, had discovered me on the back stairs after hours with one hand dangling a Newport Light and the other inside Billy Doyle's jeans. She knew and respected my three older sisters, and though I suspected she wouldn't rat me out, I couldn't face the judgment that was sure to be coiled upon the old lady's face if she saw me. So I sent my mother to get *Travels with Charley* for my ninth-grade Steinbeck project. By accident or by ruse—I'll never know— Mrs. Barger sent her home with Graham Greene's *Travels with My Aunt*.

The book's breezy conceit—eccentric elderly woman plucks her virgin nephew from his life tending dahlias and off they go to exotic ports of call—was the perfect foray into Greeneland and I was beguiled by the author's literary charms. By the time I sat down with *The Comedians*, five books later, I still loved the tableaux of colonials clinking pink gins while rebels plotted in the shadows, but what got me into the tent isn't what kept me there. I allied myself with Greene's autobiographical heroes—men at once bound to, haunted by, and estranged from the Catholic Church, whose teachings run through their veins. At fifteen, I wasn't really much of a sinner, but like Billy Doyle and pretty much everyone else I knew in suburban Boston, I was a Bad Catholic. Saddled with the twin encumbrances of lust and guilt, yet fully knowing what was right and holy, I took a sharp left away from catechism and what the nuns at Sunday school had tried to impart. Like lepidopterists or Francophiles, conflicted Catholics have a way of finding each other, as if to share the burden of juggling transgression and confession while trying to live a life. It is the constant tug of these extremes that only a person doused from birth in sacramental incense and holy water can fully comprehend, and one best endured in similar company.

The Comedians isn't Greene's most Catholic novel—that is probably *The Heart of the Matter*. But narrator Mr. Brown's Jesuit upbringing is always at the forefront of his brain, whether in his frequent remembrances of his first (and only) fuck with the married teacher twice his age, who picks him up at the betting tables in Monaco where he was a seminary student, or in his guilt over his own guiltlessness in the arms of his present-day lover. "'Man has but one virginity to lose,' and I lost mine that winter afternoon in Monte Carlo," Brown, the owner of the Hotel Trianon, ruminates in another casino, this time in Port-au-Prince, Haiti, on the night he meets Martha Pineda, the young wife of a fat South American ambassador. Even when he collects his winnings, Brown can't dodge the shadow of the Catholic priests who raised him, as he discusses whether ambassadors—then husbands—are necessary evils.

"'You believe that evil is necessary?'" he says to the cashier. "'Then you're a Manichean like myself.' Our theological discussion could go no further, for he had not been educated at the College of the Visitation, and in any case the girl's voice interrupted us." The "girl" being the married woman with whom he's about to sleep.

Brown strays and adheres simultaneously; he conveys that being a Catholic means that although you will never shake your history or the rituals that constitute its core and backbone, you're also doomed to pursue sin, no matter what the cost. But he isn't talking murder here, just sex. As a teenager, what wasn't I to admire in this? I could think of no bigger turn-on than a person for whom seduction always prevails. The Greene hero knows he is damned, but he also knows that sensual pleasure is what grounds us in this short life, and anyway, there is absolution (or at least personal accountability) in the confessional. Greene was the most masculine of writers—all that whiskey, all that sweat-drenched lovemaking with either younger women or married ones or both—but I am convinced he really wrote for us ladies. Greene's characters are troubled by their own detachment from women but they still respect them. The author gives them brains, and never condescends to the prostitutes in the brothels the heroes frequent in back alleys from Saigon to northern Argentina. In the Haiti of *The Comedians*, as usual, such women are smarter, braver, and more politically switched on than the johns. Greene wrote for men who like women, but also for women who like men—especially unencumbered loners who take big risks, are always in the mood, and, sexier still, are tortured Catholics.

In *The Comedians*, as in other books, Greene is not one for spouting papal encyclicals but rather for making Catholicism the undercurrent of all else, the fulcrum upon which everything tilts. It's hard not to see the irony—and the Church's omnipresent mantle—when the lovers' moonlight assignations take place under the statue of Christopher Columbus in Port-au-Prince. (Back in Boston, we panted in the backseat of our parents' station wagons behind St. Eulalia Church). The explorer who brought Catholicism (and its traveling companions, the enslavement and murder of the natives) to Haiti lords above the adulterers while the country descends into madness, thus mingling and bringing to light the many hypocrisies of the Church. The theme gets another layer as the new president, Haitian nationalist and Catholic Papa Doc Duvalier, leads the country into terror, and infuriates Rome not for his practice of torture and executions but for expelling all foreign-born priests. Brown discusses his religion at every turn—with Dr. Magiot, the dignified Marxist rebel leader, and later, with Captain Concasseur, the terrifying Tonton Macoute, while the latter holds the hotelier at gunpoint, making him pee his trousers. Evil has taken over and even the so-called faithless recognize hell when they see it.

This is notable during Brown's first and only voodoo ceremony, which he attends in solidarity with his hotel's trusted bartender, Joseph. Scared, and maimed from an encounter with Papa Doc Duvalier's security force, Joseph turns to the pagan gods when all else—prayer and the government, for starters—has failed. Brown is skeptical. "'You are a Catholic,'" he says to Dr. Magiot. "'You believe in reason.'" "'The Voodooists are Catholic too, and we don't live in a world of reason,'" Magiot responds.

In Haiti, you have to be Catholic to take part in a ceremony, whose Latin refrains—*Líbera nos a malo, agnus dei*—are lifted from liturgy and provide Brown with a familiar reference point. But every religion and every deity, Brown seems to say, end up disappointing us: "I told myself I hadn't left the Jesuits to be the victim of an African god," he muses.

And yet, for Brown, his religion, both its presence and its absence, dominates his every breath. The constant interplay of sin and penance is the ingrained curse of the born Catholic, and luckily there is such a thing as reason, even if it comes only in flashes. One night, with the Trianon nearly abandoned in the political terror engulfing Haiti, Brown lies with Martha by the pool, where a government minister has recently slit his own throat to prevent Duvalier's henchmen from doing it for him. After making love to her (Greene, not accidentally, endows Brown with both prodigious sexual appetites and occasional impotence), he denies his faith to Martha ("'Do you think I still believe?'") but later, obliquely, acknowledges the long shadow cast by the priests in Monaco. Mrs. Smith, one of two remaining Trianon guests, has seen and taken note of Brown's rendezvous with Martha. "'Was it my guilt which had deciphered disapproval on her face the other night?'" the self-professed remorseless one wonders. Sex with his mistress is a necessary pleasure, even if he can't dodge the harshest judge: himself.

For a Catholic, the Church always forces its way in, tries to be noticed, begs to be ignored. Brown—with all his faults and in spite of himself—is a more spiritual man than he wants us to believe, no matter how many prostitutes or married women he beds or how forcefully he tries and is unable to deny his faith. Although Brown neither chose nor escapes the cross he was born bearing, the subsequent abandonment of his faith is an intellectual exercise at best. His Catholicism is too deeply embedded as both scar and moral fiber. Even if he renounces it, he is compelled to maintain it, which allows him to be committed not to one thing, but to everything. It renders him human.

"We [the faithless] have chosen nothing, except to go on living," he says. "I daresay it eased the never quiet conscience which had been injected into me without my consent, when I was too young to know, by the Fathers of the Visitation."

In other words, Greene seems to say, you don't need religion to be a Good Catholic. For me, as a teenager with many thousands of sins yet to commit, this was very good news indeed.

ON LEONARD GARDNER'S

Fat City

AARON GILBREATH

When Farrar, Straus and Giroux first published Leonard Gardner's *Fat City* in 1969, the novel created a bit of a stir. A reviewer for the *Atlanta Journal* said the book was "destined to become a classic," calling it "a novel more moving than any I can recall in a decade." The *Cleveland Plain Dealer* called Gardner "a craftsman of the first magnitude." There were comparisons to Twain and Melville. The novel was nominated for a National Book Award, and in 1972, John Huston directed Gardner's screen adaptation of *Fat City* into a well-received film. Then Gardner fell off the radar. Sure, in 1988 he turned one of his short stories—from a 1965 issue of the *Paris Review*—into a low-budget movie called *Valentino Returns*, and he had a cameo in Francis Ford Coppola's *Tucker*, playing a character known only as the "Gas Station Owner." But if Gardner kept writing literary fiction, he published none of it. While Gardner's visibility shrunk, *Fat City* grew into one of the great sleeping giants of modern literature, a slim volume that evokes as much reverie in its devotees as Charles Portis's *Norwood*, Barry Hannah's *Ray*, and Frederick Exley's *A Fan's Notes*. If there's any justice in this crazy world, *Fat City* will secure Gardner's place in that legendary pantheon of one-book authors alongside Harper Lee, Ralph Ellison, and Emily Brontë.

Fat City is, on the surface, the braided narratives of two boxers in Stockton, California: Ernie Munger, an eighteen-year-old greenhorn who hopes his natural talent will lead to a professional career, and Billy Tully, a worn-out twenty-nine-year-old whose glory days are behind him. Working odd farm jobs and sleeping in fleabag hotels, Tully drinks in order to endure the painful realization that "the peak of his life . . . had gone by without time for reflection, ending while he was still thinking things were going to get better." Conversely, Ernie's future lies unformed ahead of him; if Ernie represents all the squashed hopes and delusions of Tully's youth, in Tully, readers see the disappointments looming in the young man's future.

You can tell from the first pages that this isn't going to be a buoyant book. It starts inside Tully's flophouse room—the fifth hotel room he's inhabited in the year and a half since his wife left him—and the story unfolds in equally dismal locations: musty gyms, dark bars, gas stations, Greyhound buses. The gritty settings enrobe the story in a desultory fuzz reminiscent of John Fante's *Ask the Dust* and Denis Johnson's *Jesus' Son*, except, unlike those books, here the motel life has neither the air of blithe nostalgia nor the ethereal sheen of a morphine dream. Whatever redemption Gardner's characters find comes in the form of their resolve. Perseverance is success in *Fat City*, not a championship belt or escape from the poorhouse. These troubled souls don't ask for pity, and therefore one does not pity their desperate stations so much as celebrate their tenacity. This sympathetic reading stems from the author's skillful rendering—Gardner doesn't pander. His touch is tender, his treatment compassionate, yet his vision remains as dutifully realistic as any camera.

Subtlety and tenderness aren't qualities one might expect from a so-called "boxing novel." Then again, to label this a boxing novel would be no more accurate than calling John Coltrane "just a sax player." Boxing is the window dressing. *Fat City*'s true subject is the way life pits a person's hopes against his abilities, and the ways in which people deal with the ensuing disappointment, which is to say, the book is about endurance, that peculiar drive innate not strictly to men with powerful uppercuts, but to all living things: the will to survive. *Fat City* meticulously depicts the way we all fight—or succumb to—what Gardner calls "the desolate reality of defeat." That's no simple boxing metaphor; that's the universal truth of blood and bone, the essential nature of our shared human experience.

Like so many of my favorite things, I discovered *Fat City* by accident. During my mid-twenties I became fascinated by the region in which Stockton sits: California's Central Valley. Following my first visit in 1995, I had to read and know everything about the place: natural history, Spanish exploration history, early settlers' accounts, native plant names. Sometimes my intellectual interests border on loony, or at least, their ferocity resists explanation. It isn't like the Central Valley is some overlooked Big Sur. This flat, smelly, rural landscape is scorching in summer, foggy in winter, and devoid of significant topography—what most interstate travelers consider a four-hundred-and-thirty-mile-long roadside bathroom break. It's the largest raisin-producing region in the world, if that tells you anything. Yet while other college kids guzzled margaritas on Mexican beaches, I spent some of my spring breaks hiking tiny, derelict natural areas between Bakersfield and Sacramento. *Highway 99: A Literary Journey through California's Great Central Valley*, one of the many anthologies I took to help pass time in motel rooms and truck stops, includes an excerpt from Gardner's novel. I never read it. I was so busy devouring John Muir's and William Henry Brewer's historical exploration accounts that I routinely neglected fiction. When I bought *California Heartland*, another anthology, I came across one of Gardner's short stories, entitled "Christ Has Returned to Earth and Appears Here Nightly," originally published in 1965 in the *Paris Review*. I ignored that, too.

Fourteen years later, I got a job at Powell's Books. Other interests joined my Valley obsession and opened me up to the pleasures of fiction. Then *Fat City* popped up on the sidebar of the Powell's Web site. The University of California Press had republished *Fat City* as part of its California Fiction series, which includes such novels as Carolyn See's *Golden Days* and James D. Houston's *Continental Drift*. Joan Didion's blurb says Gardner's novel affected her "more than any new fiction I've read in a long while." That sold me, but it was the Stockton setting that grabbed my attention. I kept thinking: *Stockton? Nobody set novels in Stockton. It's a sprawling, back-bay Valley town known mostly for its high crime rate and deep-water ship channel.* It seemed this Leonard Gardner shared my obscure regional interest. Were it not for this Valley connection, I would never have noticed the book. But I bought it and became a Gardner disciple, only later realizing that all these years a selection had been with me in *Highway 99*.

In addition to making Gardner a perfect fit for the infamous one-book pantheon, *Fat City* also fits squarely within the Central Valley literary canon, a regional body of work that few people, even Californians, know exists. Composed of work written about the Valley, as well as work written by Valley residents, this canon includes poets such as Philip Levine, Lawson Fusao Inada, and Larry Levis; the fiction writers William Saroyan, William

Haslam, and Gary Soto; and nonfiction writers such as Maxine Hong Kingston, David Mas Masumoto, and Richard Rodriguez. It also includes historical pieces such as Thomas Jefferson Mayfield's *Indian Summer* and Mark Twain's "The Eternal Summer of Sacramento" (from *Roughing It*). Frank Norris's 1901 historical novel, *The Octopus*, is arguably one of three Valley opuses, though Steinbeck's *The Grapes of Wrath* is unquestionably king. Even Didion contributed to the Valley canon, with her incredible essay "Notes from a Native Daughter," about growing up in Sacramento.

Despite the gritty streets and the characters' many failures, most everyone in *Fat City* hunts for the small pleasures that make life's turbulent froth bearable, whether it's a bottle of Thunderbird or a liaison on a levee. Even when they have only feeble sports aphorisms and flawed logic to propel them, the sense of tenacity—the absolute hunger of their need to carry on—rings true, as when the teenage boxer Buford Willis tells Ernie, "'If you want to win bad enough you win.'" It's so foolish to believe that hope alone can make our desires manifest, yet there's an affecting resonance to such locker room talk, something terrifyingly familiar: hope, and the need to cling to it at all cost. Had Gardner written the story of his literary career into one of his novel's characters, we might find it tragic: One book from such a talent? That's it? Such is the mystifying legacy of the one-book author. Spilling praise and allusions to his promising future, it's too easy to perceive Gardner as a sui generis talent who should have gone on to write numerous follow-up works of equal power. But to me, writing one book this powerful is accomplishment enough. Maybe Gardner, like Ernie, still clings to hope. Or maybe what Gardner wanted "bad enough" was to write one perfect novel. As the *Kansas City Star* said, "Probably there isn't a living novelist who, if he were honest with himself, would not be proud to have written *Fat City*. That's how good it is."

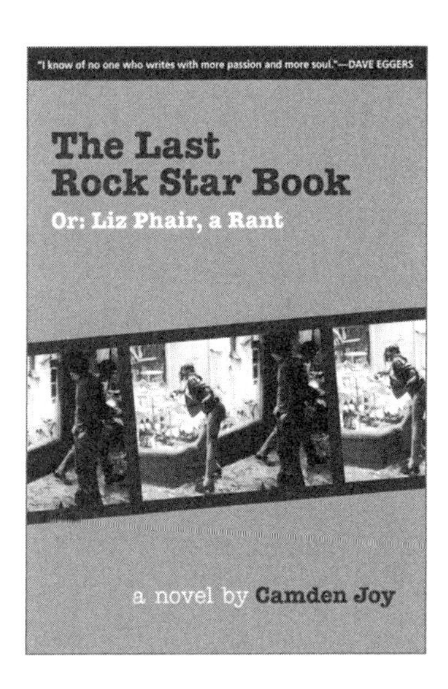

ON CAMDEN JOY'S

The Last Rock Star Book or: Liz Phair, A Rant

JOSEPH MARTIN

It takes just a plod through Don DeLillo's *Great Jones Street* or the manic tedium of Lester Bangs's short story "Maggie May" to reveal contemporary fiction's worst-kept secret: rock 'n' roll tends to die on the page. Bubbling with adolescent romance, near-religious mythology, and in-the-moment viscera, rock is less a musical genre than a perpetual youth "attitude"; given its teenage kicks and yen for novelty, the stories it inspires often defy thoughtful critical exegesis. Rock plots, like their drug-plot counterparts, offer characters a precious few unpleasant options: either stay in a go-nowhere band and itemize its strife and delusions (Jonathan Lethem's *You Don't Love Me Yet*); become famous and socioeconomically out of touch (DeLillo, parts of Jennifer Egan's *A Visit from the Goon Squad*); or get old and acknowledge previous accomplishments as frivolous (Jonathan Franzen's *Freedom*, Egan). Writers can shove tabloid hijinks or frank analyses into those base narratives, but even then, the results seldom create a buzz louder than the subject matter.

Of course, riffing on rock (so to speak) isn't always a recipe for disaster—Egan, Lethem, and Franzen have gathered plenty of acclaim, and others, like Nick Hornby, Bryan Charles, and Irvine Welsh, have portrayed the pop-addled, self-destructive impulses of the music's audience to great effect. When played in a realist mode and focused squarely on character development, rock can be absorbed into literary fiction's environs just like anything else. But few writers have captured the potential for passionate listener misinterpretation and long-term soul deformation inherent in the music, its ability to prey on its fans' most reptile-brained desires. It's this trick—this ability to gesture toward rock's relationship between distant musician and projective audience—that allows Camden Joy's fiction debut, *The Last Rock Star Book Or: Liz Phair, A Rant* (1998), a resonance both more affectionate and less affected than its topical peers.

Rant follows a small-time music writer named Camden Joy, lately conferred "critic" status thanks to being "a little sick in the head" and wheat-pasting music reviews on New York City walls—all of which is true of the author and provides the first sign of *Rant*'s blurry reality. This scrawling habit leads to periodicals publishing his work without consent, a violation that quickly builds Joy's renown and results in a "Where Are They Now?" book gig about Liz Phair. It's a hack job, the kind of photo dump where "no one reads the words," but Joy takes it for the money; his editor underscores the project's artless spirit by insisting Joy dictate the book to expedite the writing process. When our fictive hero decides early on to treat his Dictaphoned notes as a journal, his musings begin to conflate memory and pop crit, reconstructing his task as an exploration of rock's most self-serving dictum—"never compromise"—and that dictum's personal fallout.

Much of that fallout circles around relationships, and much of the book presents the fictional Joy as emotionally stunted; as both a boyfriend and a pop fan, he leans hard on the "romance" of ownership and adolescent obsession. Ostensible subject Liz Phair unpacks into a myriad of objects, among them a myth, a woman, and a diaristic talisman not unlike theorist Dick Hebdige in *Rant*'s spiritual sister, Chris Kraus's *I Love Dick*. The narrator's recollections of his ex-girlfriend Shaleese, purportedly the daughter of dead Rolling Stone Brian Jones, begin to bleed into other interests: his research on Phair, the story of a daughter taken from his parents, a *Life* photograph of a woman taken during the sixties Quebecois riots, a personal history of teenage terrorism. By the time Joy sets up an interview with Ms. Phair, his dalliance with rock criticism has obliterated already patchy boundaries; after two hundred pages recounting Shaleese's diaries alongside his analyses of Phair's *Exile in Guyville*, the two women are pathologically convolved in the narrator's head, resulting in a dangerous, deluded climax.

At the time of its publication, both *This American Life*'s Sarah Vowell and *Spin* pegged Joy's work as "stalker"-like because of its eerie blend of narrative narcissism and paparazzi detail. To a degree, they were right: alive to Generation X's use of and romance with pop culture, *Rant* presents the post-MTV musical landscape as an invitation to greater obsession, and, by christening his disturbed protagonist "Camden Joy," the author perhaps indicts himself (or, at least, his pseudonym—Joy's real name is Tom Adelman) as an agent of that obsession. But these criticisms miss the point. Joy's basic method, which posits both writer and pop musician as cultural constructs, has plenty of precedent; stretching back to Norman Mailer's *Armies of the Night* and Max Apple's *Oranging of America* on through David Foster Wallace's *Girl with Curious Hair* and *Twilight* fanfic, the traditions of using meta self-representation to comment on narrative and absorption of celebrities to explore celebrity have become old postmodern standbys. "Stalker" claims aside, even the ickiest, most invasive elements of Joy's style— his narrator's narcissism, for example, a Nabokovian "referential mania" by any other name—are old hat in the realm of literary fiction, time-honored methods of entry into an unstable narrator's mind.

Perhaps more interesting than this focus on style-as-content, however, is the blind eye Joy's critics turned to *Rant*'s real moral project: a book-length interrogation of how pop culture's narrative of celebrity has invaded the civilian world. Long before John D'Agata and David Shields began to champion their soup of fiction and memoir, Generation X had already developed an Information Age sense of self-mythology. For the author and others writing in the twentieth century's final moments, pop culture and day-to-day life had merged, fame now offering the most prized, mysterious version of class mobility around: even a persona as minor as Liz Phair, a twentysomething with a guitar and a small-time record deal, could end up on the cover of *Rolling Stone* and become untouchable, a point of projection, through celebrity. Mastering (and parsing) pop culture became a coping device, a way somehow both to connect to others and to own the contents of an endless media barrage. But Joy was wise to this problem of ownership—to believe that you own something is to idealize it, place unreasonable expectations upon it, invest dreams in it, and smother it. In *Rant*, he zeroes in on these emotionally stunted, dehumanizing elements of pop obsession and, by pushing them to their "stalker" extreme, teases out the adolescent psyche afflicting an entire generation raised on rock 'n' roll—and, worse, on people talking about rock 'n' roll. Thirteen years and a whole self-branded webscape later, Joy's accidental critic still tells that awful truth. As a result, *Rant* remains a bracing read—a lipstick-smeared mirror held up to America's hyper-romantic, self- and celebrity-obsessed youth culture.

FICTION

TOSCA

Ready!

Aim!

On command, the firing squad aims at the man backed against a full-length mirror. The mirror once hung in a bedroom, but now it's cracked and propped against a dumpster in an alley. The condemned man has refused the customary last cigarette but accepted as a hood the black slip that was carelessly tossed over a corner of the mirror's frame. The slip still smells faintly of a familiar fragrance.

Through his rifle sight, each sweating, squinting soldier in the squad can see his own cracked reflection aiming back at him.

Also in the line of fire is a phantasmal reflection of the surprised woman whose black slip now serves as a hood (a hood that hides less from the eyes looking out than from those looking in). She's been caught dressing, or undressing, and presses her hands to her breasts in an attempt to conceal her nakedness.

The moment between commands seems suspended to the soldiers and to the hooded man. The soldiers could be compared to sprinters poised straining in the blocks, listening for the starter's gun, though of course, when the shot is finally fired, it's their fingers on the triggers. The hooded man also listens for the shot even though he knows he'll be dead before he hears it. I've never been conscripted to serve in a firing squad or condemned to stand facing death—at least, not any more than we all are—but in high school I once qualified for the state finals in the high hurdles and I know that between the "Aim" command and the shot there's time for a story.

Were this a film, there'd be time for searching close-ups of each soldier's face as he waits for the irreversible order, time for the close-ups to morph into a montage of images flashing

Stuart Dybek

back through the lives of the soldiers, scenes with comrades in bars, brothels, et cetera, until one of the squad—a scholarly looking, myopic corporal—finds himself a boy again, humming beside a pond, holding, instead of a rifle, a dip net and a Mason jar.

There's a common myth that a drowning man sees his life pass before his eyes. Each soldier taking aim imagines that beneath the hood the condemned man is flashing through his memory. It's a way in which the senses flee the body, a flight into the only dimension where escape is still possible: time. Rather than a lush dissolve into a Proustian madeleine moment, escape is desperate—the plunge through duration in "An Occurrence at Owl Creek Bridge," or through a time warp, as in "The Secret Miracle," Borges's *ficcion* in which a playwright in Nazi-occupied Prague faces a firing squad.

In this fiction, set in an anonymous dead-end alley, the reflection of a woman, all the more beautiful for being ghostly, has surfaced from the depths of a bedroom mirror. Those soldiers in the firing squad, who can see her, conclude that she is a projection of the hooded man's memory, and that her flickering appearance is a measure of how intensely she is being recalled. Beneath the hood, the man must be recalling a room in summer where her bare body is reflected beside his, her blond-streaked hair cropped short, both of them tan, lean, still young. The mirror is unblemished, as if it, too, is young.

"Look," she whispers, "us."

Was it then he told her that their reflection at that moment is what he'd choose to be his last glimpse of life?

The question prompts each soldier to ask himself: given a choice, what would I ask for *my* last glimpse of life to be?

But actually, the hooded man would have never said something that mawkishly melodramatic. As for having the unspoken thought, well, to that he pleads guilty. So shoot me, he thinks.

Back from netting tadpoles, the scholarly corporal, sweating behind his rifle again, imagines that rather than recalling random times in bars, brothels, et cetera, the hooded man is revisiting all the rooms in which he undressed the woman in the mirror.

One room faces EL tracks. The yellow windows of a night train stream across the bedroom mirror. After the train is gone, the empty station seems illuminated by the pink-shaded bed lamp left burning as he removes her clothes. Beneath the tracks there's a dark street of jewelry shops, their display windows stripped and grated. Above each shop, behind carbonized panes, the torches of lapidaries working late ignite with the gemstone glows of hydrogen, butane, and acetylene. Her breasts lift as she unclasps a necklace, which spills from her cupped hand into an empty wineglass beside the bed. Pearls, pinkish in the light, brim over like froth. A train is coming from the other direction.

In the attic she calls his tree house, the bed faces the only window, a skylight. The mirror is less a reflection than a view out across whitewashed floorboards to a peeling white chair draped with her clothes and streaked by diffused green light shafting through the leafy canopy. The shade of light changes with the colors of thinning maples. At night, the stars through bare branches make it seem, she says, as if they lie beneath the lens of a great telescope. Naked under a feather tick, they close their eyes on a canopy of constellations light years away, and open them on a film of first snow. Daylight glints through the tracks of starlings.

The question prompts each soldier to ask himself: given a choice, what would I ask for *my* last glimpse of life to be?

In a stone cottage near Lucca, rented from a beekeeper, they hear their first nightingale. They hear it only once, though perhaps it sings while they sleep. At twilight, the rhapsodic push-pull of an accordion floats from the surrounding lemon grove. To follow it seems intrusive, so they never see who's playing, but on a morning hike, they come upon a peeling white chair weathered beneath a lemon tree. When he sits down, she raises her skirt and straddles him. The accordion recital always ends on the same elusive melody. They agree it's from an opera, as they agreed the birdcall had to be a nightingale's, but they can't identify the opera. It's Puccini, he says, which reminds her they have yet to visit Puccini's house in Lucca. Tomorrow, he promises.

Recognize it—the aria playing even now, the clarinet, a nightingale amid twittering sparrows. Sparrows twitter in the alley from power lines, rain gutters, and the tar-paper garage roofs onto which old ladies in black toss bread crusts, and this entire time the aria has been playing in the background. Not pumped from an accordion, probably it's a classical radio station floating from an open window, or maybe some opera buff—every neighborhood, no matter how shabby, has one—is playing the same aria over, each time by a different tenor—Pavarotti, Domingo, Caruso—on his antiquated stereo.

The clarinet introduces the aria's melody and the tenor echoes it as if in a duet with the woodwind: *E lucevan le stelle,* he sings—*And the stars were shining. E olezzava la terra—the scent of earth was fresh . . .*

Stridea l'uscio dell'orto,
e un passo sfiorava la rena.
Entrava ella, fragrante,
mi cadea fra le braccia . . .
The garden gate creaked, and a step brushed the sand. She entered, fragrant, and fell into my arms . . .

Admittedly, "E lucevan le stelle" is a predictable choice for an execution. So predictable that one might imagine the aria itself is what drew this motley firing squad with its unnecessarily fixed bayonets and uniforms as dusty as the sparrows brawling over bread crusts.

Who loves life more, the guy on the Outer Drive riding without a helmet or the guy with his eyes closed playing "Moonglow"?

On closer inspection, doesn't the soldiers' appearance, from their unpolished boots to the hair scruffing from beneath their shakos, verge on the theatrical, as if a costume designer modeled them on Goya's *The Disasters of War*. A role in the firing squad doesn't require acting; their costumes act for them. They're anonymous extras, grunts willing to do the dirty work if allowed to be part of the spectacle. Grunts don't sing. In fact, the corporal will be disciplined for his ad-libbed humming by the pond. They march—*trudge* is more accurate—from opera to opera, hoping to be rewarded with a chorus, a chance to emote, to leave on stage some lyrical record of their existence beyond the brutal percussion of a final volley. But their role has always been to stand complacently mute. This season alone they've made the rounds from *Carmen* to *Il Trovatore*, and when the classics are exhausted, then it's on to something new.

There are always roles for them, and the promise of more to come. In Moscow, a young composer whose grandfather disappeared during Stalin's purges labors over *The Sentence*—an opera he imagines Shostakovich might have written, which opens with Fyodor Dostoyevsky, five days past his twenty-eighth birthday, facing the firing squad of the czar. Four thousand three hundred miles away, in Kalamazoo, Michigan, an assistant professor a few years out of Oberlin who has been awarded his first commission, for an opera based on Norman Mailer's *The Executioner's Song*, has just sung "Froggy Went A-Courtin" to his three-year-old daughter. She's fallen asleep repeating, *Without my Uncle Rat's consent, I would not marry the president*, and now the house is quiet, and he softly plinks on her toy piano the motif that will climax in Gary Gilmore's final aria.

And here in the alley, the firing squad fresh from Granada, 1937, where they gunned down the poet Federico García Lorca in Osvaldo Golijov's opera, *Aínadamar*, has followed the nightingale call of *E lucevan le stelle* and stands taking aim at a man hooded in a slip.

If you're not an opera buff, "E lucevan le stelle" is from the third act of *Tosca*. The opera's hero, Mario Cavaradossi, a painter and revolutionary, has been tortured by Baron Scarpia, the lecherous, tyrannical chief of the secret police, and waits to be shot at dawn. Cavaradossi's final thoughts are of his beloved Tosca. He bribes the jailer to bring him pen and paper so that he can write her a farewell, and then, overcome by memories, stops writing and sings his aria, the most famous in the opera, a showstopper that brings audiences to applause and shouts of *Bravo* before the performance can continue. Besides the sheer beauty of the music, the aria is a quintessential operatic moment, a moment both natural and credible—no small feat for opera—in which a written message cannot adequately convey the emotion, and the drama soars to its only possible expression: song.

She entered, fragrant, and fell into my arms, Oh! sweet kisses, Oh! lingering caresses. Trembling, I unveiled her beauty, the hero sings—in Italian, of course. But in American opera houses, subtitles have become accepted. *My dream of love has vanished forever, my time is running out, and even as I die hopelessly, I have never loved life more.*

That final phrase, *Non ho amato mai tanto la vita*, about loving life always reminds me of Ren. He was the first of three friends I've had who would, over the years, say that he was living his life like an opera. We were both nineteen when we met that day Ren stopped to listen to me playing for pocket change before the Wilson el station and proposed a trade—his Kawasaki 250 with its rebuilt engine for my Leblanc clarinet. Usually, I played at el stops with Archie, a blind accordion player, but it was thundering and Archie hadn't showed. I thought Ren was putting me on. When I asked why he'd trade a motorcycle for a clarinet, he answered: Who loves life more, the guy on the Outer Drive riding without a helmet, squinting into the wind, doing seventy in and out of traffic, or the guy with his eyes closed playing "Moonglow"?

Depends how you measure loving life, I said.

Against oblivion, Ren said, then laughed as if amused by his own pretension, a reflex of his that would become familiar. A licorice stick travels light, he explained, and he was planning to leave for Italy, where, if Fellini films could be believed, they definitely loved life more. He'd had a flash of inspiration watching me, a vision of himself tooting "Three Coins in the

Fountain" by the Trevi Fountain and hordes of tourists in coin-tossing mode, filling his clarinet case with cash. He'd rebuilt the 250cc engine—he could fix anything, he bragged—and even offered a warranty: he'd keep the bike perfectly tuned if I gave him clarinet lessons.

A week later, we were roommates, trading off who got the couch and who got the Murphy bed and sharing the rent on my Rogers Park kitchenette. From the start, his quip about loving life set the tone. The commonplace trivia from our lives became the measure in an existential competition. If I ordered beer and Ren had wine, it was evidence he loved life more. If he played the Stones and I followed with Billie Holiday, it argued my greater love of life.

The university we attended had a center in Rome, and Ren and I planned to room together our junior semester abroad. Neither of us had been to Europe. A few weeks before our departure, at a drunken party, Ren introduced me to Iris O'Brien. He introduced her as the Goddess O'Iris, which didn't seem an exaggeration at the time. He assured me there was no "chemistry" between them. Lack of chemistry wasn't my experience with Iris O'Brien. In a state that even in retrospect still feels more like delirium than like a college crush, I decided to cancel my trip so that once Ren left, Iris could move in. I'd never lived with a girlfriend before.

When I told Ren I wasn't going, he said, I suppose you think that giving up Europe for a woman means you win?

Iris isn't part of the game, I said, and when I failed to laugh at my own phony, offended honor, Ren did so for me—uproariously.

Living with Iris O'Brien lasted almost as long as the Kawasaki continued to run, about a month. Although Ren and I hadn't kept in touch, I figured that if he wouldn't return my clarinet, he'd at least fix the bike once he got back. But when the semester ended, he remained in Europe.

From a mutual friend who had also gone to Rome, I heard Ren had dropped out. He spent his time playing clarinet at fountains across the city, and fell in love, not with a woman, but with opera. That surprised me, as the love of jazz that Ren and I shared seemed, for some reason, to require us to despise opera. With the money he'd made playing arias on the street, he bought a junked Moto Guzzi, rebuilt it, and took off on an odyssey of visiting opera houses across Italy. That spring I got a note scrawled on the back of a postcard of the Trevi Fountain: *Leaving for Vienna. Ah! Vienna! Non ho amato mai tanto la vita—Never have I loved life more. Living it like an opera—well, an opera buffa—so, tell the Goddess O'Iris, come bless me.*

It was the last I ever heard from him.

I didn't catch the allusion to *Tosca* in Ren's note until years later, when I was enrolled in grad school at NYU. I was seeing a woman named Clair who had ducked out of a downpour into the cab I drove part-time. Nothing serious, we'd agreed, an agreement I kept reminding myself to honor. Clair modeled to pay the bills—underwear her specialty. She'd come to New York from North Dakota in order to break into musical theater and was an ensemble member of Cahoots, a fledgling theater on Bank Street, which billed itself as a fusion of cabaret and performance art. Cahoots was funded in part by an angel, an anonymous financier whom Clair was also sleeping with. Through Clair, I met Emil, the founder and artistic director of Cahoots, and the two of them, flush with complimentary tickets, became my tutors in opera.

Clair worried that Emil's addiction to male dancers was more self-destructive than the drugs.

Their friendship went back to Juilliard, where Emil had been regarded as a can't-miss talent until he'd become involved in what Clair called "Fire Island Coke Chic." She'd been Emil's guest at a few of the parties he frequented, including a legendary night when he sang "Somewhere" with Leonard Bernstein at the piano. Clair worried that Emil's addiction to male dancers was more self-destructive than the drugs.

Emil worked as a singing waiter at Café Figaro, a coffeehouse in the Village with marble-top tables and a Medusa-hosed Italian espresso machine that resembled a rocket crossed with a basilica. Each steamed demitasse sounded like a moon launch and the waiters, singing a cappella, were all chronically hoarse. Emil felt even more contempt toward his job than Clair had for modeling. The one night he allowed us to stop in for coffee, Emil sang "Una furtiva lagrima," the famous aria from *The Elixir of Love*. His voice issued with an unforgettable purity that seemed at odds with the man mopping sweat, his Italian punctuated by gestures larger than life. The room, even the espresso machine, fell silent.

In the opera, that aria is sung by Nemorino, a peasant who has spent his last cent on an elixir he hopes will make the wealthy woman he loves love him in return. Nemorino sees a tear on her cheek, and takes it as a sign that the magic is working. Watching Emil sing his proverbial heart out at a coffee house, Clair, too, looked about to cry. He's singing for us, she said. Until that moment, I hadn't recognized the obvious: she'd been in love with Emil since Juilliard—years of loving the impossible.

Emil's voice rose to the climax and Clair mouthed the aria's last line to me in English, *I could die! Yes, I could die of love,* while Emil held the final *amor* on an inexhaustible breath.

The espresso machine all but levitated on a cushion of steam, and patrons sprang to a standing ovation that ended abruptly when Emil, oblivious to the blood drooling onto his white apron from the left nostril of his coke-crusted nose, flipped them off as if conducting music only he could hear.

After Figaro's became the third job Emil lost that year, Clair decided to risk desperate measures. Emil was broke. His doomed flings with danseurs had left him without an apartment of his own. The actors in Cahoots had grown openly critical of his leadership. Refusing to crash with increasingly disillusioned friends, Emil slept at the theater, whose heat was turned off between performances.

In Emil's script, the town is Winesburg, Ohio, an all-American community of secret lusts and repressed passion.

He's out of control, we're watching slow-mo suicide, Clair said, enlisting me in a small group of theater people for an intervention. It was an era in New York when the craze for interventions seemed in direct proportion to the sale of coke. Emil regarded interventions as a form of theater below contempt. To avoid his suspicion, Clair planned for it to take place at the private cast party following the opening of a show Emil had worked obsessively over—a takeoff on *The Elixir of Love*.

In the Donizetti opera, Dr. Dulcamara, a salesman of quack remedies, arrives in a small Basque town and encounters Nemorino, who requests a potion of the kind that Tristan used to win Isolde. Dulcamara sells him an elixir that's nothing more than wine.

In Emil's script, the town is Winesburg, Ohio, an all-American community of secret lusts and repressed passion. A chorus of townsfolk sings of their need for a potion to release them from lives of quiet desperation. Emil played the traveling salesman—not Dr. Dulcamara, but Willy Loman. As Willy sings his aria "Placebo," sexually explicit ads for merchandise flash across a screen, attracting the townsfolk. They mob Nemorino, and the bottle of bogus elixir is torn from hand to hand. Its mere touch has them writhing lewdly, unbuttoning their clothes, and when the bottle breaks, they try to lap elixir from the stage, pleading for more, threatening to hang Willy Loman by his tie if he doesn't deliver.

Alone, Willy finds a wine bottle beside a drunk slumped against a dumpster. As scripted, the bottle is half filled with wine, and Emil is only to simulate urinating into it. But that night, onstage, he drained the bottle, unzipped his trousers, and, in view of the audience, pissed.

"Here's your elixir of love!" he shouted, raising the bottle triumphantly as he stepped back into the town square.

The script has the townsfolk passing the elixir, slugging it down, and falling madly, indiscriminately in love. Willy demands to be paid, and they rough him up instead. The play was to end with the battered salesman suffering a heart attack as an orgy swirls around him. In an aria sung with his dying breath, he wonders if he's spent his money-grubbing life unwittingly pissing away magic.

Script notwithstanding, opening night was pure improv, pure pandemonium. When the actors realized Emil had actually given them piss to drink, the beating they gave him in return wasn't simulated either. Emil fought back until, struck with the bottle, he spit out pieces of tooth, then leapt from the stage, ran down the center aisle, and out of the theater. The audience thought it was the best part of the show.

The cast party went on backstage without Emil. Stunned and dejected, the actors knew it was the end of Cahoots and on that final evening clung to each other's company. Around midnight, Clair pressed me into a corner to say, You don't belong at this wake. We stood kissing, and then she gently pushed me away and whispered, Go. One word, perfectly timed to say what we had avoided saying aloud, but both knew: whatever was between us had run its course. Instead of goodbye, I said what I'd told her after our first night together and had repeated like an incantation each time since: thank you.

Emil showed up as I was leaving. He still wore his bloodied salesman's tie. His swollen lip could have used stitches, but he managed to swig from a bottle of vodka.

Drunk on your own piss? Glen, who'd played Nemorino and had thrown the first punch on stage, asked him.

Shhh, no need for more, Clair said. She took Emil's arm as if to guide him. Sit down with us, she told him. Emil shook off her hand. Judas, he said, and Clair recoiled as if stung.

Keeping a choke hold on the bottle, Emil climbed up on a chair.

I've come to say I'm sorry, he announced, and to resign as your artistic director. I guessed you all might still be hanging around, given that without Cahoots none of you has anywhere else to perform.

Clair, blotting her smeared makeup, began to sob quietly, hopelessly, as a child cries. Emil continued as if, like so much else between them, it was a duet. Sweat streaked his forehead as it did when he sang.

Did you think I didn't know about the pathetic little drama you'd planned for me tonight by way of celebration? he asked. So, yes, I'm sorry, sorry to deprive you of the cheesy thrill of your judgmental psycho-dabbling. But then what better than your dabbling as actors to prepare you to dabble in others' lives? Was it so threatening to encounter someone willing to risk it all, working without a net, living an opera as if it's life, which sometimes—tonight, for instance—apparently means being condemned to live life as if it's a fucking opera.

The last friend of mine to say he was living life like an opera was Cole.

He said it during a call to wish me a happy birthday, one of those confiding phone conversations we'd have after being out of touch—not unusual for a friendship that went back to high school. Twenty years earlier, Cole had beat me in the state finals, setting a high school record for the high hurdles. We were workout buddies that summer between high school and college, which was also the summer I worked downtown at a vintage jazz record shop. Cole would stop by to spin records while I closed up. He'd been named for Coleman Hawkins and could play Hawkins's famous tenor solo on "Body and Soul" note for note on the piano. Cole played organ each Sunday at the Light of Deliverance, one of the oldest African American churches on the South Side. His grandfather was the minister. I'd close the record shop and we'd jog through downtown to a park with a track beside the lake, and after running, we'd swim while the lights of the gold coast replaced a lingering dusk. His grandfather owned a cabin on Deep Lake in Northern Michigan, and Cole invited me up to fish before he left for Temple on a track scholarship. It was the first of our many fishing trips over the years to come.

Cole lived in Detroit now, near the neighborhood of the '67 riots, where he'd helped establish the charter school that he'd written a book about. He'd spent the last four years as a community organizer and was preparing to run for public office. When he'd married Amina, a Liberian professor who had sought political asylum, "Body and Soul" was woven into the recitation of their vows. The wedding party wore dashikis, including me, the only white groomsman.

He called on my birthday—our birthdays were days apart—to invite me up to Deep Lake to fish one last time. His grandfather had died years earlier and the family had decided to sell the cabin. When I asked how things were going, Cole paused, then said, I'm living my life like an opera. I knew he was speaking in code, something so uncharacteristic of him that it caught me by surprise. I waited for him to elaborate. Before the silence got embarrassing, he changed the subject.

We'd always fished after Labor Day, when the summer people were gone. By then evenings were cool enough for a jacket. The woods ringing the lake were already rusting, the other cottages shuttered, the silence audible. Outboard engines were prohibited on Deep Lake, although the small trolling motor on the minister's old wooden rowboat was legal. Cole fished walleye as his grandfather had taught him: at night—some nights under a spangle of Milky Way, on others in the path of the moon, but also nights so dark that out on the middle of the lake you could lose your sense of direction.

I cracked the seal on a fifth of Jameson's and passed it to Cole; tradition demanded that I arrive with a bottle.

The night was dark like that. There was no dock light to guide us back, but the tubed stereo that had belonged to his grandfather glowed on the screened porch. Cole's grandfather had had theories about fishing and music: walleyes rose to saxophones. His jazz collection was still there, some of the same albums I had sold in the record shop when I was eighteen. We chose *Ballads* by Ben Webster. The notes slurred across the water as I rowed out to the deep spot in the middle. Cole lowered the anchor, though it couldn't touch bottom. I cracked the seal on a fifth of Jameson's and passed it to Cole; tradition demanded that I arrive with a bottle. We'd had a lot of conversations over the years, waiting for the fish to bite.

I been staying at the cabin since we last talked, Cole said.

What's going on? I asked.

Remember I told you I was living life like an opera? You didn't say boo, but I figured you got my meaning, seeing you'd used the phrase yourself. Never know who's listening in. Cole laughed as if kidding, but, given the surveillance on Martin Luther King, he worried about wiretaps.

Cole, I said, I *never* used that phrase.

Where do you think I got it? he asked.

Not from me.

Maybe you forgot saying it, he said, maybe you finally forgot who you said it about. Anyway, whoever said it, I'm at a fund-raiser in Ann Arbor, everyone dressed so they can wear running shoes except for a woman I can't help but notice. You know me, it's not like I'm looking—just the opposite—there's always someone on the make if you're looking. She's out of *Vogue*. I hate misogynist rap, man, but plead guilty to thinking: rich bitch—which I regret when she comes up with my book and a serious camera that can't hide something vulnerable about her. Photojournalist, her card reads, and could she take one of me signing my book, and make a donation to the school, and how could she get involved beyond just giving money, and where's my next talk, and do I have time for a drink? Two weeks later at a conference in DC, she's there with Wizard tickets. And this time I go—we go to the game. In Boston it's the symphony, in Philly, I show her places I lived in college and take her to the Clef, where 'Trane played, and in New York we go to the Met. I'd never been to an opera; we go three nights in a row. Was I happy—happiness isn't even the question. Remember how running a race you disappear like playing music? She could make that happen again. One night, I'm home working late, Mina's already asleep, and the phone in my office rings. I'd never given her that unlisted home number. You need to help me, she says, and the line goes dead. Phone rings again. Where are you? I ask. Trapped in a car at the edge, she says. Her calls keep getting dropped, her voice is slurred: Come get me before I'm washed away. I keep asking her, Where are you? Finally she says: Jupiter Beach—I drove to see the hurricane. I say, You're a thousand miles away. The phone goes dead, rings, and Mina asks, Who keeps calling this time of night? She's in her nightgown, leaning in the doorway for I don't know how long. Too long for lies. I answer the phone, but no one's there.

She's talking crazy since she's stopped taking the meds you never noticed, and when she said she loved you, that was craziness, too.

She have a husband? Mina asks. You got to call him now.

The business card she gave me in Ann Arbor has private numbers she listed on the back, one with a Florida area code. A man answers, gives his name. I say, You don't know me, but I'm calling about an emergency, your wife's in the storm in a car somewhere on Jupiter Beach.

I know you, he says. I know you only too well. Don't worry, she doesn't tell me names, I don't ask, but I know you.

Mina presses speakerphone.

You teach tango or Mandarin or yoga or murderers to write poetry, film the accounts of torture victims, rescue greyhounds. I know the things you do, the righteous things you say, and I know you couldn't take your eyes off her the first time you saw her, and how that made you realize you'd been living a life in which you'd learned to look away. And like a miracle she's looking back, and you wonder what's the scent of a woman like that, and not long after—everything's happening so fast—you ask, what do you want, and she says, to leave the world behind together, and you think beauty like hers must come with the magic to allow what you couldn't ordinarily do, places you couldn't go, a life you'd dreamed when you were young. But now, just as suddenly, she can destroy you by falling from the ledge she's calling from, or falling asleep forever in the hotel room where she's lost count of the pills. She's talking crazy since she's stopped taking the meds you never noticed, and when she said she loved you, that was craziness, too—you're a symptom of her illness. So you called me, not to save her, but yourself, and it's me who knows where she goes when she gets like this, and I'll go, as I do every time, to save her, calm and comfort her, bring her home, because I love her, I was born to, I'll always love her, and you're only a shadow. I've learned to ignore shadows. She made you feel alive; now, you're a ghost. Go. Don't call again.

I told you on the phone, Cole said, that I was living my life like an opera, but he's the one who sang the aria.

FIRE!

A borrowed flat above a plumbing store whose back windows looked out on a yard of stockpiled toilets filled with unflushed rain. Four AM, still a little drunk from a wake at an Irish bar, they smell bread baking. Someone's in the room, she whispers. It's only the mirror, he tells her. She strips off her slip, tosses it over the shadowy reflection, and then follows the scent to the open front windows. A ghost, she says as if sighing. Below a vaporous street lamp, in the doorway of a darkened bakery, a baker in white, hair and skin dusted with flour, leans smoking. FIRE!

A bedroom lit by fireflies, one phosphorescent above the bed, another blinking in the mirror as if captured in a jar. The window open on the scent of rain-beaded lilacs. When the shards of a wind chime suspended in a corner tingle, it means a bat swoops through the dark. Flick on the bed lamp and the bat will vanish.

FIRE! DAMN YOU! FIRE!

Whom to identify with at this moment—who is more real—Caruso, whose unmistakable, ghostly, 78 rpm voice carries over the ramparts where sparrows twitter, or Mario Cavaradossi?

Or perhaps, with an extra in the firing squad, who—once Tosca flings herself from the parapet—will be free to march off for a beer at the bar around the corner, and why not, he was only following the orders barked out by the captain of the guard, who was just doing what the director demanded, who was in turn under the command of Giacomo Puccini.

Or with the hooded man, his mind lit by a firefly as he tries to recall a room he once attempted to memorize when it became increasingly clear to him that he would soon be banished.

FIRE! I AM GIVING YOU A DIRECT ORDER.

How heavy their extended rifles have become. The barrels teeter and dip, and seem to be growing like Pinocchio's nose, although it's common knowledge that rifles don't lie. Still, just to hold one steady and true requires all the strength and concentration a man can summon.

Turn on the bed lamp to better illuminate the target. On some nights the silk shade suggests the color of lilacs and on others of areola. See, the bat has vanished, which doesn't mean it wasn't there.

FIRE! OR YOU'LL ALL BE SHOT!

The lamp rests on a nightstand with a single drawer in which she keeps lotions and elixirs and stashes the dreams she records on blue airmail stationery when they wake her in the night—an unbound nocturnal diary. She blushed when she told him the dream in which she made love with the devil. He liked to do what you like to do to me, she said. Then she rephrased that to what *we* like.

In the cracked mirror each member of the squad sees himself aiming at himself. Only a moment has passed since the "Aim" command, but to each member of the squad it seems they've stood with fingers ready on their triggers, peering down their sights, for so long that they've become confused as to who are the originals and who are the reflections. After the ragged discharge, when the smoke has cleared, who will be left standing and who will be shattered into shards?

PLEASE, FIRE!

I can't wait like this any longer.

Non ho amato mai tanto la vita.

WILLING TO PAY

It's your face I wanted. Spent
All day at the dentist hoping
He'd hammer the smile right.
Your face and that thing
You do with your eyes
When I get you livid. Don't be
Flattered. Don't be afraid.
It's 1979 or so. I'm known
To lie about my age. My parents
Are trying again. How's that
For language, the moans
They made making me. If only
One of them lasted longer,
If they preferred the dog to some
Other position, then maybe I'd be
The same on both sides or
A babyface the rest of my life.
This is the night of a thousand
Noses. You want entertainment,
But how can I watch TV knowing
A guy cuter than me is getting paid

To wink, and I'm the one
Willing to pay? I wonder a while
At football. At least, I'd have had
A lovely set of calves. Everybody
Who eats loves an athlete
Naked and recently showered.
What's fair? You got the face
And the body and the cameras
Calling while I got you
Waiting for me to put the W
Behind the O in words like
Now. Look, I bought you
Something else. Something perfect
For hanging on that wall you wanted
Up. The painter did the damnedest
Job pulling your lips close to mine.

ESSAY

GLUTTON FOR PUNISHMENT

Benjamin Percy

Fourth and Goal in Cholesterol's Red Zone

In high school, in the backseat of my Jeep Wrangler, in the parking lot behind the Pine Tavern, I slipped out a box of condoms. I did this because I believed the half-naked young woman who had snuck out of her house to meet me at midnight wanted to have sex with me. For the past few weeks, we had been doing everything else, everything that is possible to do, but not that, not yet.

I had never bought condoms before, and earlier that night I spent a long time wandering the health-care aisle at Safeway, studying the many packages, before strategically deciding on Ultra Pleasure. I also purchased a red apple, which I laid wobblingly on the black conveyer belt at the register and later chewed down to the core while waiting for her ghostly figure to appear at the street corner where she had told me to meet her with my engine idling, my headlights off.

The Pine Tavern had closed hours ago, its lot empty, and we parked in a dark, quiet corner. One thing led to another. The windows fogged over except where we smeared the fog away. When I held out the box of condoms, she did not respond, and when she did not respond, I smiled in what I

thought was a becoming way and gave the box an excited shake, as if it were a maraca.

My hand remained in the air long after she knocked the box from it. I watched her scoop her breasts into her bra, pull on her shirt, and clamber into the front seat, where she said, so softly I could barely hear, "Take me home."

We drove in silence. No, that's incorrect. I said, "I'm sorry," over and over and over, and she said nothing. When she ran for her house—and yes, she ran, as if worried I might pursue her—she kept her arms crossed, as if to hug herself, to comfort herself, which made me feel overcome with wretchedness.

The next day she wrote me a poem on a piece of lined notebook paper. I can still remember two lines from it: "How could such a paragon / become such a problem?" I had to look up *paragon*, believing at first she meant to compare me to some kind of falcon, a bird of prey. But the word did not mean what I thought it meant.

She forgave me a few days later, when I finally stopped saying, "Sorry," and—fed up—said, "Why are you blaming me for wanting you?" That wasn't it at all, I discovered. My desire was not the problem. She was furious because I had not listened to her. During one of our milkshake-and-burger dates, she had told me she would remain a virgin until her wedding night, a conversation I perhaps willfully did not recall.

There was a solution, she said. A way I could earn back her trust. One afternoon, while my parents were out, she would come over to my house and we would take a shower together. I could kiss her, and I would clean her, but I should not—no chance, no way and no how, not now and not ever—have sex with her.

I readily agreed.

I knew this would be a definitive moment of torture. But I also knew this was the rare, impossible chance for me to study—at length, in the light of day—a naked female body. A welcome, purposeful suffering.

One afternoon, while my parents were out, she would come over to my house and we would take a shower together.

We peeled off our clothes and heaped them on the floor. The water hissed, the room swirled with steam. For twenty minutes I massaged shampoo into her hair, scraped a bit of dirt from beneath her thumbnail, ran a bar of soap along the inside of her elbow. She stared at me the entire time.

Of course I began to get carried away—my hands taking in every inch of her—and when I did, she turned off the water and studied me through her wet bangs and said, "Now dry me off."

He is studying a sheet of paper, the results of my blood tests. He looks like a doctor should—silver-haired, bespectacled, with the long lean body of a marathon runner. Above us the fluorescents buzz and cast a sickly white light. He heaves a sigh and folds the paper in half and in half again and tells me to explain myself.

I am not overweight. Three times a week I throw metal around the gym. I can pound out ten sets of ten pull-ups. Every day I hammer out ten miles on the bike, riding back and forth between my house and the office where I work.

My grandfather, too, appeared fit. But in his early sixties he died of a massive coronary while mowing the lawn. His blood runs through my veins. Cut me and I bleed gravy.

He used to soak up bacon grease with Wonder Bread, guzzle vodka hidden in his greenhouse, smoke a pipe until his beard yellowed around his mouth. I have inherited his excessive habits. If a plate is set before me, I clean it. I drain the coffee pot. I empty the tumbler, the bottle, the liquor cabinet. So too do I leap out of planes, hang glide off mountains, climb 250-foot trees for a shot of adrenaline. So too do I roll around in bed with my wife. I am a man of great appetites.

I can't help it, I say to my doctor. I am always . . . desiring.

He lays it out for me, jabbing my knee with his finger to punctuate his sentences. My triglycerides clock in at 365. My HDL is ridiculously high and my LDL pathetically low—the bad and good cholesterol, as they're known. The red zone, my doctor calls it. I am thirty-two years old and in the red zone. If I don't do something, I will end up with cirrhosis, fatty liver disease, eventually a heart attack, a stroke.

"Enough," he says.

If I don't do something, I will end up with cirrhosis, fatty liver disease, eventually a heart attack, a stroke.

Some things about the liver:

It was once believed to house the darkest emotions of man—greed, wrath, jealousy.

Long ago, seers fingered through animal livers for answers, a form of divination called haruspicy.

I have pleasured in the muddy-flavored livers of duck, deer, elk, turkey, cow, chicken, quail, and grouse, lightly floured and fried with onions in bacon grease.

The first line of Dostoevsky's *Notes from Underground*, one of my favorite lines in all of literature, a line worthy of getting tattooed across my back, reads, "I am a sick man . . . I am a spiteful man . . . I believe my liver is diseased."

The liver is the body's vital filter. It detoxifies, metabolizes. It synthesizes nutrients, stores glycogen, produces hormones. It is a reddish brown color, though I suspect mine is sleeved in gummy yellow fat. There is no way to survive without it.

It is also the only organ capable of regenerating itself. I know a woman who had two-thirds of hers removed and it grew back.

I am told that if I give my liver a break—if I effectively clean it—it will be the equivalent of a reset button for my body.

For three weeks, I decide, I will drink nothing but water and eat nothing except fruits and vegetables. That means no bourbon, no beer, no coffee, no steaks or pizza or cheeseburgers, no Triscuits, Fruit Loops, Almond Joys, no cheese curds or prosciutto or any of the other dozen things I reach for in a day. No legumes, either. And no nuts, no grains. Nothing that commonly inflames the liver and the digestive system. No medicine, either. An unconditional purification.

Several people advise me to ease into the diet. I do not listen to them. And though I can't say exactly why, I want to hurt. I in fact look perversely forward to the punishment I will endure.

The night before I am to detox I go to a baseball game and swill four beers and snarf down two hot dogs, a platter of nachos, a bag of popcorn. The next morning I am gnawing on a carrot and chugging two glasses of water until my stomach feels full even if it is not.

By midafternoon I can feel my pulse in my temple and fingertips. The edges of my vision flutter with black wings of exhaustion. My body seems to be eating itself. That night I cannot sleep. During the day I cannot concentrate. But my body is shrinking. In three days, I lose five pounds—and then a pound a day thereafter. Purplish smears appear beneath my eyes. My ribs rise from my skin like claws coming together. My pants fall off me as I go down three belt notches. When I step from the shower and wipe my towel across the mirror, I don't recognize the body before me, the veins worming down my arms, my stomach like stones stacked one on top of the other.

I don't realize how often I snack until I catch myself walking into the kitchen, reaching for the cupboard for no reason. I don't miss booze, I don't miss meat or cheese, as I expected I would, because my body *needs* so many other things I am denying it. I crave coffee. And carbs. I cannot seem to satisfy my appetite without them. I dream about mountains of toast smothered with marmalade, about Olympic-sized pools splashed full of chocolate milk and Honey Nut Cheerios. One morning, when I walk past a man eating a cinnamon roll, I seriously consider ripping off his arm and beating him to death with it. Everyone keeps saying I will find a second wind, renewed energy, but I do not. Everyone keeps saying I can cheat—enjoy a sip of coffee, a bite of chocolate—but I do not. I eat heaping piles of steamed broccoli. I rip open bananas, suck pears dry. I spoon out avocados, grapefruits, kiwis. I drink strawberry shakes. My wife makes me ratatouille and eggplant curry, setting them down before me and stepping back as I attack my meals, shoveling forkfuls into my mouth until the tines scratch an empty plate. I take whey extract for protein. I take organic supplements packed full of things that seem better suited for a magician's potion: red yeast rice, tuna oil, buckwheat, milkweed thistle.

And all this time I am pushing my body to its limit. Sprinting my bike. Hefting metal on the bench. Squeezing out crunches on my living room floor. My appetite somehow lessens the more I hurt myself, my body distracting my mind. I am at war with myself.

One night, two weeks in, I stand in front of the fridge with the door open. It emits a pale light. Its cold breath plays across my skin. A minute goes by, and when my wife asks what I am waiting for, I tell her I do not know.

Two days later I unpeel a chocolate bar and open my mouth and hold it inches from my tongue—before setting it down and stabbing my thumb with a steak knife.

I grew up on a hobby farm outside Eugene, Oregon, twenty-seven acres of woods, blueberry bushes, plum trees, a pond, a henhouse. Once, the chickens exploded in a panicked clucking—and by the time my father raced to the coop, his flashlight cutting through the dark, the whirl of feathers, he found broken eggs littering the floor and a half-dead hen in the corner missing a wing and a clump of its throat. So he set up a trap, a cage with a spring-loaded door that crashed closed. He baited it with overripe bananas. By the next night he had his possum. It hissed and paced the length of the cage and threw itself against the bars and chewed at them with its needled teeth and reached forth a claw to rake the air.

Sometimes I feel like my ribs are a cage. Sometimes I feel as though some beast is trapped inside me, pacing, rattling my bones, trying to find a way out.

Ways in which I have enjoyed punishing myself:

Driving fifteen minutes in 100-degree heat—windows up, no air-conditioning—so that the ice-cream cone I was about to buy would taste better.

Sleeping outside during a rainstorm, though I had packed a tent.

Hitting the gym whenever ill or hungover, believing I must sweat out the poisons.

Eating a thirty-two-ounce steak, at Bigfoot's Tavern, in less than an hour, so that I got it for free.

Powering my car along the freeway, all through the day and night, sucking down gas-station coffee and white-knuckling the wheel, rather than stopping at a Super 8, because I wanted to get home.

Buying a run-down house with the express purpose of fixing it up—and then spending the next year ripping down the wallpaper, ripping up the floors, ripping off the roof, ripping out the outlets and fixtures and switches.

Climbing a 100-foot seawall along the Oregon coast with no gear.

Hiking twenty-four miles at eight thousand feet in one day with no food or water.

Rationing out episodes of *The Wire* on Netflix over a four-year period rather than bingeing all at once on its gritty goodness.

Wobbling my bike along ice-cobbled streets in zero-degree weather.

Drinking an entire bottle of hot sauce on a bet.

Dropping my gloves and letting my sparring partner hit me full in the face to know what it felt like.

Sometimes, when I am hunched over the stationary bike, sweating through my shirt, watching the football game, pedaling hard and going nowhere, I think about *Conan the Barbarian.* In the 1982 John Milius film, a snow-swept village is attacked, its huts burned, its people murdered. The children are enslaved, among them a boy who is lashed to a wheel—the wheel of pain, it is called—that may grind grain or pump water, its purpose irrelevant. A time-lapse sequence shows the wheel turning and turning and turning, pushed by dozens of children who grow into teenagers and then adults, all of them eventually dying of exhaustion, except for Conan—Schwarzenegger—whose shoulders surge with muscle and whose feet have tromped a deep furrow into the earth. His eyes are hooded, accepting of the pain, because the pain is good.

The pain is good.

Everyone tells me his or her purification story. The vegan diet. The juice diet. The lemon-water-and-cayenne-pepper diet. They suffered for a weekend, maybe a week. When I tell them about my detox, they seem confused. But what about coffee? No, not coffee. But what about____? No, not that either. And how long am I doing this for? Three weeks; twenty-one days; five hundred and four hours.

"Oh," they say.

Then they tell me two things. When the diet ends, I will retain my healthy eating habits because I will be so pleased with the way I look and feel. And if I test myself, if I regress to my old ways, if I go on a bender, if I order everything on the menu, my body will punish me. They don't understand. I'm not chasing a lifestyle—I'm chasing a feeling—the rare, pure feeling available only in the borderlands. Drop me in the woods without a compass. Feed me a marble-sized dose of wasabi. Race me until my vision blackens and my legs feel separate from me. The pain is as fleeting as the pleasure, and when they fade, they're replaced by a question: what next? How next will I punish myself?

I'm not chasing a lifestyle—I'm chasing a feeling—the rare, pure feeling available only in the borderlands.

On Day 22, the morning after my detox ends, a nurse pricks me with a needle and sucks 16 ccs of blood out of the crook of my elbow. She says my vein was easy to find, and when she tapes a cotton ball over the welling blood, I tell her thank you.

I run from the medical center and drive at a perilous speed to the Grove Café, where I drum my knuckles on the table and order a stack of pancakes, an omelet, hash browns, bacon, sausage, toast, and coffee.

"Will somebody be joining you?" the waitress asks and I say, "No. Just me."

My numbers have turned out perfectly, my triglycerides dropping from 365 to 100, my HDL and LDL evening out. My liver enzymes are stable, healthy. I am, my doctor says, in the green zone. He offers his congratulations.

But at this point I don't really care. My blood work, I've come to realize, was simply an excuse for what in the end amounted to an elaborate trial, punishment, purification of a very different sort. I feel most vitally alive when I bleed, shake off a punch, walk away from a car accident, stand perilously close to the edge of a chasm. This fast—three weeks of self-denial, enduring temptation—amounts to a dark door leading to a bright room.

When the table fills with food, I sit there for a long minute, leaning in, letting the steam tease my face, taking in the smell and sight of it all, and I am once more in the shower with my high school girlfriend, painfully suspended before what I desire most.

Then I drown my pancakes in syrup and season my omelet with salsa and begin to eat. I do this slowly, carving away a forkful at a time, allowing each bite to melt on my tongue. The bacon snaps between my teeth. Each piece of toast I lavishly coat with grape jelly. I drink the coffee as if it were wine, taking in tiny sips, sloshing it around in my mouth, before swallowing.

When the waitress splashes my mug full for the third time, I tell her she can leave the pot. I spend the next hour eating. And as I fill the void inside me, the sensation—a cramping joined by a trembling heat that spreads outward and ultimately leaves me languid and spent—is equivalent to orgasm.

NEW VOICE POETRY

THIS IS THE REMIX

No wonder I keep walking into the blizzard of my own
    making cold weather systems designed to hold me
back from you. My bad. Each thought is shaped exactly

like the thought-shaped duffle bag I was told I had won.
    If I was late it's because I must have misread
your text a translation of what the leaves have been doing.

Still. The fact you're the only person who called me
    all day makes me imagine your name written over
and over my mind a billboard graffiti bombed in the dark.

Everything is the worst but worse than what I can't figure out.
    What's next for us? Today I put up the flyer
they gave me to put up. I felt fine all alone in another brightly lit

flyer-less street. Someone at work showed me another
    viral video. Now lions eating giraffe has
over ten million hits. There's a little girl you can't see

crying from the backseat. There's a father saying this is
    just what they do. After work I show it to you on the
couch
and try to kiss you. Later when you're in bed I'll look up

what the dream encyclopedia says about streaming
    online videos in your sleep. It will say this is the remix
to that song stuck in your head that you decided to get

stuck in mine. It will say it's some cure you're always singing
    into a tunnel built so unavoidably wide
I won't have to squeeze my tacky heart into its thesis.

PHARMACEUTICAL AD, TAKE ONE

Every time this happens I wake to a sky blue sky that is pure stock footage. Uncanny how every time my mind begins copy-righting clouds each shape becomes my own. At this point a man with a ski mask has a flower pressed to my head *Frolic or die* he threatens and scoops two purple pills from the eyeholes in his skull. *They work like seeds inside you* he whispers. Etched into each pill in a font so small I must read it with a spyglass is something romantic, some endless song rapidly listing possible side effects: *May cause feelings of euphoria along with nausea diarrhea an effusion of metaphors issuing forth from every orifice and pore. Do not take if you already enjoy sunsets.* Already the dusk has been turned on. Mothers call children back in from the edge of the woods, from the fires they were planting there. The dramatic music of the evening news cues the dead air. I tilt my head back to swallow my dose and an airplane unzips the sky causing every cloud shape to enter then dissolve at the back of my mouth. That's when my body flips inside out like an anatomical map, vital organs exposed to the wind. That's when I start running maniacally over the daisy-strewn meadow and throw myself into the lake like I'm on fire. That's when, pulled up through layers of water, the light knifes its way towards me and my lungs reach for any night possible, drowned-out stars or no.

FICTION

House Heart

THE HOME REMAINS. EVEN IF THE HOUSE WERE RAZED, THE FOUNDATION SCORED AND broken and the pieces carried away, a spiritual outline of the home in which people cooked dinner or lay down exhausted or looked out the window at the garbage truck rumbling down the road would persist. The story of our home is the story of a city's shift from industry. The space was once the preparation wing of a garment factory, the room in which material was cooked with chemicals to change its color and character. We found this information in a reference book. Hints to the room's previous function can be found in the scars on the concrete where machines were once bolted and an industrial ventilation system thick like an artery across the high, open ceiling, feeding veins of air to each white-walled room. The larger warehouse has since been destroyed and replaced with stinking-new lofts, but our home remains as a testament to utility.

My partner and I have lived in this house for many years, though we see ourselves as temporary residents of the space and of the land beneath it. We believe in leaving no trace when we are gone. We bring our own containers to the grocery and our clothes dry in the sun. We are very interested in hemp products. Every object has a purpose, but with care and attention, one can find multiple purposes, a range of functions found in reuse. Once, my partner brought me an old child's tricycle, the rubber wheels hardened with age, and I scrubbed the rust away and attached a cage to the front handles and turned it into a planter.

Amelia Gray

It was my idea to purchase the girl. I had decided that would be a fine way to pass an afternoon and my partner agreed. He called a service and asked the receptionist if their business practices included the concept of fair trade. He said it was important to him as a consumer to have a sense of the origin of the products he used. He told her he realized that it was an issue of privilege, but that the least he could do was to utilize his privilege in a way that might benefit others, even in some small way.

The girl came over the next morning. She was wearing jeans and a T-shirt and rang the bell twice while we took turns admiring her from the peephole. Her hair was blond and ironed straight and she was falsely tanned. She glanced at something written in a pink notebook and took a step back to look up and down the street, shading her eyes with her hand. While we watched her, my partner asked me if we could educate her on the physical dangers of using chemically bleaching products and I said No, none of that.

The girl pounded on our door with her little fist, leaning in so close that we could see her eyes, pale and clear, the sclera like water in a bowl. She looked surprised, shocked even, when my partner unlocked the door and we were both standing there, smiling at her, but she entered our home anyway and put down her notebook and her purse. She said she had just come from class and I asked her what class she was taking and she told me and I said Ah, yes. Her fingers were manicured with a pink polish. She smelled like a bowl of sugar that had been sprayed with disinfectant. She told us her name; even her name sounded processed. My partner held the girl's shoulders and told her that he was happy she had come. She started to say something but he embraced her and she frowned and put her tanned arms across his back and said Okay, okay. We were all a little nervous.

My partner suggested that the girl change into something comfortable. We led her to the bathroom and she stripped naked before us and we anointed her with oil while she stood on the bath mat. Her muscles were tense under my hands, but I rubbed her feet and legs and back and she began to relax. There seemed to be a thin layer of glowing light just under her skin.

The oil was a jojoba blend to which I had added fresh sage and rosemary. The power in our hands inspired her to relax. I began to feel calmer as well, and was able to hear more of the conversation my partner was having with the girl. He led us all to the hallway and the air-conditioner intake duct. I gave him a screwdriver and he began to remove the duct's grate. He handed me each small screw and I held them in a cupped palm. He was asking the girl what her goals were and she said that she would like to be a medical assistant and he said that becoming a medical assistant was very much like playing House Heart with someone you trust and she said that she didn't understand. She stood between us with her arms crossed over her breasts, each hand holding an opposite shoulder. She shivered though it was quite warm. Her skin glistened and the oil made a small pool around her feet. I held her hips and kissed her face and tried to tell her a joke about an elevator repairman but she didn't laugh. She asked what we were doing in the hallway and I told her that my partner and I have a game we like to play called House Heart and it's a special game to us, very special, but we had never had a chance to share it with someone else and that was a big goal for us as a couple, and it would mean so much for us to meet that goal. She asked a few obvious questions and was taking a few hesitant steps away, but my partner was prying the grate from its spot and so I hushed the girl and patted her round bottom.

We led her to the bathroom and she stripped naked before us and we anointed her with oil while she stood on the bath mat.

Because our home is a converted industrial space, the duct area is large enough for a crouching man to spend a few productive hours. There would be plenty of space for our small girl. When we kissed her and coaxed her in, she barely had to crouch to get inside and then stood comfortably. There was no room to sit. Her feet were bare, but I had swept out the floor's grime many times before, and that morning had scrubbed the floor with a vinegar-soaked rag. When my partner started to replace the grate, she made a whine of protest, but we explained that it would help us complete the game, and that we would be so pleased if she would help us finally achieve our goal as a couple, a romantic goal for which she would be well compensated, and finally she was silent and the grate was replaced. I handed my partner the tiny screws quickly and in silence.

For a while, nothing happened. My partner and I stood facing the grate, holding hands. The girl was quiet as well, though after a few minutes we heard her scraping around, feeling the boundaries with her feet and hands. My partner told her that she would find another duct at her head and one at her feet. Those main arterial ducts would branch into smaller openings that would lead to different rooms. One would end up in a vent over the kitchen and another would terminate in the living room, one near the chandelier in the dining room and the other three in the bathroom, bedroom, and office. She would be able to hear us speaking to her at different points of the ductwork, thanks to the happy accidents of design that allow for echoes. In a small voice, the girl asked if we could maybe just let her out, but my partner shushed her and I fed a few dollars through the grate. The money stayed there for a moment before it vanished and we heard her folding it on the other side.

She was crying softly. My partner knocked on the grate and told her to calm herself, that she would earn five times the amount of money than if she had made love to us in a traditional way. He said there was no danger to playing House Heart, that there was a secret way out of the maze if she could find it. Her noises became more frantic as she felt along the corridor.

I dipped my head down onto my partner's genital, savoring the girl's energy as I worked.

We heard her clamber up to the high duct, finding a place for her bare feet in the metal's niches. I put my eye to the grate and saw her legs dangling before they vanished upward. She stopped crying after a while, the effort of movement distracting her enough to focus on her task. My partner held my hips and we did it right there in the hallway. We licked each other's faces. We could hear the girl crawling through the vein above us, looking for a way out. At that moment, she was learning that she could crawl on her hands and knees in the main duct, and in the smaller ducts, she would have to slide on her belly, pulling herself forward blindly, arms outstretched. At the system's narrowest points, the metal would surround and press her body from all angles.

After we were done in the hallway, my partner and I retired to the bed, where he rubbed the oil into my body. He rolled out of bed, arranged a stepladder under the vent, and stretched up to feed money through the slats, folding it so it would stay. He knocked on the grate so she would know there was some activity there. After a few minutes, the money disappeared and we heard her moving backward, her thin body shaking with adrenaline and making the metal shudder above us. I dipped my head down onto my partner's genital, savoring the girl's energy as I worked.

My partner left for work and I practiced with my doors. As I opened and closed the bathroom door, I wondered idly if the girl above had a boyfriend who would be worried about her. She might even be thinking of him at that moment, willing him to take to the streets, to search for her. I knew there would be no value in her fantasies.

For me, no real romantic bond materialized until I began to accept love in a more practical sense. In past relationships, my brain had been diseased with fantasy. I would imagine a shared future, one in which my partner cradled a little boy. My invasive mind settled comfortably into a corner chair, a voyeur into a manifestation. The child so resembled his father in this fantasy that I saw the two of them as a paired image representing the man at varied stages of his life. They were stages of my partner's life in which it made no sense for me to be present. Of course, the reality of the relationship would ruin the fantasy of it, but I had ruined it from the start by act of the fantasy itself.

True happiness came when I left those dreams behind. Within each moment, I found a struggle to be fully unattached to the past or the future. I needed not only to exist at a point on a vector but also to destroy the vector and inhabit that solitary point, akin to living inside a meteor without knowledge of its movement. Obviously it took some time to gain this ability, but eventually, it was possible to disengage. The image of the fantasy growing old vanished into a haze. Daily tasks were more difficult, but with practice and attention, I couldn't picture my partner sitting at work or driving a car. I have gotten to the point where I cannot quite describe what he looks like when he has left the room.

With thoughts of him erased from my mind, I became free to attend to my daily practice. After he leaves for work, I throw open the bedroom door and declare what a fine day it is, how the sun is glinting so kindly off available glinting things. Opening the door to the pantry, I speak of the green lawn. I hold my palm up in the bedroom closet and note that it is about to rain. In this way, I have repurposed the home and found new utility in its rooms.

The girl slept up there each night, turning over every few hours. There was no space for her to curl her legs up to her chest. In the morning, we heard her noises change as she lifted her elbows and slid on her belly. My partner rolled atop me and whispered that the girl was trusting the surfaces she was coming to know. It was very exciting for him, which made it very exciting for me.

He left for work and I opened and closed the pantry door before putting on water for tea. I could hear the girl slide above me in the kitchen. She stopped with her face above the vent. I could feel her eyes on me. She said Could you let me out of here? I told her that the world that had been created for her was out of my control. She said that wasn't true, that if I could call an authority, everything would be solved.

I wanted to cut the duct open with a knife and plunge that knife into her heart. Instead, I pointed out that she had made all the choices that brought her to that moment, that if she had been forced to do anything in her life, it had not been in our presence and we could not be held accountable. As I spoke, a drop of liquid landed on my shoulder. I told her she would be generously compensated for her lost time. Another drip landed on the stove. She confessed that she wanted to be let out because she didn't know where to urinate. Pee, she said. Without another word to her, I took my tea into the living room. I was annoyed at her for cheapening our transaction. She banged away for a while but lost interest after a while. A few hours passed and I cleaned the mess up from where it had landed on the kitchen floor.

From then on, the girl made waste in that portion of the duct and we couldn't convince her otherwise, even when my partner did his best to startle her as she did it. We suspected it was her small idea of insurrection. As he pounded the duct with a broom handle, my partner shouted that she was lucky to be where she was, that the world was a terrifying place for anyone and particularly terrifying for a girl like her, and that when she toughened her softer parts and grew out some more of the hair on her body, she could come out and live with us in strength and power. She continued her daily protest. Without a word to me about it, he rigged up a tarp and bucket under the vent in the kitchen.

We were sleeping late one morning when the girl began to knock on the duct. The knocking sound grew louder and she cried out without words. My partner got out of bed and left the room for some time. When he returned he spoke to her, saying he had opened the vent over the office and left an expensive watch inside. She stopped knocking and slid away.

It was his father's watch, I knew. His father was a company man who worked all his life to afford a house for his family. He never cared much for the size of his carbon footprint and would drive the family across the country every few months to observe the passing seasons. They watched turning leaves and local rock formations and various beaches. My partner's father snapped a picture, then herded the family back into the car. He drank gas station coffee from Styrofoam cups and when he finished the coffee, he would bite into the cup itself, chewing it thoughtfully, usually eating the whole thing before the next destination. On one of his later birthdays, he bought himself a fine watch and enjoyed it for a few years before he died. It was one of those things that my partner had long wanted to get rid of without knowing exactly why.

A scraping noise from the far side of the house meant that the girl had found the watch. I imagined her spreading her fistfuls of cash in front of her, slipping the watch over her thin wrist and tucking the singles into its silver band.

She confessed that she wanted to be let out because she didn't know where to urinate. Pee, she said.

I could hear her crawling above the bathroom while I washed my hair in the morning. She said she had heard the water running and asked if she could come down for a quick soap scrub. I responded that we use only baking soda and white vinegar to bathe and that I could make her a cup with which to wash in the duct if she liked. She declined but was polite about it. She had become more polite as the days wore on. I suspected she had created a fantasy of winning me over to her side through feminine duplicity.

While she was over the kitchen, I dragged the stepladder into the office and climbed up with a ham sandwich and a handful of radishes from the local harvest box. I said that lunch was served if she could find it and that I had opened a window so she could have a little air. I liked her, this other girl, but I would not be fooled.

The girl created a method by which she could live with relative order. A few times a day, she would crawl into the standing-room area where she had first entered the system, finding the footholds and lowering herself into the space. She could store her money and empty dishes there, or stand and stretch her legs. A scraping sound when she crawled suggested she was wearing the watch around her wrist or ankle. I discovered her routine while opening and closing the bathroom door, which stood next to the entry portal to the system. My continued practice against fantasy was making it harder to imagine what green grass would look like up close. My best image was of a sea of green like what one finds in a stagnant pond, but this image was fading along with my knowledge of ponds. The work was to convince myself that this was an improvement. The girl and I did not speak to each other most days, and after a while, I noted that the girl had quit speaking entirely. It was a welcome discovery.

My partner arrived home with groceries, and I put them away in their proper places. I fixed dinner and climbed the stepladder to serve the girl after we had eaten our share. Playing her part in the game, the girl ate quickly and then crawled to the standing-room area to store her dish. We all had our individual function and hers was to be the life inside the house, which had begun to smell like a hot scalp.

The girl started her period and a few drops of blood fell onto the floor by our bed. With that action, the ductwork veins of the house became actual veins pushing life through every room. The veins began to expand and contract and the house itself could breathe. Every room of our home was replete with veins.

I felt concerned about the girl's silence and brought it up to my partner while he was feeding me from a bowl of cottage cheese. He spooned curds into my mouth and said it was only natural that the girl had become comfortable with her surroundings. He reminded me that I had not challenged the boundaries of my own life in many years, nor had he challenged his. Even though we all feel quite free, he remarked, every life has its surrounding wall. He wiped my chin with a napkin and kissed the napkin.

My partner phoned the girl's employer, then held the phone to the grate over the bedroom while I was cleaning dishes in the kitchen. Over my noise, I could hear the girl say that she had decided to quit. There was a long silence in the room. At first I stopped my movement and strained to hear, and then I couldn't avoid the silence and began to hate it. I opened a cabinet to put away the clean dishes. In the back of the cabinet, over the plates, there was a portal through which I could view a wide, dark field. There was no wind.

Later, after my partner and I made love, we lay in bed and I sang a song about loving the world you know. The song encouraged all of us to live within the boundaries that were created for us by the people who love us and care for our safety. I had learned the song long ago and remembered it well. The girl was quiet at first but then we heard her sweet voice rise with the harmony.

THE KILLING FIELDS

Because it has been days it has been years
Of new space new space being water
Organisms feel it work it
Moist growths of a new head space conjunctions of a skull
Are here—they are right here

We look at skulls and feel unsettled—skulls are right here
Anything we don't need to step outside ourselves to be in the company of
Unsettles us from the thing we have left
The thing we are looking at
Smoke over a field

I wrote a book with a white cover it went to the hill of the poisonous trees
Children were following my retarded stepbrother around the fields
He very shallowly appreciated them following him I observed
And felt to be worse than outright disgust
Here's a broom—Pick it up Drag it across your hands and feet
He should have given at least
A corner of the truth then
Sat me down and asked if I loved him
I am the broom I said I do not know you pulling your pants down
Will not help me to know you—He asked me

To explain a poem I had written about my father
He had found fussing in my father's sock drawer
For snacks—I gazed through his eyes to the gleam
Of the metal plate in his head, said simply
Read the poem but then realized
His defect—he did not believe in a world outside of the world of the present
Moment and therefore in the possibility of being
In two places simultaneously not only
Did he not but he barely
Possessed the courage to believe
In the world of the present moment
Therefore in the possibility of being in even one therefore in anything
Imagination is driven by
An an-heroic sliver—not always light always light
An acid element suffocating that which is other than
Precisely what is and barely even
That therefore everything real
In its first however fatal dimension—acid element forged
By hand to fit
As wide as possible the head, and in that sense I actually loved him
Though I wanted to put him
Wholesale into a blender and drink him

On the day my father and mother married—August 25, 1972
Grindelwald, Switzerland, the Alps they celebrated

With a tin of anchovies and a bottle of orange soft drink
On a hill overlooking the village, that is
The world I believe in the world I replicate in the world that is passing
Where also a Cambodian princess
Mauled by a dog is falling eternally in love with my retarded stepbrother
I convinced her to she was falling in love with me
I did not need her love then I did not need love then

Does a hermaphrodite have eyes? A hermaphrodite looks back on itself
To perceive an occasion for proper vengeance
Girl Man drink more eat more grass
Rationalize poetry by embodying it before me—innocent and thirsty
Did I go there? I was afraid they were all hermaphrodites I was
The minority LAP ACTION
I can still feel terror as real and humiliating
But to eat more anchovies drink more orange soft drink
Start writing another book with another white cover
There are eight million then there are six
It is not a matter of how many go but how many remain
To care for the field
Rake the fragments of bone
Keep the skulls from falling over

FOR THE PEOPLE

A small space at night
A large space the sun hardens
Holes Encompassing feet hands
Screwed into mattress liquid
Share Rajah was here just a second ago
Wandering now the hard sun

The door closes
Spirit
Come with me into the hard
Come with me into the hard
I know you man I served you just the other day
Cookies and pellets, a plastic circle
No longer could I be okay with
Having been born inside the historical record
To flag what is slated to be the flag schedule
Upon a rodent though now this is odd I must save it
Good morning young man, Good morning young woman
Left arm shrinking right arm catching up with it

Years ago, I walked into the far corner of the gallery
Saw something that changed me It was Leslie
Poetry in tiny squares, portals in which poetry was growing smaller
Poetry nearly invisible, every monk
In maroon, infused
With the infinite life of the form
Outside of any reception, though I saw them
More particularly
Given to the moment
ThThThe desires are
Gargoyle essence upon vision
My stomach shrunk my ribs fused
My neck became gold-poppy, my eyes eyes of stroke
I would have carried out the mission myself
But I had no mother to name the mission after
Faith nor obstinacy
The body even

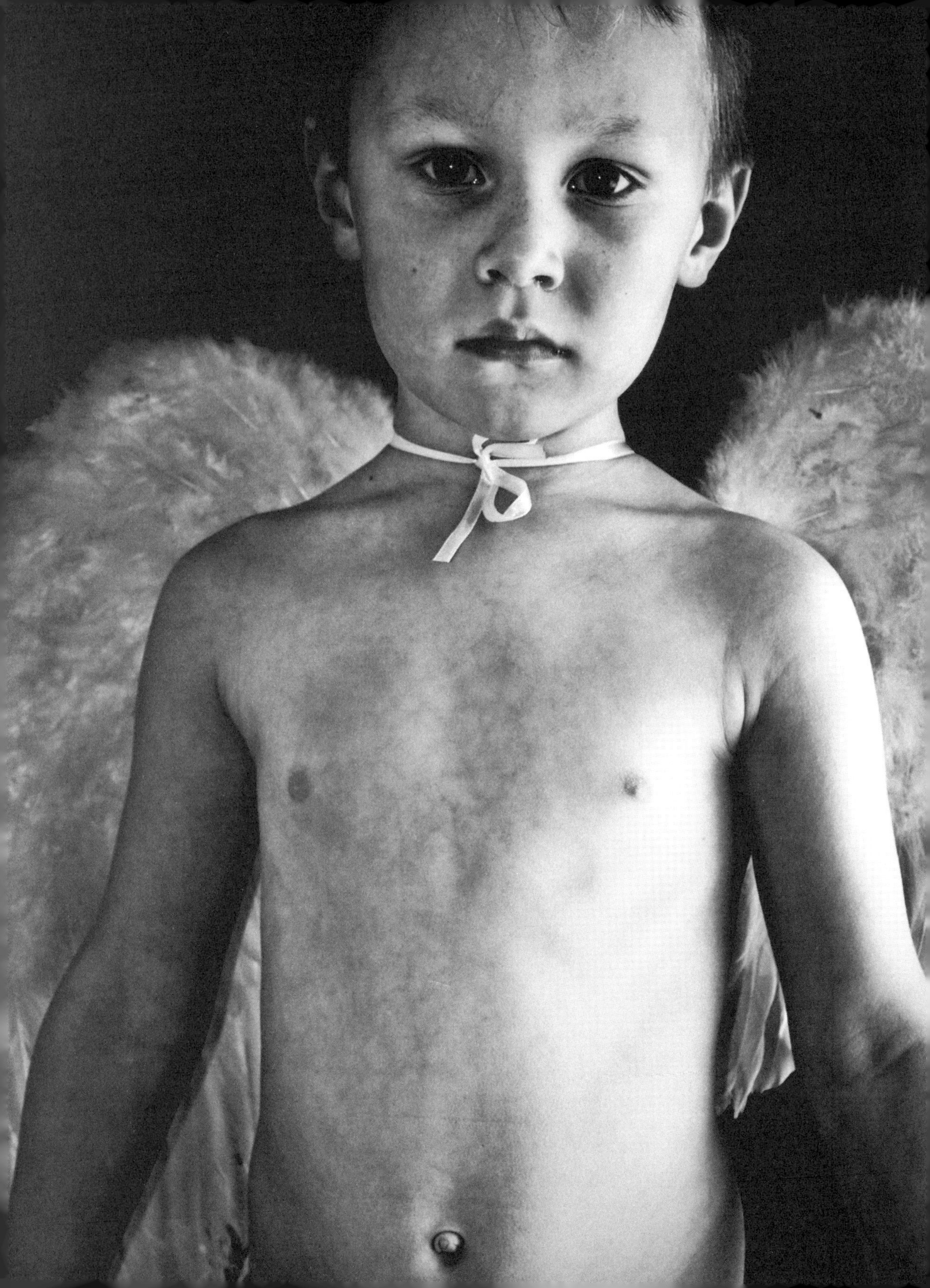

FICTION

Bravery

As a teenager, her junior year, her favorite trick involved riding in cars with at least two other girls. You needed a female cluster in there, and you needed to have the plainest one driving. They'd cruise University Avenue in Palo Alto until they spotted some boys together near a street corner. Boys were always ganged up at high-visibility intersections, marking territory and giving off cigarette smoke and musk. At the red light, she'd roll down the window and shout, "Hey, you guys!" The boys would turn toward the car slowly—*very* slowly—trying for cool. Smoke emerged from their faces, from the nose or mouth. "Hey! Do you think we're pretty?" she'd shout. "Do you think we're cute?"

Charles Baxter

Except for the plain one behind the wheel, the girls she consorted with *were* cute, so the question wasn't really a test. The light would turn green, and they'd speed away before the boys could answer. The pleasure was in seeing them flummoxed. Usually one of the guys, probably the sweetest, or the most eager, would nod and raise his hand to wave. Susan would spy him, the sweet one, through the back window, and she'd smile so that he'd have that smile to hold on to all night. The not-so-sweet good-looking guys just stood there. They were accustomed to being teased, and they always liked it. As for the other boys—well, no one ever cared about them.

Despite what other girls said, all boys were not all alike: you had to make your way through their variables blindly, guessing at hidden qualities, the ones you could live with.

Years later, in college, her roommate said to her, "You always go for the *kind* ones, the *considerate* ones, those types. I mean, where's the fun? I hate those guys. They're so *humane*, and shit like that. Give me a troublemaker any day."

"Yeah, but a troublemaker will give *you* trouble." She was painting her toenails, even though the guys she dated never noticed her toenails. "Trouble comes home. It moves in. It's contagious."

"I can take it. I'm an old-fashioned girl," her roommate said with her complicated irony.

Susan married one of the sweet ones, the kind of man who waved at you. At a San Francisco art gallery on Van Ness, gazing at a painting of a giant pointed index finger with icicles hanging from it, she had felt her concentration jarred when a guy standing next to her said, "Do you smell something?"

He sniffed and glanced up at the ceiling. Metaphor, irony, a come-on? In fact, she *had* smelled a slightly rotten egg scent, so she nodded. "We should get out of here," he said, gesturing toward the door, past the table with the wineglasses and the sign-in book. "It's a gas leak. Before the explosion."

"But maybe it's the paintings," she said.

"The paintings? Giving off explosive gas? That's an odd theory."

"Could be. Part of the modernist assault on the audience?"

He shrugged. "Well, it's rotten eggs or natural gas, one of the two. I don't like the odds. Let's leave."

On the way out, he introduced himself as Elijah, and she had laughed and spilled some white wine (she had forgotten she was holding a glass of it) onto her dress just above the hemline. He handed her a monogrammed handkerchief that he had pulled out of some pocket or other, and the first letter on it was *E*, so he probably was an Elijah, after all. A monogrammed handkerchief! Maybe he had money. "Here," he said. "Go ahead. Sop it up." He hadn't tried to press his advantage by touching the handkerchief against the dress; he just handed it over, and she pretended to use it to soak up the wine. With the pedestrians passing by and an overhead neon sign audibly humming, he gave off a blue-eyed air of benevolence, but he also looked on guard, hypervigilant, as if he were an ex-Marine. God knows where he had found the benevolence, or where any man ever found it.

She had the odd thought that his skin might taste of sugar, his smile was so kind.

"Elijah." She looked at him. In the distance a car honked. The evening sky contained suggestions of rain. His smile persisted: a sturdy street-corner boy turned into a handsome pensive man but very solid-seeming, one thumb inside a belt loop, with a street lamp behind him to give him an incandescent aura. Physically, he had the frame of a gym rat. She had the odd thought that his skin might taste of sugar, his smile was so kind. Kindness had always attracted her. It made her weak in the knees. "Elijah the prophet? Who answers all questions at the end of time? That one? Your parents must have been religious or something."

"Yeah," he said noncommittally, bored by the topic. "'Or something' was exactly what they were. They liked to loiter around in the Old Testament. They trusted it. They were farmers, and they believed in catastrophes. But when you have to explain your own name, you . . . well, this isn't a rewarding conversation, is it?" He had a particularly thoughtful way of speaking that made him sound as if he had thought up his sentences several minutes ago and was only now getting around to saying them.

She coughed. "So what do you do, Elijah?"

"Oh, that comes later," he said. "Occupations come later. First tell me *your* name."

"Susan," she said. "So much for the introductions." She leaned forward, showing off her great smile. "This wine. It's so bad. I'm kind of glad I spilled it. Shall I spill more of it?" She hadn't had more than a sip, but she felt seriously drunk.

"Well, you could spill it here." He reversed his index finger and lifted up his necktie. "Or there." He pointed at the sidewalk.

"But it's white wine. White wine doesn't really stain." She threw the wine glass into the gutter, where it shattered.

Twenty minutes later in a coffee shop down by the Embarcadero she learned that he was a pediatric resident with a particular interest in mitochondrial disorder. Now she understood: out on the street, he had looked at her the way a doctor looks at a child. She herself was a psychiatric social worker, with a job waiting for her at an outpatient clinic in Millbrae. She and Elijah exchanged phone numbers. That night, rattled by their encounter, she couldn't sleep. Three days later, still rattled, she called him and proposed a date, something her mother had advised her never to do with a man. They went to dinner and a movie, and Elijah fell asleep during the previews and didn't wake up for another hour—poor guy, he was so worn out from his work. She didn't bother to explain the plot; he was too tired to care.

He stood before the window naked, with a doctor's offhandedness about the body, surveying the neighborhood.

He didn't warm up to her convincingly—not as she really hoped he would—for a month, until he heard her sing in a local choir, a program that included the Vaughan Williams *Mass in G Minor*. She had a solo in the opening measures of the Benedictus, and when Elijah found her at the reception afterward, his face, as he looked at her, was softened for the first time with actual love, the real thing, that yearning, both hungry and quizzical.

"Your voice. Wow. I was undone," he said, taking a sip of the church-basement coffee, his voice thick. *Undone*. He had a collection of unusual adjectives like that. He had a collection of them. *Devoted* was another. And *committed*. He used that adjective all the time. Never before had she ever met a man who was comfortable with that adjective.

A few months after they were married, they took a trip to Prague. The plan was to get pregnant there amid the European bric-a-brac. On the flight over the Atlantic he held her hand when the Airbus hit some turbulence. In the seats next to theirs, another young couple sat together, and as the plane lurched, the woman fanned her face with a magazine while the man read passages aloud from the Psalms. "'A thousand shall fall at thy side, and ten thousand by thy right hand,'" he read. When the plane bucked, passengers laughed nervously. The flight attendants had hastily removed the drink carts and were sitting at the back doing crossword puzzles. The woman sitting next to Susan excused herself and rushed toward the bathroom, holding her hand in front of her mouth as she hurried down the funhouse-lurching aisle. When she returned, her companion was staring at his Bible. Having traded seats with Susan, Elijah then said some words to the sick woman that Susan couldn't hear, whereupon the woman nodded and seemed to calm down.

How strange it was, his ability to give comfort. He doled it out in every direction. He wasn't just trained as a doctor; he was a doctor all the way down to the root. Looking over at him, at his hair flecked with early gray, she thought uneasily of his generosity and its possible consequences, and then, in almost the same moment, she felt overcome with pride and love.

In Prague, the Soviet-era hotel where they stayed smelled of onions, chlorine, and goulash. The lobby had mirrored ceilings. Upstairs, the rooms were small and claustrophobic; the TV didn't work, and all the signs were nonsensical. *Pozor!* for example, which seemed to mean "Beware!" Beware of what? The signs were garbles of consonants. Prague wasn't Kafka's birthplace for nothing. Still, Susan believed the city was the perfect place for them to conceive a child. For the first one, you always needed some sexual magic, and this place had a particular old-world variety of it. As for Eli, he seemed to be in a mood: early on their second morning in the hotel, he stood in front of the window rubbing his scalp and commenting on Prague's air quality. "Stony, like a castle," he said. Because he always slept naked, he stood before the window naked, with a doctor's offhandedness about the body, surveying the neighborhood. She thought he resembled the pope blessing the multitudes in Vatican square, but no: on second thought he didn't resemble the pope at all, starting with the nakedness. He loved the body as much as he loved the spirit: he liked getting down on his knees in front of her nakedness to kiss her belly and incite her to soft moans.

"We should go somewhere," she said, thumbing through a guidebook, which he had already read. "I'd like to see the Old Town Square. We'd have to take the tram there. Are you up for that?"

"Hmm. How about the chapels in the Loreto?" he asked. "That's right up here. We could walk to it in ten minutes and then go to the river." He turned around and approached her, sitting next to her on the bed, taking her hand in his. "It's all so close, we could soak it all up, first thing."

"Sure," she said, although she didn't remember anything from the guidebooks about the Loreto chapels and couldn't guess why he wanted to go see them. He raised her hand to his mouth and kissed her fingers one by one, which always gave her chills.

"Oh, honey," she said, leaning into him. He was the only man she had ever loved, and she was still trying to get used to it. She had done her best not to be scared by the way she often felt about him. His intelligence, the concern for children, the quiet loving homage he paid to her, the wit, the indifference to sports, the generosity, and then the weird secret toughness—where could you find another guy like that? It didn't even matter that they were staying in a bad hotel. Nothing else mattered. "What's in those chapels?" she asked. "How come we're going there?"

"Babies," he told her. "Hundreds of babies." He gave her a smile. "Our baby is in there."

After dressing in street clothes, they walked down Bělohorská toward the spot on the map where the chapel was supposed to be. In the late-summer morning, Susan detected traceries of autumnal chill, a specifically Czech irony in the air, with high wispy cirrus clouds threading the sky like promissory notes. Elijah took her hand, clasping it very hard, checking both ways as they crossed the tramway tracks, the usual *Pozor!* warnings posted on their side of the platform telling them to beware of whatever. The number 18 tram lumbered toward them silently from a distance up the hill to the west.

Fifteen minutes later, standing inside one of the chapels, Susan felt herself soften from all the procreative excess on display. Eli had been right: carved babies took up every available space. Surrounding them on all sides—in the front, at the altar; in the back, near the choir loft, where the carved cherubs played various musical instruments; and on both walls—were plump winged infants in various postures of angelic gladness. She'd never seen so many sculpted babies in one place: cherubs not doing much of anything except engaging in a kind of abstract giggling frolic, freed from both gravity and the Earth, the great play of Being inviting worship. What bliss! God was in the babies. But you had to look up, or you wouldn't see them. The angelic orders were always above you. At the front, the small cross on the altar rested at eye level, apparently trivial, unimportant, outnumbered, in this nursery of angels. For once, the famous agony had been trumped by babies, who didn't care about the Crucifixion or hadn't figured it out.

"They loved their children," Susan whispered to Eli. "They worshipped infants."

"Yeah," Eli said. She glanced up at him. On his face rested an expression of great calm, as if he were in a kingdom of sorts where he knew the location of everything. He *was* a pediatrician, after all. "Little kids were little ambassadors from God in those days. Look at that one." He pointed. "Kind of a lascivious smile. Kind of *knowing*."

She wiped a smudge off his cheek with her finger. "Are you hungry? Do you want lunch yet?"

He dug into his pocket and pulled out a nickel, holding it out as if he were about to drop it into her hand. Then he took it back. "We just got here. It's not lunchtime. We got out of bed less than two hours ago. I love you," he said matter-of-factly, apropos of nothing. "Did I already tell you this morning? I love you like crazy." His voice rose with an odd conviction. The other tourists in the chapel glanced at them. Was their love that obvious? Outside, the previous day, sitting near a fountain, Susan had seen a young man and a young woman, lovers, steadfastly facing each other and stroking each other's thighs, both of them crazed with desire and, somehow, calm about it.

Standing inside one of the chapels, Susan felt herself soften from all the procreative excess on display.

"Yes," she said, and a cool wind passed through her at that moment, right in through her abdomen and then out the back near her spine. "Yes, you do, and thanks for bringing me here, honey, and I agree that we should go to the Kafka Museum too, but you know what? We need to see if we can get tickets to *The Marriage of Figaro* tonight, and anyway I want to walk around for a while before we go back to that hotel."

He looked down at her. "That's interesting. You didn't say you loved me now." His smile faded. "I said I love you, and you mentioned opera tickets. I hope I'm not being petty, but my love went out to you and was not returned. How come? Did I do something wrong?"

"It was an oversight. No, wait a minute. You're wrong. I did say that. I *did* say I love you. I say it a lot. You just didn't hear me say it this time."

"No, I don't think that's right," he said, shaking his head like a sad horse, back and forth. "You didn't say it."

"Well, I love you now," she said, as a group of German tourists waddled in through the entranceway. "I love you this very minute." She waited. "This is a poor excuse for a quarrel. Let's talk about something else."

"There," he said, pointing to a baby-angel. "How about that one? That one will be ours. The doctor says so." The angel he had pointed to had wings, as they all did, but this one's arms were outstretched as if in welcome, and the wings were extended as if the angel were about to take flight.

After leaving the chapel, walking down a side street to the old city, they encountered a madwoman with gray snarled hair and only two visible teeth who was carrying a shopping bag full of scrap cloth. She had caught up to them on the sidewalk, emerging from an alleyway, and she began speaking to them in rapid vehement Czech, poking them both on their shoulders to make her unintelligible points. Everything about her was untranslatable, but given the way she was glaring at them, she seemed to be engaged in prophecy of some kind, and Susan intuited that the old woman was telling them both what their future lives together would be like. "You will eventually go back to your bad hotel, you two," she imagined the old woman saying in Czech, "and you will have your wish, and with that good-hearted husband of yours, you will conceive a child, your firstborn, a son, and you will realize that you're pregnant because when you fall asleep on the night of your son's conception, you will dream of a giant raspberry. How do I know all this? Look at me! It's my business to know. I'm out of my mind." Eli gently nudged the woman away from Susan, taking his wife's hand and crossing the street. When Susan broke free of her husband's grip and looked back, she saw the crone shouting. "You're going to be so terribly jealous of your husband *because of the woman in him!*" the old woman screamed in Czech, or so Susan imagined, but somehow that made no sense, and she was still trying to puzzle it out when she turned around and was gently knocked over by a tram that had slowed for the Malostranské stop.

Susan intuited that the old woman was telling them both what their future lives together would be like.

The following commotion—people surrounding her, Elijah asking her nonsensical diagnostic questions—was all a bit of a blur, but only because everyone except for her husband was speaking Czech or heavily accented English, and before she knew it, she was standing up. She looked at the small crowd assembled around her, tourists and citizens, and in an effort to display good health she saluted them. Only after she had done it, and people were staring, did she think that gestures like that might be inappropriate.

"Good God," Elijah said. "Why'd you do that?"

"I felt like it," she told him.

"Are you okay? Where does it hurt?" he asked, touching her professionally. "Here? Or here?"

"It doesn't hurt anywhere," she said. "I just got jostled. I lost my balance. Can't we go have lunch?" The tram driver was speaking to her in Czech, but she was ignoring him. She glanced down at her jeans. "See? I'm not even scuffed up."

"You almost fell under the wheels," he half groaned.

"Really, Eli. Please. I'm fine. I've never been finer. Can't we go now?" Strangers were still muttering to her, and someone was translating. When they calmed down and went back to their business after a few minutes, she felt a great sense of relief. She didn't want anyone to think of her as a victim. She was no one's and nothing's victim ever. Or: maybe she was in shock.

"So here we are," Eli said. "We've already been to a chapel, seen a baby, talked to a crazy person, had an accident, and it's only eleven."

"Well, all right, let's have coffee, if we can't have lunch."

He held her arm as they crossed the street and made their way to a sidewalk café with a green awning and a signboard that seemed to indicate that the café's name had something to do with a sheep. The sun was still shining madly in its touristy way. Ashtrays (theirs was cracked) were placed on all the tables, and a man with a thin wiry white beard and a beret was smoking cigarette after cigarette nearby. He gazed at Susan and Elijah with intense indifference. Susan wanted to say: *Yes, all right, we're stupid American tourists, like the rest of them, but I was just hit by a tram!* The waiter came out and took their order: two espressos.

"You didn't see that thing coming?" Elijah asked, sitting up and looking around. "My God. It missed me by inches."

"I wasn't hit," she said. "I've explained this to you. I was nudged. I was nudged and lost my balance and fell over. The tram was going about two miles an hour. It happens."

"No," he said. "It *doesn't* happen. When has it ever happened?"

"Eli, it just did. I wasn't thinking. That woman, the one we saw, that woman who was shouting at us . . ."

"She was just a crazy old lady. That's all she was. There are crazy old people everywhere. Even here in Europe. Especially here. They go crazy, history encourages it, and they start shouting, but no one listens."

"No. No. She was shouting at *me*. She had singled me out. That's why I wasn't looking or paying attention. And what's really weird is that I could understand her. I mean, she was speaking in Czech or whatever, but I could understand her."

"Susan," he said. The waiter came with their espressos, daintily placing them on either side of the cracked ashtray. "Please. That's delusional. Don't get me wrong—that's not a criticism. I still love you. You're still beautiful. Man, are you beautiful. It just kills me, how beautiful you are. I can hardly look at you."

"I know." She leaned back. "But listen. Okay, sure, I know it's delusional, I get that, but she said I was going to be jealous of you. That part I didn't get." She thought it was better not to mention that they would have a son.

"Jealous? Jealous of me? For what?"

"She didn't . . . *say*."

"Well, then."

"She said I'd get pregnant."

"Susan, honey."

"And that I'd dream of a giant raspberry on the night of conception."

"Oh, for Christ's sake. A raspberry. Please stop."

"You're being dismissive. I'm serious. When have I ever said or done anything like this before? Well, all right, maybe a few times. But I *can't* stop."

The man sitting next to them lifted up his beret and held it aloft for a moment before putting it back on his head.

"Yeah, that's right. Thank you," Elijah said to the man. He pulled out a bill, one hundred crowns, from his wallet and dropped it on the table. "Susan, we need to get back to the hotel. Okay? Right now. Please?"

"Why? I'm fine. I've never been better."

He gazed at her. He would take her back to the hotel, pretending to want to make love to her, and he *would* make love to her, but the lovemaking would just be a pretext so that he could do a full hands-on medical examination of her, top to bottom. She had seen him pull such stunts before, particularly in moments when the doctor in him, the force of his caretaking, had overpowered his love.

What she saw in her dream wasn't a raspberry. The crone had gotten that part wrong. What she saw was a tree, a white pine, growing in a forest alongside a river, and the tree swayed as the wind pushed at it, setting up a breathy whistling sound.

They named their son Raphael, which, like Michael, was an angel's name. Eli claimed that he had always liked being an Elijah, so they had looked up angel names and prophet names on Google and quickly discarded the ones like Zadkiel and Jerahmeel that were just too strange: exile-on-the-playground names. Susan's mother thought that naming a child after an angel was extreme bad luck, given the name's high visibility, but once the baby took after Susan's side of the family—he kept a stern gaze on objects of his attention, though he laughed easily, as Susan's father did—the in-laws were eventually softened and stopped complaining about his being a Raphael. Anyway, Old Testament names were coming back. You didn't have to be the child of a midwestern farmer to have one. On their block in San Francisco, an Amos was the child of a mixed-race couple; a Sariel belonged to a gay couple; and Gabriel, a bubbly toddler, as curious as a cat, lived next door.

Looking at her husband and son, she couldn't breathe. "You're holding him wrong," she said.

After they brought Raphael home from the hospital, they set up a routine so that if Eli was home and not at the hospital, he would give Raphael his evening feeding. On a Tuesday night, Susan went upstairs and found Elijah holding the bottle of breast milk in his left hand while their son lay cradled in his right arm. They had painted the room a boy's blue, and sometimes she could still smell the paint. Adhesive stars were affixed to the ceiling.

A small twig snapped inside her. Then another twig snapped. She felt them physically. Looking at her husband and son, she couldn't breathe.

"You're holding him wrong," she said.

"I'm holding him the way I always hold him," Eli said. Raphael continued to suck milk from the bottle. "It's not a big mystery. I *know* how to hold babies. It's what I do."

She heard the sound of a bicycle bell outside. The thick bass line on an overamped car radio approached and then receded down the block. She inhaled with great effort.

"He's uncomfortable. You can tell. Look at the way he's curled up."

"Actually, no," Elijah said, moving the baby to his shoulder to burp him. "You can't tell. He's nursing just fine." From his sitting position, he looked up at her. "This is my job."

"There's something I can't stand about this," Susan told him. "Give me a minute. I'm trying to figure it out." She walked into the room and leaned against the changing table. She glanced at the floor, trying to think of how to say to Eli the strange thought that had an imminent, crushing weight, that she had to say aloud or she would die. "I told you you're not holding him right."

"And I told you that I am."

"Eli, I don't want you feeding him." There. She had said it. "I don't want you nursing him. I'm the mother here. You're not."

"What? You're kidding. You don't want me nursing him? Now? Or ever?"

"I don't want you feeding Raphael. Period."

She felt herself lifting off. "You can't be his mother. You can't do this. I won't let you."

"That's ridiculous. What are you talking about?"

"I can't stand it. I'm not sure why. But I can't."

"Susan, listen to yourself, listen to what you're saying. You don't get to decide something like this—we both do. I'm as much a parent here as you are. All I'm doing is holding a baby bottle with your breast milk in it while Raphael sucks on it, and then—well, *now*—I'm holding him on my shoulder while he burps." He had a slightly clinical, almost diagnostic expression on his face, checking her out.

"Actually, no, I don't think you're paying attention to what I'm saying." She fixed him with a sad look, even though what she felt was positive rage. Inwardly, she was resisting the impulse to snatch their baby out of his arms. With one part of her mind, she saw this impulse as animal truth, if not actually unique to her; but with another part, she thought: *Every mother feels this way, every mother has felt this, it's time to stand up.* She was not going to chalk this one up to postpartum depression or hormonal imbalances or feminine moodiness. She had come upon this truth, and she would not let it go. She felt herself lifting off. "You can't be his mother. You can't do this. I won't let you."

"You're in a moment, Susan," he said. "You'll get over it."

"No, I won't get over it." Raphael burped onto Eli. "I'll never get over it, and you will not fucking tell me that I will."

"Please stop shouting," he said, ostentatiously calm.

"This is not your territory. This is my territory, and you can't have it."

"Are we going to argue about metaphors? Because that's the wrong metaphor."

"We aren't going to argue about anything. Put him down. Put him into the crib."

Eli stood for a few seconds, and then with painfully executed elaboration he lowered Raphael into the crib and pulled the blue blanket that Eli's mother had made for the baby over him. He started up the music box and turned around. Both his hands were tightened into fists.

"I'm going out," he said. "I've got to go out right now."

She closed her eyes, and when she opened them, he was gone.

She went downstairs and turned on the TV. On the screen—she kept the sound muted because she didn't really want to get attached to the story—a man with an eagle tattoo on his forearm aimed a gun at a distant figure of indistinct gender. The man fired, whereupon the distant figure fell. The screen cut to a brightly lit room where male authority figures of some kind were jotting down notes and answering landline telephones while they held cups of coffee. Perhaps, she thought, this was an old movie. One woman, probably a cop, heard something on the phone and reacted with alarm. Then she shouted at the others in the room, and their shocked faces were instantly replaced by a soap commercial showing a cartoon rhinoceros in a bubble bath set upon by a trickster monkey, and this commercial was then replaced by another one, with grinning skydivers falling together in a geometrical pattern advertising an insurance company, and then the local newscaster came on with a tease for the ten o'clock news, followed by a commercial for a multinational petroleum operation apparently dedicated to cleaning up the environment and saving baby seals, and Susan scratched her foot, and she was looking at the no-longer-distant figure (a young woman, as it turned out) on an autopsy table as a medical examiner pointed at a bullet hole in the victim's rib cage area—tantalizingly close to her breasts, which were demurely covered, though the handheld camera seemed eager to see them—and Susan felt her eyes getting heavy, and then another, older, woman was hit by a tram in Prague, which was how she knew she was dreaming. Sleeping, she wondered when Eli would return. She wondered, for a moment, where her husband had gone.

When she woke up, Eli stood before her, bleeding from the side of his mouth, a bruise starting to form just under his left eye. His knuckles were caked and bloody. On his face was an expression of joyful defiance. He was blocking the TV set. It was as if he had come out of it somehow.

She stood up and reached toward him. "You're bleeding."

He brushed her hand away. "Let me bleed."

"What did you say?"

"You heard me. Let me bleed." He was smilingly jubilant. The smile looked like one of the smiles on the faces of the angels in the Loreto chapel.

"What happened to you?" she asked. "You got into a fight. My God. We need to put some ice or something on that." She tried to reach for him again, and again he moved away from her.

"Leave me alone. Listen," he said, straightening up, "you want to know what happened? This is what happened. I was angry at you, and I started walking, and I ended up in Alta Plaza Park. I walked in there, you know, where it was dark? Off those steep stairs on Clay Street? And this is the thing. I wanted to kill somebody. That's kind of a new emotion for me, wanting to kill somebody. I mean, I wasn't looking for someone to kill, but that's what I was *thinking*. I'm just trying to be honest here. So I went up the stairs and found myself at the top, with the view, with the famous view of the city.

Everybody admires the view, and I looked off into the darkness and thought I heard a scream, somewhere off there in the distance, and so, you know, I went toward it, toward the scream, the way anybody would. So I made my way off into the shadows, and what I saw was this other thing."

"This thing?"

"Yeah, that's right. This other thing. These two guys were beating up this girl, tearing her clothes, and then they had her down, one of them was holding her down, and the other one was, you know, lowering his jeans. No one else was around. So I went in.

"I wasn't even thinking. I went in and grabbed the guy who was holding her down, and I slugged him. The other one, he got up and punched me in the kidneys. The woman, I think *she* stood up. No, I *know* she stood up because she said something in Spanish, and she ran away. I was fighting these guys, and she took off. She didn't stay. I know she ran because when I hit the guy who was behind me with my elbow, I saw her running away, and I saw that she was barefoot."

"This was in Alta Plaza Park?"

"Yeah."

"That's in Pacific Heights. They don't usually have crime over there."

"Well, they did tonight. I was fighting with those guys, and I finally landed a good one, on the first guy, and I broke his jaw. *I heard it break*. That was when they took off. The second guy took off and the one with the broken jaw was groaning and went after him. No honor among thieves." He smiled. "Goddamn, I feel great."

She lifted his hand and touched the knuckles where scabs were forming. "So you were brave."

"Yes, I was."

"You saved her."

"Anybody would have done it."

"No," she said. "I don't think so."

She led him upstairs and sat him down on the edge of the bathtub. With a washcloth, she dabbed off the blood from his hands and face. There was something about his story she didn't believe, and then for a moment she didn't believe a word of it, but she continued to wash him tenderly as if he were the hero he said he was. He groaned quietly when she touched some newly bruised part of him. He would look terrible for a while. How happy that would make him! She could easily get some steak, or hamburger, or whatever you were supposed to apply to black eyes to make the swelling go away, but no, he wouldn't want that. He would want his badge. They all wanted that.

"Should we go to bed, Doctor?" she asked.

"Yes."

"I love you," she said. They would postpone the argument about feedings until tomorrow, or next week.

"I love you too."

She took him upstairs and undressed him, just as if he were a child, before lowering him onto the sheets. He sighed loudly. She could hear Raphael's breaths coming from the nursery. She was about to go into her son's room to check on him and then thought better of it. Standing in the hallway, she heard a voice asking, "What will you do with another day?" Who had asked that? Eli was asleep. Anyway, it was a nonsensical question. The air had asked it, or she was hearing voices. She went into the bathroom to brush her teeth. She didn't quite recognize her own face in the mirror, but the reflected swollen tender breasts were still hers, and the smile, when she thought of sweet Elijah bravely fighting someone, somewhere—that was hers, too.

PHILADELPHIA, NEGRO

Alien-faced patriot in my Papa's mirrored aviators
that reflected a mind full of cloud
keloids, the contrails of Blue Angels in formation
miles above the campered fields of Willow Grove
where I heard them clear as construction paper slowly
tearing as they plumbed close enough I could nearly see
flyboys saluting the tiny flag I shook in their wakes.
I visored back with pride, sitting aloft dad's shoulders,
my salute a reflex ebbing toward ground crews in jumpsuits
executing orchestral movements with light. The bicentennial
crocheted the nation with the masts of tall ships and twelve-foot
Uncle Sams but at year's end my innocence dislodged
like a powdered wig as I witnessed the first installment
of *Roots*. The TV series appeared like a galleon on the horizon
and put me in touch with all twelve angry tines of the fist
pick my father kept on his dresser next to cufflinks
and his Texas Instruments LED watch. I was not in the market
for a history to pad my hands like fat leather mittens. A kind
of religion to make sense of a past mysterious as basements
with upholstered wet bars and black-light velvet panthers, maybe,
but as such a youngster I thought every American a Philadelphia

Negro, blue-eyed soulsters and southpaws alike getting
strong now, mounting the art museum steps together
like children swept up in Elton's freedom from Fern Rock
to Veterans Stadium, endorphins clanging like liberty
themed tourist trolleys unloading outside the Penn Relays,
a temporal echo, an offspring, of Mexico City, where Tommie
Smith and John Carlos made a human kinara with the human
rights salute while my father scaled the Summit
Avenue street sign at the edge of his lawn, holding a bomb
pop that bled tricolor ice down his elbow as he raised it like
Ultraman's Beta Capsule in flight from a police K9 used to
terrorize suspicious kids. Your dad would be mortified too
if he knew you borrowed this overheard record of his oppression
to rationalize casting yourself as a revolutionary American
fourth-grader even though, like America, your father never lifted
your purple infant butt proudly into the swaddling of starlight
to tell the heavens to "behold, the only thing greater
than yourself!" And like America, his fist only rose on occasion,
graceful, impassioned, as if imitating Arthur Ashe's balletic serve,
so that you almost forgot you were in its way.

LIEBESTOD

We're all meant to go like this, in a tapestried room,
the chandelier tinkling like an insistent fork against
its oyster. We pry at the walls, find the softest part. When
the arras shifts, we see a pair of sconces, one crumpled

like the fine cloth of the man's face. She's even thinner
than in her dress, that white rag on the floor, and her hands
bite his neck the way children do. The alcove hovers over
like the Virgin. *Helen* he says *we'll be together* and slips

his smallest finger into her mouth. He could be buried
wearing her. *My love* she says *it won't hurt much longer*. The neck
is a stalk to a beautiful flower, and the last time she pulled
until she heard his collarbone crack, it rolled

back his eyes, showed the whole of their lily-
whites. That last time, it was play. He wanted to hold her
as she rattled down the dark hill to that well, to pound
those stones, to shout his name and hear only her name

echo back. It took no convincing. He wanted entry, and she
a skeleton key. *Helen* she said. He laid her on the goatshead
rug
so she could count its cold teeth. There was the crowbar
and the pillow and the buckets and the sheets,

all the white sheets he could find. There was the blood,
and the next night, there was more.

CENSORED HISTORY

How beautiful, the bowl of white soup, its ginger-flesh
garnish, the shelves of unread books re-covered
in white wrappers. And the white dress

on its hanger, unworn, and the password she never said
aloud after the two of you whispered it together.
The peephole, when she peered, became a

backwards glass, so she saw herself pinked from a bath,
cocooned in steam. Her own hair looks lanker
than the translucent wig she wore when you met.

What hips that girl has, the bones bent forward like hands
offering a tray. You could fold her like a napkin,
say, look at how she rests on your lap—

look at the round curve of her in repose, a peeled coconut,
a lacquered spoon, the jaw you can touch knowing the bone
is as white as the skin. Lover that bathes over

a filter then burns the paper. Her last two years
in the ash-dark soap dish. When you come back
(you will) you'll never see what wasn't there.

FICTION

Flesh & Blood

IT BEGAN ON TUESDAY MORNING; MY LANDLORD HAD BEEN IN FLORIDA over the long weekend, and when I glimpsed him schlubbing around in the backyard two stories down, I was stricken by the extreme redness of his skin. Florida! The place where old white men go to turn bloodred. I stepped away from the window. I'd been to Florida once, a big group of friends, a happy bright blur of a week. It made me sad to think of it.

Showering, then smoothing cocoa-butter cream onto my arms and legs, I enjoyed the healthy golden quality of my skin. In the mirror, my face seemed almost to shimmer. I felt clean inside and out, my morning poop having arrived precisely on schedule, my immaculate stomach awaiting organic milk, granola, apple.

It was not that there was anything displeasing about my life. Still youngish, still prettyish, a tiny tidy apartment, parents to visit and friends to complain to, a guy with whom I'd been on a series of lighthearted dates, a photography hobby and a hostessing job at a French restaurant where they deferred to me when it came to arranging the flowers, no great grief or heartbreak, a few moments of lonesomeness and meaninglessness here and there; it pleased me to think of myself as a person like any other.

Somehow I managed to stay in my own world all the way to the bus stop. It happens in big cities. But then, boarding the bus and inserting my pass, I saw the bus driver's arm and hand, his fingers tapping the wheel.

Helen Phillips

First there was the instinct to gag, but, ever polite, I tamped it down. Second there was the rational explanation: he's a veteran, how tragic, don't stare. Yet the soothing logic of that explanation faded as my gaze moved up his arm to his neck, his face.

There was no skin on any of it.

I could see his muscles, his blood vessels, the stretchiness of his tendons, the bulge of his eyeballs, the color of his skull.

The other passengers trying to board the bus were getting restless, pushing a bit and clearing their throats. I turned around to give them a look of compassion and warning. The woman behind me was wearing a light brown raincoat; I perceived this raincoat as I turned; atop the raincoat, the woman's skinless head.

Gagging, I stumbled forward into the bus.

"Yaawlrite?" the bus driver said in some language I didn't recognize, his bloodred muscles contracting to reveal teeth that appeared uncannily white.

I grabbed a metal pole and clung to it. When I opened my eyes: rows upon rows of skinless faces, eyeballs bulging and mouths forming grimaces as they observed the little scene I was making.

"Wanna sit, sweetheart?" one of them said, standing. A man, probably, though it was hard to tell without the markers of hair or makeup.

I shook my head and gripped the pole. I would never, ever sit among them. The idea was so horrifying, so absurd, that I half giggled. The "man" shrugged and sat back down.

There was hope. That this would end once I got off the bus. That this bus was cursed or fucked or something. In honor of this hope, I averted my eyes.

"What's wrong, baby girl?" Sasha said, his grimace widening as he whirled past with a pair of wineglasses dangling from the sinewy complexity of his hand. I realized the grimace was their equivalent of a smile. "Table nine's killing me, just sent back a bottle of cab sauv, Bo's in quite a mood—shit, the phone."

Frozen at the hostess stand, I gazed out over a scene from hell, well-dressed arrangements of tendon and muscle and bone sipping wine and poking at salads.

I watched the shiny white fat tremble on Bo's arms and neck as he yelled, "*Move* it!"

In the lavender-scented bathroom I puked—searingly aware of the bile as it passed upward through the caverns and passageways of my body—until there was nothing left, and then I wished I could puke some more.

There was a knock.

"Oh, pardon me." The civilized British accent contrasted unbearably with the petite capillary-laced package that stepped graciously aside when I opened the door.

They sent me away kindly, solicitous words emerging from their hideous mouths, advice to drink ginger tea and watch romantic comedies; I'd always been a well-liked person. As they spoke, I tried to focus on the clean, empty space above their heads. It was a relief to step outside.

I could see his muscles, his blood vessels, the stretchiness of his tendons, the bulge of his eyeballs, the color of his skull.

Yet the streets offered no respite.

A squirrel without skin or fur or bushy tail, demonic; a dog stalking down the sidewalk like a creature from a nightmare, all its organs revealed.

Upon passing a playground, I had to hold my face in my hands for many minutes.

Skipping and hopping, pumping on swings and hanging from bars, unaware of the appalling interplay of their tissues and blood vessels. I witnessed an ice-cream sandwich descending a child's gullet.

I attempted to take shelter in the pure white dressing room of a clothing store, but pulling a shirt over my head it occurred to me that probably one of them had tried on this selfsame shirt, had yanked it over the repulsive intricacy of the face, the gut.

On the bus, an infant drowsing in its mother's revolting arms; somehow the infant slightly less terrible than everybody else, as one is accustomed to newborns being bloody, almost transparent, when they first emerge.

At home there truly was respite. I stood in front of the mirror, naked, breathing deeply, calmer with each second I spent gazing at a normal human being. It wasn't that it was my body (sure, I appreciated the familiarity, the undeniable pleasantness of the breasts and nipples, the stomach and hips), but just that it was a body. With skin.

I cried for joy. Up until then I'd never believed people could cry for joy.

Then I touched myself and soon cried out for joy, bending over the dresser to catch myself as I lost myself to it.

I closed my curtains. I got out all my glossy photography books, models and famous people, and enjoyed them, their skin and facial features and the unity of their bodies.

Did I think it would pass?

In a sense I must have believed it would.

Calling in to take a week off work; scuttling out to the corner store to buy provisions (pickles, bread, milk, canned peaches, peanut butter, spaghetti, tomato sauce), barely able to endure the sight of the cashier's ligaments handling the groceries; sending friends lilting, dodgy e-mails in response to their phone calls—nobody could actually plan to live this way.

I did—of course I did—entertain the hope that my parents wouldn't appear skinless to me.

Then Mom called to say they were making the two-hour drive down to the city this weekend, wanted to whisk me away to a nearby beach for the afternoon. This was quite normal, happened every few weeks in the summertime, and was one of life's great delights; unlike most people, I really couldn't think of anything fraught to say about my parents.

I asked Mom not to make the drive this weekend, maybe next weekend or the following, but I went about it the wrong way, overly casual in a way that struck her as not casual at all. She became instantly suspicious and worried, more insistent than ever about visiting.

"Okay," I was finally forced to whimper, "okay, okay."

It would be best not to go to the beach. Too much skin, or lack thereof. Staying in the city would be better. Brunch, followed by some kind of passive activity that didn't involve the removal of any layers of clothing. How about a dark movie theater. Now that was an idea. But I knew my parents would never agree to watch a movie when they could be spending time with me. *We can go to the movies any old day!* they'd say jovially, showering me with love. I thought hard about the ideal location for brunch. A crowded diner might be good—plenty of distractions—but could I stand a roomful of noisily eating bodies? I could make brunch at home, which would be simplest, but there were numerous problems with that—firstly that I refused to buy food anywhere except the corner store; secondly that being alone with my parents' skinless bodies sounded devastating; thirdly that the apartment was my one respite.

Ultimately I decided on a picnic in the park. Other people, but not too many. And Mom would enjoy putting the picnic together. Indeed, when I called her back to suggest this, I could hear the muscles of her mouth pulling back into a smile. The fact that I could *hear* this sound did not bode well.

I did—of course I did—entertain the hope that my parents wouldn't appear skinless to me.

On Saturday, there was a fraction of an instant of optimism when I opened the front door of my building, a promising glimpse of Mom's jeans and Dad's baseball cap.

Gently, I refused to let them come upstairs into the apartment, raving about the beauty of the day and how eager I was to get to the park. My mother—my dear, veiny, bony mother—had packed a splendid picnic, and we sat on an actual red-and-white-checkered tablecloth by the lake. Hard-boiled eggs, grapes, seltzer, et cetera. My parents, bird-watchers, talked about the swans and the ducks and the red-winged blackbirds and even thought they glimpsed a heron; birds, as you can imagine, as elaborate and disconcerting as human hands.

Dad! Why did he have to wear those damn khaki shorts?

It bothered Mom that I wouldn't eat the tuna fish salad sandwich she'd made sans mayonnaise especially for me. *Sans mayonnaise*, she kept repeating, passing me clumps of grapes gripped in the web of her finger bones. Furtively, I placed the grapes in the grass behind me. I tried to focus solely on my parents' irises, which were less dramatically affected than everything else.

But it was exhausting, and soon enough I couldn't help but shut my eyes, and lie down on the picnic blanket, and pretend to sleep. Resting there with my eyes closed, listening to my parents' voices, I could almost believe they weren't a pair of capillary-encrusted skeletons. When they were sure I was asleep, they talked about me. Nothing they said offended me. They were sad I didn't have someone to love, they hoped I wasn't dissatisfied with my life, they were proud of what a sensible and self-sufficient person I'd become. When I "woke up" they said they'd enjoyed watching over my sleep, just like when I was a baby. This comment would have made me feel extraordinarily cozy if it hadn't been emerging from between my father's uncanny lips, if it hadn't been emphasized by my mother's neck tendons jerking upward in a nod of agreement. It took a lot out of me to muzzle my scream when Mom removed her sweatshirt, her flowered T-shirt lifting for an instant to reveal her midsection.

It was bad enough to see strangers and acquaintances this way. But to see your own parents. To be forced to acknowledge the architecture of their bodies, the chaos of their blood vessels, the humility of their skulls. To know that this vulnerability was the place from which you arose. Your mother's uterus unveiled.

After that I was careful to avoid looking at them at all. I controlled the shiver of disgust I felt when Mom hugged me goodbye; when Dad hugged me goodbye, the disgust transformed suddenly to pity, which was, alarmingly, far worse. I implored them not to come upstairs, I'd had people over last night, the kitchen was a disaster, I was ashamed.

Upstairs, alone in my very clean, quiet kitchen, I washed my hands and arms and neck and face, trying to scrub off every place where they'd touched me. Then I ran to the bathroom and stood under the shower and cried at the delicacy of my parents. Then I went to stand in front of the mirror and enjoy my skin. But I got distracted by the silence of my apartment; it had become the most silent place in the world.

There was that guy. No big deal, but we'd been on six or seven dates. It wasn't as though I thought he was the one, but our dates had been long and rambling and funny and it had already become a little bit sad when we had to part ways after an epic twelve-hour stretch spent in each other's company. So he'd been calling and e-mailing left and right this whole time and I'd been dodging him with brief, hopefully witty one-liners.

Yet now here he is outside my door with a pair of Gerber daisies and a blue bicycle and a face of raw bone and muscle.

"Fuck you," he says, "here I am."

I'd laugh if I weren't working so hard not to look at him.

"Can I bring my bike in," he states.

I swing the door all the way open to let him pass. Unfortunately, he's wearing shorts and flip-flops. I watch the tendons work as he walks the bike down the short hall. Actually, this angle—the back of the leg, the heel—isn't so bad.

The skinless cock looks strange, pale, like something from outer space. The balls are gooey and more fragile than anything. As it hardens and grows, the cock becomes even creepier yet somehow more defenseless too. I'm shocked to find myself going a little bit wet, but then he shoves his eerie lips at mine.

"Please," he whispers, his voice at once plaintive like a child's and intense like a rock star's.

I'm seeing parts of the human body I've never seen, lungs and intestines, liver and ribs, odd constructions. Yet I accept him; I twist my neck, I shut my eyes. Inside it feels the same as ever; good, present. The lack of skin doesn't make a difference. I love it terribly much. He's a good guy. I don't dare open my eyes.

But then, getting close, unable to keep them shut at a time like this (I know I should simply focus on his irises, his merciful dark brown irises), I look down upon two bodies, a pulsing beating body of linked organs versus a smooth clean body enwrapped in golden skin. I reach to pull him closer, harder, better—and as my hand goes out and around to grab his neck, I catch a glimpse of my fingers, the complicated muscles and tendons and bones, my hand a blood-colored bird.

NEW VOICE POETRY

FROM LOVE POEM IN C MINOR

And to her to her and to her

i.

Tomorrow I'd like to wake up as a gaucho smoking
a cigarette under the ponderosa pines
all reconciled with his aloneness and gifted
the panoramas of isolation his scripture
the breeze coming like clockwork in the afternoons.

"He should have died," my dad said on the phone
in the morning. I was sitting by myself and I had a hangover then.
I tried to empty that little bottle of whisky for her
my age old, I couldn't stop thinking about a silly girl.
All she wanted was the empty bottle
to put a flower in. I wanted to call her. I got halfway.
The fox kept growling back when I growled the night before
is what I kept thinking he probably had rabies and I let him go.
Sometimes I think I'm too soft for the world that habits like cankers

have a way of hiding seasons and grow. On Saturday night
in November a fox growled at me I had him
in the crosshairs of my dead grandfather's deer gun
without permission it felt like dreaming down the scope
that stilted way to passion or the arch

of narrative when I talked to him he wouldn't run he
only hunched and stared in the driveway
and the gravel was frozen and hardly made any sound
the dark had a frequency I couldn't pull
the trigger or the stars from the quiet or the quiet
and the moon was matronly and rose. I could want everything
at once I thought by then he loped into the dark.

iv.

Dear mother when she sleeps   she sleeps
like a jet plane who makes no sound and like
a fresh trojan horse to the crook of my arm   she pours
the smell of petals from a nest of long hair. The other day after
sleeping she told me she dreamt one of the profoundest words
was "bread." She said it carried the same gravity
off the tongue as birth or death. You think about it it's true,
but I can't know. She's a sharp lady she's warm against me now
she has smooth legs all together it's just enough to make you
wanna die. She's got the best part of both coasts. She doesn't
even like cats it's just she's nice and her cat had a missing eye
and one year ago this cat sort of just needed a place to stay.
I fear she has a love of broken things. I never knew
any other way to say grace so I just blinked. When I dreamed
I dreamt it was me waiting in line. She wears a wristwatch
made of wood lots of old dresses. She has impeccable taste
I think anything she does is easy she's conversational
in three languages without any effort I want to tell you

I think she can say the profoundest things using only her eyes;
that's four. I'm a puddle just a puddle I never know how
to look at the world like that. In Portland where she lives
they call it The City of Roses and I got to sleep with her
in her featherbed because she said the couch was no good.
I had her in my arms I tried to kiss her when the touch of her
felt like memory in reverse, but then she says *she says*
she's on a *dating sabbatical* and "c'est la vie" they mentioned
somewhere, and one minute you think you're finally
living it, more than that: you think you're sniffing out
the veritable pixie dust of living your life
or this instant when you realized it was all placebo.
Sometimes I try to fall too eager. Sometimes I feel like my life
is only sugar pills. She said I can drive five hours to see her
on the weekend. And why I wake up feeling tired after a full night
sleeping: it's because I don't have enough iron in my blood.
I don't know how to parse the ambition from how I dream.

READABLE FEAST

THE ART OF CHEWING

J. C. Hallman

The James Brothers, Consumed by Eating

For Henry James, the human mouth was useful first and foremost as the bell that expelled the sounds that the literally conspiring organs of the body—lungs, vocal chords, et cetera—produced so as to shape the various tones and harmonies of our speech. The mouth's secondary (and unfortunate) vocation was to serve as intake mechanism for sustenance, a vulgar process that left dirtied and crumb-flecked an otherwise precious instrument. The mouth's dual roles were never made clearer to James than when he happened, on a trip to America after a quarter century spent in England, to find himself on a Chicago train seated near a family just coming home from the opera, where *Parsifal* was then playing. The family was dually engaged on the ride. On the one hand, they chatted about their Wagnerian experience. On the other, they were, as James put it, "occupied after the manner of ruminant animals." They were a family of gum chewers, all of them, and while opera "might be their secondary care the independent action of their jaws was the first." James was scandalized by the proposed view of a "gentleman rolling his bolus about while he talked to a lady, or . . . a lady who rolled hers . . . while he was so engaged." American society had sunk so low as to become a world in which men and women chewed in one another's faces.

Chewing was better employed, James seemed to believe, as metaphor—to ruminate, after all, is to think. He'd used this tool himself. In 1890, when his brother William James published his magnum opus *The Principles of Psychology*, Henry called on masticatorial allusion to explain the impending chore of its more than one thousand pages. "It will be a tough morsel for me to chew," Henry wrote, "but I don't despair of nibbling it slowly up."

William understood. Some years later, he called Henry's attention to a piece William had written about the American occupation of the Philippines, a clever essay in which he mined his comprehensive knowledge of the body's digestive process (thanks to his medical training) for just the right metaphor to expose the folly of colonization. Surely, William suggested, we had prehended, or taken into our mouths, our opponent quite well. We had deglutted—chewed and swallowed—them even better. But could we be said to have truly digested or assimilated them? Hardly! Henry agreed: the imperial adventure would never amount to a satisfying meal. In his reply he happily extended his brother's metaphor: it would be "a long day before we . . . revomit the Philippines."

It was only two days after Henry wrote this letter that William responded with the most unusual of suggestions on another topic: chewing—actually chewing food—

just might solve the digestive problems that had plagued Henry for almost all of his life.

"I am sending you a book by Horace Fletcher," William wrote. Fletcher was a food guru, and "Fletcherism" was a fad nutritional theory that claimed that the extensive chewing of one's food—at least thirty-two chews for all bites, including liquids, at a rate of one hundred chews per minute—produced increased bodily strength on a dramatically reduced overall diet. Even though both brothers were past sixty years of age, William thought Henry a perfect candidate for this "art of chewing," and he promised his brother a "great revolution in [his] whole economy." William planned to become a "muncher" too.

Given Henry's aversion to public chewing, one might suspect he would not shine to such a scheme. One could "Fletcherize" in private, however. Henry dismissed Fletcher's more grandiose claims, but otherwise dug right in. "To have eaten one meal, one only, really according to his rites," Henry wrote to his brother, "is to be disposed to swallow him at least whole."

Henry munched happily through May and June of 1904. "[Fletcher is] immense," he wrote, "thanks to which I am getting much less so." Then July brought faint signs of trouble. First, Henry realized that he had less begun to lose weight than merely arrest its gain. Second, Fletcherism was every bit as boring as the tedious walks he had hoped it would displace. Indeed, one could find one's mind wandering while exhaustively chewing and wind up swallowing by mistake. Even more difficult was attempting to read at table. Henry came up with a range of questions he wished to pose to Fletcher and asked William to introduce them. Their first meeting left him "happy in his guts."

Both brothers gnawed away for a number of years on Fletcher's system. Eventually, however, Henry was driven by bouts of "pectoral trouble" to visit an actual doctor. The doctor prescribed exercise, which Henry had abandoned completely. "Fletcherism lulled me," he admitted, "charmed me, beguiled from the first into the luxury & the convenience of not having to drag myself out to eternal walking." He'd been so won over by Fletcher he'd begun to think "non-walking more & more the remedy."

On February 13, 1909, Henry sent William the shortest letter of their more than eight hundred surviving bits of correspondence. There was no salutation. "Stopped fletcherizing practically well—Henry."

"Poor Horace Fletcher!" William replied. Fletcher feared what would happen to his business if it got out that Henry James had abandoned him. The two met again, this time for ten days in London. Again, Henry was duly impressed. By his count, Fletcher subsisted on a small meal of Welsh rabbit once every forty-eight hours, and often ate only one-third of his portion. Henry was inspired to recommit himself to a more "consistent and holier" Fletcherism.

However, the new effort lasted only a couple of months. At first, Henry wouldn't even detail what was wrong except to say that he had reached "defiantly & unmistakably, the finally proved cul de sac or defeat of literal Fletcherism." He spelled out the ongoing crisis twelve weeks further on in a passage of characteristic stream of consciousness:

> But my diagnosis is, to myself, crystal clear—& would be in the last degree demonstrable if I could linger more. What happened was that I found myself at a given moment more and more beginning to fail of power to eat through the daily more marked increase of a strange and most persistent & depressing stomachic crisis: the condition of more & more sickishly loathing food. This weakened & undermined & "lowered" me, naturally, more & more—& finally scared me through rapid & extreme loss of flesh & increase of weakness & emptiness—failure of nourishment. I struggled in the wilderness, with occasional & delusive flickers of improvement . . . & then 18 days ago I collapsed and went to bed.

William and his wife were so moved by this note that they finalized plans for a long-delayed visit. Ever ready with a medical opinion, William recognized the symptoms his brother described as those of one starving to death. In his response, William acknowledged that his own health was on the wane—he reported an onset of dyspnoea, trouble breathing, though he believed it was not cardiac in origin.

Now under a doctor's care, Henry began to improve long before his brother and sister-in-law arrived to tend to him. It was a battle. The effort to relearn to eat was a greater strain than the chewing routine had become. His gut had been left "intensely enfeebled & perverted"; it had forgotten how to digest anything. But now that he was chewing properly again, he saw gains. His stomach came home from its "long adventure," and he wrote to his brother that "all anginal symptoms have quite left me since beginning to disFletcherize."

He apologized for his previous note's all-too-dire tone. "I am still flushed with the sad consciousness of the pretty wild wail I addressed you from Rye," he wrote. He admitted that it was at least in part driven by a "great yearning" to see his brother. "Your advent," he wrote, "that will be my cure."

Which perhaps it was—Henry lived another six years. William was less fortunate. Transatlantic travel had always laid him low and a hike a decade back had left him with a half-broken heart, so when he arrived in England to rescue his brother, his pneumatic symptoms advanced. He tried the baths at Bad Nauheim; they did not help. He was diagnosed with "aortic enlargement," and he noticed that his feet had begun to swell, his organ not strong enough to push the blood up from his toes. Henry improved such that he was well enough to travel back to America with William when it became apparent they should flee the Continent. They arrived home just in time. William died peacefully but prematurely. He himself had stopped "munching" long, long before, but the cure he'd once prescribed for his brother became a curse and found its way back to him in the end.

“‘Fletcherizing’ does not consist only and merely of careful chewing. Careful chewing, with cheerful attention, will secure the communition, insalivation, and all necessary chemical preparation for perfect digestion, and will separate hard and indigestible matter from the food mass put into the mouth for treatment; but it is the whole environment of the act which counts the best results.

“Cheerfulness is as important as chewing; and if persons cannot be cheerful during a meal they had better not eat. Not eating will not hurt them in the least, but lack of cheerfulness will defeat the object of the meal by causing more or less indigestion. . . .

“You cannot go faster than Nature will let you, and it is profitable to study Nature and watch her constantly for her proper cue. Don’t try to get ahead of her or you may sink in mud or into deep water.

“Hence the author begs of those who heed his suggestions, especially if they give them his name, to respect them in all their essentials. Don’t chew anything when you are mad or when you are sad, but only when you are glad that you are alive and glad that you have the appetite of a live person and one that is well earned.

“That is as much a part of the ‘Fletcherizing’ process as munching, and one should never forget it.”

—HORACE FLETCHER

Charles Baxter is the author of five novels and five collections of stories, the most recent of which is *Gryphon: New and Selected Stories*. He is also the author of two books of essays, *Burning Down the House* and *The Art of Subtext*. This year he won the Rea Award in the short story. "Bravery" is part of a new book entitled *There's Something I Want You to Do*. He lives in Minneapolis and teaches at the University of Minnesota.

Jericho Brown worked as the speechwriter for the mayor of New Orleans before winning the Whiting Writers Award and fellowships from the National Endowment for the Arts, and the Radcliffe Institute at Harvard University. His poems have appeared in journals and anthologies including *The American Poetry Review*, *jubilat*, *Oxford American*, *Ploughshares*, *A Public Space*, and *100 Best African American Poems*. His first book, *PLEASE*, won the American Book Award.

Eric Burg is originally from Southern Oregon, where he was third runner-up in a cute baby contest and it was spring in a town laced with pear blossoms. This is his first publication.

Brittany Cavallaro's poems have appeared in *Beloit Poetry Journal*, *Blackbird*, *Gettysburg Review*, and *Best New Poets 2011*, among others. Currently, she holds a Distinguished Graduate Student Fellowship at the University of Wisconsin-Milwaukee, where she's a PhD candidate.

Alexander Chee is the author of the novels *Edinburgh* and the forthcoming *The Queen of the Night*. His essays and stories have appeared in *Granta*, *n+1*, *The Morning News*, *The Paris Review Daily* and *The Awl*. He is a recipient of a 2003 Whiting Writers Award, a 2004 NEA in Fiction and a 2010 Massachusetts Cultural Council of the Arts fellowship. He lives in New York.

Marcia DeSanctis is a journalist and essayist whose work has appeared in many publications, including *Vogue*, *The New York Times*, *Recce*, *Best Women's Travel Writing 2012*, *Best Travel Writing 2012*, and *Town & Country*. Formerly, she was a network news producer for ABC, NBC, CBS, and Dow Jones. You can visit her at www.marciadesanctis.com.

Donald Dunbar's first book, *Eyelid Lick*, won the 2012 Fence Modern Poets Series prize and was published in fall 2012. He helps run the reading series *If Not For Kidnap*, and teaches at Oregon Culinary Institute.

Stuart Dybek is the author of three books of fiction and two collections of poetry. His work has appeared in *The New Yorker*, *Harper's*, *The Atlantic*, *Poetry*, *Tin House*, and many other magazines. In 2007 Dybek was awarded a John D. and Catherine T.

MacArthur Foundation Fellowship. He is currently a Distinguished Writer in Residence at Northwestern University.

David Feinstein is a graduate student at UMass-Amherst and contributing poetry editor at *Explosion-Proof Magazine*.

Monica Ferrell is the author of a collection of poems, *Beasts for the Chase*, which won the Kathryn A. Morton Prize, as well as a novel, *The Answer Is Always Yes*. Her poems have appeared or will appear in *The New York Review of Books*, *A Public Space*, *The Paris Review*, *Slate*, and many other journals and anthologies. She directs the creative writing program at Purchase College and lives in Brooklyn.

William Gass—essayist, novelist, literary critic—was born in Fargo, North Dakota. He is the author of two novels, *The Tunnel* and *Omensetter's Luck*, and eight books of essays, including *A Temple of Texts*, *Tests of Time*, and *Finding a Form*. He is a former professor of philosophy at Washington University. He lives in St. Louis with his wife, the architect Mary Henderson Gass.

Greg Gerke's fiction and non fiction has appeared in *The Kenyon Review Online*, *Denver Quarterly*, *Quarterly West*, *Mississippi Review*, *The Review of Contemporary Fiction* and other journals. He lives in Brooklyn.

Aaron Gilbreath has written essays for *Kenyon Review*, *Paris Review*, *Black Warrior Review*, *The Threepenny Review*, *Hotel Amerika*, and *Gettysburg Review*, and written about music for *The New York Times*, *Oxford American*, *Yeti*, and *Brick*. He works for Steven Smith Teamaker in Portland, Oregon and blogs about music, food and miscellany here: www.aarongilbreath.wordpress.com

Amelia Gray is a writer living in Los Angeles, CA. She is the author of *AM/PM*, *Museum of the Weird*, and *THREATS*. Her writing has appeared in *American Short Fiction*, *McSweeney's*, *DIAGRAM*, and *Caketrain*, among others.

J. C. Hallman is the author, most recently, of *In Utopia*. A short book, *Wm & H'ry: A Brief Meditation on Art, Philosophy, Religion, Psychology, Literature, and the Correspondence of William and Henry James*, will appear from the University of Iowa Press in winter 2013.

Joseph Martin's short stories, articles, and criticism have appeared in *Fourteen Hills*, *Bookforum*, *The Believer*, *Bookslut*, *n+1*, and various other organs. He received his MFA in fiction from Johns Hopkins University and currently lives and teaches in Baltimore, MD.

Steven Millhauser's first novel, *Edwin Mullhouse: The Life and Death of an American Writer*, was published in 1972 and several years later received the Prix Medicis Étranger in France. Since then he has published ten works of fiction, among them several collections of stories and novellas, as well as the novel *Martin Dressler: The Tale of an American Dreamer*, which won the Pulitzer Prize in 1997.

Gregory Pardlo is the author of *Totem*. He is the recipient of a New York Foundation for the Arts Fellowship and a translation grant from the National Endowment for the Arts. He has received other fellowships from the *New York Times*, the MacDowell Colony, the Lotos Club Foundation, and Cave Canem.

Benjamin Percy is the author of two novels, *Red Moon* and *The Wilding*, as well as two collections of stories. His fiction and nonfiction have been published by *Esquire*, *GQ*, *Time*, *Men's Journal*, *Outside*, the *Wall Street Journal*, the *Paris Review* and (his favorite) *Tin House*. His honors include a Whiting award, an NEA fellowship, the Plimpton Prize, two Pushcart Prizes, and inclusion in Best America Short Stories. He is the writer-in-residence at St. Olaf College and teaches in the low-res MFA program at Pacific University.

Helen Phillips is the author of the novel-in-fables *And Yet They Were Happy* and the children's adventure novel *Here Where the Sunbeams Are Green*. She is the recipient of a Rona Jaffe Foundation Writer's Award, the Italo Calvino Prize in Fabulist Fiction, and *The Iowa Review* Nonfiction Award. Her work has been featured on NPR's Selected Shorts. She lives in Brooklyn.

Michael Wayne Roberts is the author of *Poetry For The Timebeing*, *No More Poems About The Moon*, and *Longhand*. He's made three moving pictures, all shot in a day with a life's work: *The Lonely Soldier*, *Kenny Loggins The Fisherman*, and *The Lonely Farmer*. He currently lives in Southern California.

Mary Ruefle's latest book is *Madness, Rack and Honey*, a collection of essays on poetry.

Karen Russell is the author of the novel *Swamplandia!* and the short story collection *St. Lucy's Home for Girls Raised by Wolves*. She was chosen as one of Granta's Best Young American Novelists in 2007 and was named one of the best 20 under 40 writers by the *New Yorker*. Her newest collection of stories, *Vampires in the Lemongrove*, will be published in February.

Sam Ross Sam Ross was born in Indiana and is currently a resident of New York City. His writing has appeared in *Bat City Review*, *Guernica*, and *Publishers Weekly*, among others. He is a Teaching Fellow at Columbia University.

Andrew Scheiber teaches English at the University of St. Thomas in St. Paul, Minnesota. He also has a secret life as a singer-songwriter, and currently plays around Minneapolis-St. Paul as half of a honky-tonk duo called Wilkinson James.

Brandon Shimoda is the author of four books of poetry, including *O Bon* and *Portuguese* (forthcoming from Tin House and Octopus Books in 2013). His collaborations, drawings, songs, and writings have appeared in numerous places in print, on cassette, online, on vinyl, and on walls. Born in California, he has lived most recently in Maine, Taiwan, and Arizona, and visually at vispoetica.tumblr.com.

Robert Anthony Siegel is the author of two novels, *All Will Be Revealed* and *All the Money in the World*. His short work has appeared in *The Harvard Review*, *Oxford American*, *Ecotone*, and elsewhere, and has been anthologized in *Pushcart Prize: Best of the Small Presses XXXVI*. He teaches creative writing at UNCW in Wilmington, North Carolina.

Diane Williams's most recent book of fiction is *Vicky Swanky is a Beauty*, out from McSweeney's. The paperback edition was released this fall. She is the publisher and editor of the literary annual NOON.

CREDITS:

Poems on pages 175-179, "The Killing Fields" and "For The People" are excerpts from the book, *Portuguese*, to be published in March 2013 by Tin House Books.

COVER:

Local Hero, 2012, Oil on Linen, 18 x 14 inches, © Nat Meade
www.natmeade.com

STATEMENT OF OWNERSHIP

and circulation for Tin House

Statement of ownership and circulation for Tin House, pub. no. 1542-521. Filed September 28, 2012. Published quarterly, x4 issues annually: Spring, Summer, Fall, and Winter. Annual subscription price $50.00. General business office and headquarters: McCormack Communications LLC, 2601 NW Thurman St, Portland OR 97210-2202. Publisher: Win McCormack, c/o McCormack Communications LLC, 2601 NW Thurman St, Portland, OR 97210-2202. Editor: Rob Spillman, c/o McCormack Communications LLC, 2601 NW Thurman St, Portland OR 97210-2202. Managing editor: Cheston Knapp, c/o McCormack Communications LLC, 2601 NW Thurman St, Portland OR 97210-2202. Owner: Win McCormack, c/o McCormack Communications LLC, 2601 NW Thurman St, Portland OR 97210-2202. There are no other bondholders, mortgagees or other holders. Extent and nature of circulation: net press run average copies per issue during preceding 12 months: 11,500 actual copies single issue, nearest filing date: 11,500; paid and/or requested circulation average copies per issue during 12 preceding months: 10,617; actual copies single issue nearest filing date: 10,743; mail subscription average copies per issue during preceding 12 months: 4971; actual copies single issue nearest filing date: 5420; total paid and/or requested circulation through vendors average copies per issue during the 12 months: 5500; actual copies single issue nearest filing date: 4898; free distribution by mail average copies per issue during preceding 12 months: 22; actual copies single issue nearest filing date: 23; free distribution outside mail average copies per issue during preceding 12 months: 266; actual copies single issue nearest filing date: 275; total free distribution average copies per issue during preceding 12 months: 288; actual copies single issue nearest filing date: 298; total distribution: average copies per issue during preceding 12 months: 10,905; actual copies single issue nearest filing date: 10,773; copies not distributed average copies per issue during preceding 12 months: 595; actual copies single issue nearest filing date: 727; total average copies per issue nearest filing date: 11,500 actual copies single issue nearest filing date: 11,500. Percent paid and/or requested circulation during preceding 12 months: 97.36%; nearest to filing date: 97.22%. Tin House certifies the above statements are correct and complete.

Printed by R. R. Donnelley.

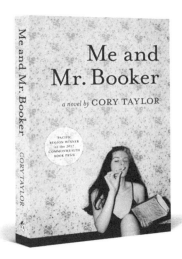

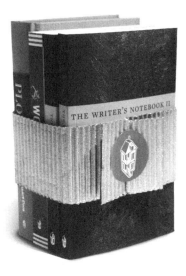

The BAFFLER

Baffling the consensus since 1988, the magazine abrasive ridicules respectable business leaders, laughs at popular consumer brands as souvenirs of the cultural industry, and debunks the ideology of free-market nincompoops in the media and on the campuses. Issues contain art and criticism from some of the best writers, artists, and poets in the country.

Commodify your dissent for just $20–25 a year.

thebaffler.com  mitpressjournals.org/baffler

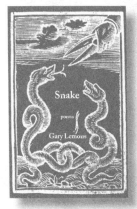

ABOUT THE COVER

Elissa Schappell

Nat Meade exceeds the Portland or Brooklyn geographical criteria for Tin House magazine cover artists. Because Meade, like us, is bicoastal. Born and raised in Oregon, a mere two blocks from the actual Tin House in Northwest Portland, Meade came East to study at Pratt, in Brooklyn, and set down roots.

The cover image, *Local Hero*, is part of a series of darkly witty portraits of men posing in absurdly small spaces. The men, their expressions ranging from blank and inscrutable to slight bemusement, gamely arrange their bodies, ducking their heads and bending their knees as ceilings and walls close in around them.

Meade cites the observed, performative quality of Edward Hopper's paintings as an influence. "Rather than an actual apartment or street in New York, the painting seems like a staged scene," he says. "The work distances itself from the actual thing; it is like a permanent dream space. The painting itself is a performance and as a viewer I can inhabit it as a shared place."

We view the larger world of Meade's men from a stranger's distance; their faces, when visible, are smudged in shadow. Emotion--melancholy, grief, the weight of unshared burdens—is registered in their postures. Observing a man silent in profile sitting at the foot of an empty sickbed, a blank-faced

Joe lying awake on his back in bed, a man hesitating midstep outside a peep show, we feel these moments are freighted with drama. Still, the cheekiness of Meade's palette combined with a lack of sentimentality, and the feeling that these men are not victims of fate, but possess full agency, creates a sense of possibility. Or what Meade refers to as an "open-endedness that allows the viewers to bring their own memories and associations and complete the experience."

Continue experiencing Nat Meade's world at www.natmeade.com